T0146455

Courtly Pleasures

Book 1

ERIN KANE SPOCK

Crimson Romance
New York London Toronto Sydney New Delhi

CRIMSON
ROMANCE

Crimson Romance
An Imprint of Simon & Schuster, Inc.
1230 Avenue of the Americas
New York, NY 10020

First Crimson Romance ebook edition DECEMBER 2017.

CRIMSON ROMANCE and colophon are trademarks of Simon and Schuster.

For information about special discounts for bulk purchases, please contact Simon & Schuster Special Sales at 1-866-506-1949 or business@simonandschuster.com.

The Simon & Schuster Speakers Bureau can bring authors to your live event. For more information or to book an event contact the Simon & Schuster Speakers Bureau at 1-866-248-3049 or visit our website at www.simonspeakers.com.

ISBN 978-1-5072-0852-6
978-1-5072-0747-5 (ebook)

This book is dedicated to my sister, Mary McKinley, without whom this book would have never been written. This book is also dedicated to my long-suffering critique partner, Raquel Byrnes, without whom this book would have never become publishable. Thank you both for your encouragement and faith in me.

Chapter One

Rule Six: It is necessary for a male to reach the age of maturity in order to love.
    —Paraphrased from "The Rules of Courtly Love" as translated in *The Book of the Courtier* by Castiglione, 1561

Commons apartment at Parliament, London, 1572

"Pray pardon, madam, but are you requesting a divorce?" The shock stamped so beautifully on Henry LeSieur's face probably should have worried Frances. He never reacted, never felt anything. Instead, the brief evidence of actual emotion made her smile.

When had she smiled last? Really smiled? Not merely lifted the corners of her lips to appear polite? She closed her eyes, unable to remember.

Schooling her features into the proper vacant, pleasant expression Frances wore so often she no longer thought of it as a mask, she shook her head slowly. "No, my lord husband, I would not wish for something so dishonorable. I was clear, I think, in my words. I would like," she looked down at the smooth parchment before her, "a separation based on the mutual agreement that both our duties have been fulfilled in regard to our marriage contract wherein you and I both acknowledge that no further conjugal relations would be required." She looked up again. "Divorce would make our children bastards and, I should think, you would find that abhorrent."

Frances waited, her gloved fingers absently tracing the beads of the rosary at her belt. It was up to him now. Yes, legally he could divorce her for denying him marital rights, but he wouldn't. Would he? In their ten years of marriage he had sired five children, three living. Given his obsession with duty, he should recognize the validity of her argument. His duty, and hers, was done. Both their parents had seen the match as advantageous. He came with property, and she came with connections of consequence. She had never expected anything different and made no argument. Neither had he. They were practically strangers then, and, thanks to his constant business in London, still were.

Why would he possibly want to continue the relationship any more than he had to? He'd never professed any affection, never spoken to her about anything other than household accounts and the like. There was no way she had broken his heart. Why the hesitation?

Looking at the fierce blaze in his deep brown eyes, she had her answer.

Pride.

Frances, not for the first time in her life, knew she had a battle before her to get what she wanted. It might be more fulfilling if she really wanted it, if she actually *wanted* anything. That wasn't true—she wanted many things. She wanted to have five living children. She wanted to forget each small coffin. She wanted to *want* to wake every morning. She was lucky Mother had arrived at her home when she did. Frances had allowed herself to fall into a deep melancholy, so far gone that it had no longer been a matter of choice. She'd lost the will to wake up, to eat, to be a mother. The guilt of the memories threatened to sink her down into that darkness again.

She sat up straight, refusing to go back to that place where no longer existing seemed like a good option.

Thank God for her mother, if not for her own sake, for her children. Her living children. And the choice to leave the countryside, it had to be only for good. At home she was part of the furniture. She no longer had any identity other than approving the menu and the linens when, in truth, the household full of servants would function, had functioned, fine without her.

And as a mother, well, she had failed. She hadn't been able to keep her baby alive, and you couldn't fail any worse than that. Her living children had grown to depend on their nurses during her... illness. They didn't need her, and she needed to be away from the constant reminder of how close she'd come to giving up.

Henry sat there, the pulse at his jaw thrumming, and Frances straightened the thumb of her worn glove. She would wait until he had something to say. It wasn't as if she had anything to lose.

Hours or seconds passed before he looked away. He stood and crossed the small room that served as his lodging when Parliament was in session. He threw open the shutters and harsh sunlight blasted through the room. Frances winced, closing her eyes to the assault, and continued to exercise patience. If this was where he chose to spend almost all his year, his aversion to home must be strong indeed. Parliament wasn't in session year round, yet he only returned home at the end of each quarter and for special events. She felt honored the birth of the twins a few months ago had warranted his attention.

Finally, *finally*, Henry walked back toward her and, laying both fists down on the polished desk surface asked, "What else is on your list?"

She covered the paper with her hands. "I would rather we come to a conclusion on the first point before I address the rest."

"By all means, then, let us stick to your schedule." He paced the length of the desk, dragging his fingertips over the spines of books scattered in the far corner. They looked like legal tomes, and Frances couldn't help but be impressed. She hadn't known he could read well at all. So much she didn't know—then again, he was rarely home.

He toed the hem of her dark skirts out of his way as he stood before her, the flare of his breeches almost touching the parchment on her lap.

"Before I tell you my answer, I wish to know why."

"Why?"

"Why you seek a separation." He leaned closer, the point of his waxed beard too close for her comfort. "Have I mistreated you in some way? What would make a woman dishonor her vows?"

"Nay, my lord husband. You have always done your *duty*," the word tasted sour on her tongue, "by me. As I have by you. We have been wed for ten years…"

"Yes, ten years during which I have met all my familial obligations. You and the children are kept in comfort and with all the prestige due our station. What makes you ill content with your lot?"

"I do not complain of your treatment," she began, mentally slapping herself when she began to chew her cheek. Yet again she schooled her face to a proper calm and straightened her shoulders.

A lady always treats her husband with all due respect.

A lady bears her responsibility with grace and dignity.

A lady does not panic at the mere thought of her husband touching her. Using her body. And a lady definitely does not tell him, face to face, that she wishes for separation. Again, she questioned herself. Why not just go on as it had been? He was hardly at home anyway. But then, when he was home… She shivered. No, he would not touch her again, and she wanted his promise. And she wanted the freedom to set up her own household if she saw fit. Maybe there she would feel needed.

"I have to wonder, my lady wife, why *now* you chose to make me privy to your disgust. Mayhap you have found another man you desire more. Tell me, Frances." When had he last used her Christian name? "Tell me, wife, am I a cuckold?"

"Nay!" She stood, unable to wipe the outrage from her face. "I would not dishonor you so."

He reached out, cupping her jaw in his hands. For an eternity his eyes locked with hers, the scent of spiced wine on his breath fanning her lips as he studied her face. When had he grown so tall? The boy she'd married had been barely a knuckle taller than she. This man seemed so different from the man she brought to mind when she thought of her husband.

The chill of the morning seeped into her skin as soon has he released her but did nothing to slow the frantic pace of her heart.

"If it is not for another man, why do this? Why not continue as we have been? What does a separation give you that you do not already have?"

She reached for the mask of calm and found it missing. With a sigh, she squeezed her eyes shut against the world. For a moment all she could feel was the darkness waiting for her, the darkness that she'd welcomed over these past months.

"I will not, I cannot," she stumbled over her words, still striving for the pleasant façade, "suffer your touch again. I do not think I can smile and do my duty as you use my body to fulfill your obligation to our marriage. I know I cannot wait out another pregnancy always in fear that this babe may not survive." She stopped to draw a shuddering breath. "I need this separation, if I wish…" She pursed her lips, well aware that her words would be thought melodramatic, if not straight out choleric. "If I wish to survive. It is all I can do to choose life now for the sake of my children. Do not make me mourn another child."

Could he feel the silence hammering around them both? Did the sunlight burn his eyes like it did hers? Did he see the depth of her desperation? Or did he only feel the slap to his pride because his needs outranked hers by privilege of being a man?

Frances LeSieur straightened to her full five foot five and met his stare. Divorcing her would only hurt the children and she dared him to be that cruel.

He let out a haggard breath and slumped against the front of his desk. "This last birth was hard on you."

"The obvious is always so profound," she blurted before she could stop herself. *By the saints, what would my mother say?*

His mustache quirked at one corner, the hint of a surprised smile more visible in his eyes than on his mouth.

"What I meant, my lord husband, is yes, birthing twins was difficult. And though I know that it is the will of God, I cannot help but grieve that only one survived." *There, that was more appropriate.*

"I, too, am sad at the loss of the babe."

"Her name was Maria." She held out a folded parchment.

He started, perhaps, at the harshness of her voice, and took the paper from her. Unfolding it he blinked at the image; a single inked footprint, hardly larger than the pad of her thumb. "Maria," he repeated and ran his fingers over the page. "It is hard to suffer the loss of a child, even for the father."

"And yet you did not return to Holme LeSieur to attend the burial. You have not come home to bless and greet the twin that survived, your daughter, Grace. She has now reached four months of age." It was a blessing the babe had thrived despite Frances's inability to mother in any way. Even if she had been able to nurse, she'd been too lost in melancholy to give the sweet babe the attention she needed. Thank God for her mother's good sense.

"My duties here have kept me…"

"Duty!" she spat. "The word makes me sick. I knew I should not have come, that it would be no good." This time she didn't even try for ladylike poise. She no longer cared. "I have been proud to be your duty, to bear your children, but I am the one who has had to bury them. Each time you touch me I will myself to accept you, to do my duty in turn, but no more. I wish your consent for a separation. You lose nothing in this arrangement. You cannot pretend love for me or your family."

"Do not presume to know me, madam."

"I do not make any such presumption, husband. What objections do you have to my request other than damage to your pride?"

"In truth?" he asked, for a moment looking more like the boy she married ten years ago than the man of twenty-five standing before her. His dark eyes, so brown they were almost black, bore into hers for a moment before glancing away. She still made him uncomfortable. That would be a sad fact if he hadn't made her feel obsolete. She wondered, if she could see his lips clearly past his shaped mustache, if he would be worrying them as he had during their vows. He was still comely, although the pretty boyishness that had given her such hope at their betrothal was gone. The hard lines of his face, the breadth of his jaw beneath the dark beard broad and firm, made her question if she had the strength to go up against him. She wondered if his hair was clipped short beneath his hat or unruly and thick. She sighed to herself, reminded by his renewed stare, no longer awkward or boyish, that none of it mattered. The look in his eyes now made *her* uncomfortable as he finally answered, "In truth, I cannot say why."

Silence hung thinner this time, less oppressive.

"I can promise that I will not cuckold you." She handed the parchment to him. "My only wish is to remain unmolested, as you see."

"And you require credit in London?" he asked, looking up from her list, brows raised.

"Aye. Mother has assured me of Her Majesty's welcome at the palace and the honor of serving as a lady of the bedchamber."

He blinked in surprise. "But you have never been at court before and will not know the way of it. It would have been an honor to the consequence of our family name for you to simply to be accepted as a guest of the Queen, allowed to be present in Her privy chamber, witness to Her entertainments. But a lady of the bedchamber, that is a position of trust; you will be one of the few closest to the Queen's person, welcome on the level of a dear friend. I know your mother is a long time friend and confidant…"

"And I have been invited upon my lady mother's recommendation," Frances interrupted, wondering at his hesitation over this. Surely he should be, if anything, proud.

He nodded. "That says much for her own standing. Bearing the title of countess is all but irrelevant when it comes to the favor of the Queen."

"Aye, and is a responsibility for me to be beyond reproach."

"That is what I am trying to explain. The behavior at court is all about diversion and entertainment. To many that involves…" He paused. That awkward look was back and, yes, he worried his lip.

"What is it that I should know before going to court?" she asked, intrigued now.

He sighed and ran a hand over his face. "The morals at court are not what you would expect."

"But the Queen expects her ladies to be above reproach…"

"Yes, and they all pretend they are. But, married or maid, there is a game at court that goes far beyond courtly flirtation. That is part of the entertainment some find as guests of the Queen. They just have to be slightly less than obvious about it."

She squared her shoulders and lifted her chin, intrigued by this new challenge. "I promised I will not cuckold you and I will maintain that, but that is not my purpose for coming to London and I refuse to let it deter me." Besides, how much did it matter? The men could flirt all they wanted. Her consent was never going to happen. "Being accepted to the Queen's entourage is an honor."

"Aye, and many women in your place would fight for it. I want you to be cautious."

"Of course," she confirmed and then cleared her throat. "Given what you have said about court, should I expect to meet any of your," she waved her hand, uncertain what word to choose and why she would care, "entertainments?"

He shook his head sharply and blinked. "What? My..." He took off his hat and smoothed his hair, thick and long enough to be secured at the back of his neck. "I do not seek my pleasure at court, if that is what you are asking. I am rarely there."

Then where are you? She couldn't bring herself to ask. She'd already decided she no longer cared.

She clasped her hands before her once more, serene. "I intend to make the most of my time at court to..." *To heal, to find meaning, to stop grieving.* "Broaden my scope." She wasn't sure what would happen, just that she wouldn't be surrounded by the same brick walls that had been her constant scenery for that past ten years. "I need change. I need something to look forward to. A reason to wake up." She raised her gaze to his, surprised to find her eyes brimming. She thought she'd run out of tears months ago.

"And despite the favorite pastime of bored courtiers, you say you do not wish to take a lover while in London." Whatever the thought did to her face made Henry laugh and ask, "Is the thought so disgusting to you?"

She shrugged as much as her corset would allow. "I have always known that the sexual act is one of my obligations as wife. Why would I pursue it for myself? It is something that I have never enjoyed."

It was Henry's turn to wince. "You never complained," he began, then shook his head. "But you would not, would you?"

Frances found her composure coming back and welcomed it like an old friend. "A lady understands her lot."

"And you have ever been the lady." He looked back at her list. "I will provide you with a seal of credit for whatever spending you see fit within London during your time with Queen Elizabeth. How long will you be in town?"

"Through the autumn. I should leave before the frost if I wish to return to Nottinghamshire before Christ's mass."

"So you do wish to return to Holme LeSieur?"

"Aye." She turned her face to the ceiling as her eyes began to brim once more. "I would not abandon our children to be raised by nurses indefinitely. You are approving the separation, then?"

Handing back the parchment, he answered, "I will not divorce you."

The pressure in the room lightened and Frances released her breath.

. . .

Henry studied his wife, surprised. For the first time since before their marriage he saw a hint of the passionate girl he'd agreed to marry. She'd done what she was told, obeyed her mother as a child her age should, but he could see the beginning of rebellion in the way she demurred with just a touch of impudence. But she'd never grown saucy with him. Not at all. She was exactly as a wife should be. She wasn't intimidated by her mother, one of the most powerful women in England, but she was wary of him. He'd convinced himself that the fire he remembered from their interactions prior to betrothal was a false memory. Either that or the act of marriage, of becoming a wife, had crushed her spirit. Until today this woman had consistently played the role of wife with docility. No spirit. No opinions or interest—nothing but duty.

This was different and, oddly, exhilarating. These demands flummoxed him, and he had an unsteady feeling he'd been there before. Felt like this…yes, on the day of their wedding. He'd been a child, fifteen. Skinny, awkward, hardly knowing his arse from his hat. Still, he did his duty and wed and bed pretty fourteen-year-old Frances Spencer. He'd liked her, loved how she never quite did exactly as was told. That impetuous spirit had made him look forward to the conjugal adventures to come. But when it came down to it, Henry thanked God he'd been able to perform at all. She'd been so lovely and so…womanly. He'd just had to tell himself that he was her husband now and rightful master. Somehow they'd gotten through it, but even now, thinking of it made him queasy. She hadn't cried, hadn't complained—just lain there with that damned pleasant expression pasted on her face. He may not have emerged from that bed feeling like a man, but he had become the legal master of his estate and, thus, duty done.

The Frances who stood before him now scared and fascinated him almost as much as his young bride. There was no reason for it—he no longer doubted himself. His service to the Crown, his service to the good people of Nottinghamshire, hell, even his service to his wife was commendable. He'd never let anyone down.

So why did he feel like his wife had just accused him of rape?

In the eyes of the law and the church, he had every right to divorce her. No one would fault him. Still, the fear and hope hiding behind her forced poise made him wonder.

"Frances…" he started, reaching to her once more.

She winced and stepped back, knocking over the bench behind her. "I simply need your yea or nay on my request."

He paused, stunned. Did she truly think him a monster? This could not stand. He cleared his throat and relaxed his posture. As unthreateningly as possible, he stepped closer and took her hand. He could feel the chill in her fingers even through the fine leather of her gloves.

His voice soft, he asked, "And if I say nay?"

She blinked, the copper tips of her lashes catching the late summer sunlight in a flash. She drew in her bottom lip, worrying at it with her teeth for an unguarded moment before she answered, "I shall have to rethink."

"Will you return to the Holme?"

Frances closed her eyes and let out a breath before raising her chin, her mouth firming into a tight line once more as if she reminded herself to be angry. She pulled her hand from his. "I will not. Not yet."

"I see."

Henry circled once more around the desk, irrationally hurt by the way her shoulders sagged in relief the moment he stepped out of her space. He pulled a sheet of parchment from the sheaf and inked his quill. The short missive, coupled with his wax seal, would serve.

"This gives you the LeSieur line of credit. I am certain you will need some more appropriate gowns if you wish to serve among the Queen's ladies."

"You are granting my request then?"

"No. Not yet."

"But…"

"You may remain in London as planned, but I will not grant you the separation at this time." He handed her the rolled parchment. "I want to understand my role in this better before I make a decision. Perhaps, I wish to redeem myself in your eyes."

"I do not see why. I am only one of your obligations. You do not desire me." Her statement held sure surety Henry couldn't help but argue.

"Do I not, madam?" Did he? Up until now he really had not desired her. She made the thought unpleasant. But this Frances, the one challenging him, was different. "Mayhap I hold you in high esteem." Which, of course, he always had. She filled her role at the manor excellently.

"Do not mock me, husband. I do not expect nor want your esteem or your love."

Love? Where had that come from? "Love is a strong word. Stronger, I fear, than the emotion that lies behind it." He'd heard courtiers play at courtly love for years and it never meant more than a tumble in a closet.

The fullness of Frances's lips curving into a smile but her eyes remained weary. "Love. We wed too young. It is known that boys do not love until they are mature."

"I am mature now," he baited, not sure why he would want to defend his potential for love. Love caused all sorts of mayhem and general stupidity.

"Of course you are, but does love ever keep you from eating or sleeping? Give your heart palpitations? I think not. Not courtly love. Not for me, at least."

The courtier in him felt like he should protest, but integrity won. "You would not wish my love. You have already told me so." The stated truth, simple and painful, felt more intimate than anything they had shared over the duration of their marriage.

"To what end?" she asked. "If love means sexual congress, I do not want any man's love. With it comes the expectation of some reciprocity, and, as I said…"

He interrupted, "You wish to remain unmolested."

"Just so."

In that moment he felt a connection with her he couldn't explain. They'd had longer conversations over crops, linens, and their son's path to Eton, but this reached deeper. He felt as if he looked upon a stranger but recognized, in the spark in her eyes, the potential for more. Maybe court would be good for her, give her an outlet to be witty or rude or whatever caught her fancy. It might even give him a better idea of who she was really. And that might lead to something new between them.

Friends? Clearly not lovers.

Molest—what sort of word was that to describe the act of love?

She still had the full lips of the girl he'd married. In fact, she was almost exactly like she'd been on their wedding day when the severe fashions of Queen Mary still lingered even past Her death. No fashionable lady at Queen Elizabeth's court covered her head so completely with the French hood and veil any longer, adopting a look with more hair, less hat. When was the last time he'd seen Frances's hair uncovered? Was it gold still or had it darkened with the years? It was hard to tell with only the slicked part at her crown visible. Her features were pleasing, but she would be eaten alive by the ladies at Court. She had the stamp of the country on her, as she should. Her duty was to the family and the estate back home.

But now she was in London. Her illness after the birth of the twins, and the loss, had changed something in her. He'd never seen her be anything less than pleasant, courteous, and calm. The consummate lady…and bland as boiled beef. Yet today's interview, well, Henry didn't know what to think. She swayed between poise, vitriol, and absolute dejection. What was a man supposed to do in these cases? The threat of tears was his undoing, though he couldn't begin to fathom her reasoning. Melancholia, as he knew it, was so far from Frances's character that he could not purport it.

The bell chimed two, calling Henry and the other members of Parliament back to the commons.

He held out his hand expectantly, and his wife, with only a little hesitation, offered hers. Leaning over her hand, politely not placing his lips on her gloved knuckles, he looked up to find her studying him, her cheeks flushed with color. A blush? It was so lovely and girlish, a sweet flush over her expression of consternation. After the shock of this meeting, the dichotomy of the two made him want to laugh. Made him want to affect her the way she affected him.

"Lady wife, this interview is not done. Take your position at court, but expect me to attend you there. You will need a friend, and I hope to show you that I can be something more than the man you think me to be."

"I do not know what you hope to…"

She gasped as he pulled her close, the proper buttons of her modest dress pressing against his chest, her skirts belling back.

"I hope to learn more about the woman I married before I agree to leave her," he leaned in, whispering against her cheek, "unmolested."

He wasn't sure if it was his injured pride that propelled him forward or the challenge. Certainly, she had emasculated him. He needed a chance to prove she was wrong. He would no longer be the awkward bridegroom with her, they both deserved that much. And he could start right now by showing her the man he'd become.

"Why?" she asked, her back turned rigid under his hand. Only the quaver of her voice gave away her discomfort. At least she no longer had that calm mask. He hoped he never saw it again.

"Because if my wife has learned the act of love is distasteful, then I have been a poor husband indeed."

"You have done all you ought and should welcome the knowledge that your duty is done." Her brow relaxed, and her mouth turned up in the pleasant half smile he now knew to be false.

He pulled her closer, and she bit her lip.

"My lady wife, I am nowhere near to done." He leaned close enough for a kiss; her breath fanned his beard. "I have much to learn and have not even begun. This is not over."

Chapter Two

Rule Eight: Only the most urgent circumstances should deprive one of love.

"What did he say?" Mary and Jane, Frances's ladies, spoke in unison.

She silenced them with a tired glance.

"Thank you, Master Rigsby. Drive onward to Hampton Court."

"Aye, Mistress LeSieur." With a click, the carriage door shut out the noise of the dirty street outside.

She closed her eyes against the dim light of the enclosed space. Six days ago they'd left Holme LeSieur in Nottinghamshire. She'd pushed her driver, her ladies, the horses, even herself, as if the faster she arrived in London and confronted her husband the sooner all this would be over. She let out a sigh as her head fell back against the squabs. This was nowhere near finished. If anything, she had made her life more complicated.

"Frances?" Mary's voice broke through the pounding in her ears.

Mary Montgomery, tall and dark, grasped hands with Jane Radclyffe, petite with a head of golden curls that would not stay confined under her proper French hood.

"You were right, as ever, Mary," Frances answered the unasked question. "He did not greet my suggestion kindly."

Jane leaned forward, placing her hand over Frances's. "Nor did you expect him to. If this is what you want, you must be prepared to fight for it."

She had no response, no words of solace for her ladies. Should her husband choose to put her out, where would Jane and Mary go? They must be as anxious as she.

"It is not a complete loss. He approved credit for my stay in London. He…" She paused, uncertain. "He seemed different somehow. Older. Larger. Something."

"Mayhap you are not familiar with the man he is in London," Mary offered with a nervous smile.

"Aye." Frances worried her lip with her teeth. She'd been so sure of how this would play out, but now… *What had she done?* At home, at least, she knew what was expected. Here…well that was the point, wasn't it? As lady of the manor she was almost part of the building. Here she would have a chance to be herself. Whoever that was.

Just as the rutted road smoothed to cobbles, the driver called the horses to a halt. A rap at the door was all the warning she had before being greeted by one of Hampton Court Palace's liveried footman.

Too tired to school her posture and expression into the norm, she let herself be dragged out and joined the current of people flowing through the palace. Too late to turn back now.

• • •

"The steward is busy, but he gave me direction to our rooms." Mary joined her once more after attending to the steward. "Your Lady Mother sent a courier ahead, and we have been provided for. If you will follow me, Frances? Jane? They are waiting for us in the gallery." Mary did not wait for an answer as she worked her way through the chaos of the main hall.

The constant motion and noise throughout the palace, even without the Queen in residence, made Frances long for the quiet of the country as she followed Mary's sure step. "You know the palace very well."

Mary nodded. "Oh yes, I was companion to Mistress Ann Cecil—"

Jane interrupted, "Oh, is she not the Countess of Oxford?" Jane's feigned awe of a fact Mary must have repeated a thousand times made Frances giggle.

Mary rolled her eyes, and Frances took up the reins. "Oh, and were you not at Hampton Court often? Sometimes with the Queen, Herself, or so I have heard."

Mary turned to face them, the smiling curve to her eyes belying the stern set of her mouth. "Fine. I suppose I have spoken of it before."

"A little," Frances agreed. "Lead on, Mistress Mary. I hope your knowledge of court will help ease our paths. If Lady Oxford is with the court, I should like to meet her."

Mary's face blanched, and the shine left her eye. "Oh, yes. Perhaps." She turned and led them down the corridor without another word until she stopped before a broad oak door. "Here we are."

The palace was like a world unto itself—Frances prayed for the fortitude to follow through in this busy place. Her husband's reluctant acceptance of her presence in London demanded that she find success. As much as she feared she'd issued him a challenge, she had one to meet as well: all she had to do was learn, well, everything.

• • •

Michaelmas had come and gone, and the palace, sparkling and full of fresh flowers, waited in a hush of anticipation. The Queen was past due and could arrive at any time. Frances, even after a fortnight, still was unused to so many people, so much bustle of activity. She groomed herself at the basin in her room and donned her best woad blue linen kirtle and umber-toned surcoat.

She checked her reflection in the glass, smoothed her slicked hair down from the center part, and secured the length of it into a caul, and pinned her French hood in place. Her face looked a little wan, so she dabbed on a bit of her all-purpose rouge and left her chamber to await the court's arrival in Henry VIII's great hall.

Frances could scarcely believe that this hub of activity and finely dressed people was the same palace she'd grown to understand in her weeks here. She looked around in amazement at the crowd of courtiers vying for attention. Somewhere beyond the crush of people the Queen, God's anointed monarch, greeted Her court. Frances did her best to calm her pounding pulse and draw a breath. The Queen, here, in the same room. She hadn't anticipated how thrilling, how overwhelming, it would be.

Standing on tiptoes, she did her best to peer through the gaps between the well-dressed courtiers only to have that view blocked by some woman's ostentatious plumage. Still trying to catch a glimpse of the Queen, Frances felt herself being pushed farther back and back to the perimeter of the room as more courtiers made room for themselves. What was she thinking to be here at court? She belonged in the country. How could she hold her own against these sparkling, and pushy, members of Her Majesty's court? This was no place for her. Flattening herself against the wall, Frances realized the immense tapestry of Abraham and Isaac partially obscured an alcove. With a sigh of relief and a little disappointment, she escaped from the crowded hall into the safe little haven.

"You're Bess's girl, yes?" The voice behind her startled a yelp out of her. Frances turned mutely to look at the speaker. An elegant woman sat calmly on a small bench. It seemed Frances had disturbed her hiding spot. "I suppose I should say 'The Countess of Spencer,' to give her rank due consequence," the older woman continued, "but I dare say she will always be Bess to me." The woman finished her statement with a sweet smile that crinkled the corners of her eyes and shone through their blue depths with genuine warmth. Disarmed by the woman's kindness and evident age, Frances was not prepared when the stranger leapt to her feet, produced a handkerchief from her sleeve, moistened it with spittle, and attacked her cheeks with unexpected strength. By the time Frances had the wherewithal to pull away, the woman was satisfied with whatever she had just done and sat down again.

"Better, but not much."

"My lady, I do not wish to be rude... Who are you? What did you do to me?" began Frances shakily with both hands on her cheeks. "And why would you do such a thing?" She hadn't decided yet if she should be affronted or see humor in the situation.

The older woman let out an infectious, merry laugh. She was probably approaching sixty, but she had the eyes and rosy cheeks of a younger woman. Her steel gray hair rose over a hairpiece that made the twist stand at least three inches from her forehead. Her black silk attifet and veil were somber, but the thick jet and hematite beading covering the entire black velvet surcoat belied the simplicity. The wealth on display before her announced that this woman was higher rank. Frances glanced down at her own less than impressive appearance and grimaced.

"I do beg your pardon, Mistress LeSieur. Your mother alerted me as to your arrival. I only just arrived myself—otherwise, I would have sought you out sooner and prepared you for court already." The older woman continued, "I am Mistress Blanche Parry. I have been in service to Queen Elizabeth since the day Queen Anne of blessed memory laid the baby princess Elizabeth in Her cradle. Then I was simply a nursemaid, a servant in truth. Now I serve out of love in Her entourage with more prestige than any titled courtier, though I hold no rank. I am here at the Queen's behest, much like you. I promised your mother that I would see to you, and so I shall. But first we must fortify ourselves to greet our Sovereign Monarch."

Frances looked out into the hall through the gap between tapestries. Sure enough, the increased clamor signaled something was definitely happening in the outer courtyard. As she turned back to ask a question, Mistress Parry held up a staying hand.

"First you must promise me that when you return to your rooms tonight you will request a bath. The Queen has set the fashion and the noble ladies are bathing at least once a month, whether they need to or not." Frances stared with shock. "You will have your hair washed and brushed and set to curl, and tomorrow I will help you begin your transformation. Oh, and never wear that horrid rouge again," Mistress Parry finished with a grimace.

Frances, flustered, merely repeated, "A bath?" She'd just bathed at the ewer in her room. Did that not suffice? The thought of requiring such a labor from the servants embarrassed her. She was too low for such a luxury.

"Aye. It will be a wondrous way to start anew. And I do not mean a hipbath in your chemise, I want you to take a full bath. Do not gripe about it being unnecessary," she waved away Frances's look of protest, "or unhealthy. Queen Elizabeth Herself bathes at least once a month." She nodded as if any argument had been preemptively addressed. "We shall work from the outside in. And your hair could use a good washing. It looks almost as if it's carved marble on your head. Egg whites?"

Frances nodded and added, "Whipped with beeswax."

"Hmph." Mistress Parry rose swiftly and made her way to the throne at the opposite end of the room to await the Queen.

Frances sat in the alcove for the rest of the evening. Too intimidated to venture out and, now, too self-conscious of her appearance to be seen, Frances stifled her excitement at the prospect of seeing the Queen and thanked God that the few courtiers who noticed paid no attention to the spineless woman within the alcove. After a lifetime that was only an hour or so, the

Queen retired to her privy chamber and most of the court either accompanied her or dispersed.

Frances, stealthy as could be, made her way back to her room. She wasn't surprised to find Jane and Mary there waiting.

Jane rushed to her, laying a well-meaning hand on her forehead. "Where have you been all evening?"

"Hiding."

When Mary raised a brow in question, Frances shook her head. "I'll explain later. For now, do you have any idea how I should go about having a bath?"

Chapter Three

Rule Fourteen: The value of love is commensurate with its difficulty of attainment.

What little dust the servants missed began to settle around Hampton Court. The newly returned Queen and Her court acclimated to the palace while all the staff and retainers settled in to their resumed roles. Henry LeSieur's duties to his constituency brought him back to London earlier than the rest of the court.

Henry adapted to court life long ago and was a sophisticated courtier in spite of his meager rank and country manor. Though the LeSieurs were not titled nobles, they were wealthy, and Henry dressed as befitted his wealth, if not his status. To succeed in the court of Queen Elizabeth one had to impress on all counts. As he surveyed his choppy reflection in a paned glass window, he wondered what his wife thought of his London appearance. He made a sour face at his image. Would the intimidating stare that worked so well to see through deceit translate well into wooing his wife?

Probably not.

That thought alone led to his decision to shave off the beard and mustache. He needed to be approachable, amiable. He should take a page from the Queen's favorites and strive to be merry and seductive. Or maybe he should just smile more.

Flashing a smile at his reflection, Henry did his best to look charming. His smile seemed too boyish and usually undermined his goal to intimidate so much that he'd trained himself against it. *Time to change that image.* His long face and firm jaw finished off with a dimpled chin, which, until this morning, had stayed hidden under his beard. He was not used to his clean-shaven appearance, but it set him apart from most of the other men at court. Perhaps a visual change would be all that it took to make his wife take notice.

Henry wondered, not for the first time, why he wanted her attention at all. No good answer came to him.

Still smiling at himself in the glass, he noticed someone standing on the other side. A woman. She preened for him as if he had been flirting. At least she didn't realize she'd caught him in a self-absorbed moment admiring his own reflection. Smiling sincerely now, he removed his hat and offered the lady a reverance, leaning back on his right leg and extending the left into a point as he lowered himself in a show of courtly respect. She reveranced in turn and then scampered back to join a cluster of giggling girls. Based on her age and style of dress, he guessed she was probably one of the Queen's maids of honor. She was young and innocent; not likely to assume his perceived attentions implied anything other than a courtly flirtation—not that he wasted time with that nonsense.

A reflection appeared just over his shoulder. Master Kit Hatton, captain of the Queen's Guard and one of Her favorites. He nodded at the comely wench giggling to her friends on the other side of the glass. "That explains why you shaved your cheeks. You look like a boy, presumably to attract the young girls surrounding Her Majesty. Now that would be courting the Queen's ire."

"Worry not," Henry replied, grasping Hatton's offered hand, "I'll leave that job to you."

"I am sure I will not let you down, though I cannot foresee when and where." He rubbed his own chin, the waxed hair fair and sparse; it was more a lad's scruff than a man's beard. "A clean chin might be a good change for me. Her Majesty may approve of the boyish appeal." He turned back to watch the young ladies on the other side of the glass and laughed. "You surprise me, Master LeSieur. You usually do not do your hunting at court."

"You assume that I hunt at all," Henry replied, then gestured to the group of girls with a tilt of his head. "My wife has come to court, and I thought I would see how she fares."

"You have a wife?" Hatton's shock reflected back at them both. "I had no idea. How long have you been wed?"

He nodded. "For the past ten years."

"Ten… You must have been a child." When Henry nodded, Hatton continued, "Why have you kept her a secret?"

"She is not a secret at all. There has never been any cause for her to come to court and no reason to discuss her. At least, not with you," Henry responded, irked that he had to talk about her even now. Why? It wasn't that she embarrassed him. No, it was more that he embarrassed himself. At five and twenty he should at least be man enough to face the woman who'd scared him so at fifteen. Surely they had both changed enough to move in the same social circles with civil regard for each other, like other married courtiers. That he wanted more than that astonished him. Perhaps it wasn't only pride that inspired him to woo her.

"Well, it must take a very dull woman to be content with you. Then again, if she came to court, she may have some fire."

Henry met his eyes in the glass. "Do not think to slur my wife. In fact, do not contemplate my wife at all."

"Strike a nerve, did I? My apologies." The suppressed laughter clear on his face belied his words. "If she has been happy wherever you have been keeping her, why come to court now?"

"I will not discuss this with you. My wife is off-limits, understood?"

Hatton clapped him on the shoulder, spinning him about. Now face to face, Hatton blanched and stepped back at whatever he saw in Henry's eyes.

"Why is that, I wonder?" Hatton continued, too arrogant to back down despite the fear in his eyes. "Do you not trust your wife to make her own choices? Is she so innocent that she will fall into the arms of any man who plies her with courtly love? Do you not trust her fidelity? I have never known you to dally and assumed you were simply too pious for it."

Henry thought the whole thing would end quickly if he just punched the man in the throat. *So tempting.* He smiled at the thought, but that just made Hatton bristle.

"Do you mock me, sirrah?"

"Nay, Master Hatton. You forget that you are the one mocking me. I am merely exercising patience and being above it."

"Are you, in truth? Or did I detect some flare of passion when I asked about fidelity? Do you not worry at all, then? Court is different from the country."

"I well know it," he answered, scanning the bustling gardens around them. How many rumor mongers had one ear open on their conversation? "And no, I have no doubts about my wife's virtue. She has come to court, yes, but I guarantee she will offer no one," not even her own husband, if she had her way, "sport." Henry turned out his leg in a reverance. "I give you good den, Master Hatton."

"Ten pounds says you will find yourself a cuckold afore Christmastide."

"Sirrah, you overstep yourself." The leather of Henry's gloves creaked against his tight fists.

"Nay, Master LeSieur, you set down the challenge."

"I merely informed you of her character. You impugn your own in this wager."

"Do I? I saw it as more of a direct insult to your," he paused, his smile anything but friendly, "prowess?"

To think, until now he'd only thought of Master Kit Hatton as frivolous. As Captain of the Guard, Hatton must know of Henry's service to Walsingham and his role in uncovering the Catholic conspiracy to assassinate the Queen. Henry might be quiet and respectable, but Hatton knew enough to realize he was playing a dangerous game here. The man must simply be stupid.

"Why do you bait me?" Henry asked, his tone soft. "Do you wish for me to call you out?"

"Would you really?" This time Hatton's smile was genuine, his teeth too white behind the dark gold of his beard.

What is he about?

"Make way for Her Majesty Queen Elizabeth Glorianna!" a herald announced from across the courtyard, and everyone jumped to attention, then promptly dropped to one knee.

Henry's hat over his heart, he held his head high as his Queen approached. A procession of guards and courtiers passed through the topiary arches and into the Queen's privy chamber beyond.

When he stood again, Hatton was gone.

Ten pounds—the price on his wife's virtue. Sad, really. How soon would half of court believe that he had wagered away the right to woo his wife?

Little Frances Chatsworth was in for some challenges at court. Henry wasn't sure if he should be amused or horrified.

Henry turned and dropped into a reverance as Mistress Parry surged toward him.

"Rise you up," she gestured for him to stand and looped her arm through his. "Walk with me."

"Is aught amiss, Mistress?" Henry had never seen the older woman so agitated.

She nodded. "As you know, your wife is here."

"I do."

"My dear friend Bess, the Countess of Spencer, asked me to watch after her, and I am doing so, but I worry."

So do I. "How so?"

"Her Majesty is just now receiving news from the French ambassador of a massacre of Huguenots in Paris."

Henry stopped, stunned. "Impossible."

"Nay, it has been confirmed. There are somewhere between hundreds and thousands dead—either way it is a great loss of life. I fear the English reaction will be to turn against those who hold to the Roman Catholic faith."

"My affiliation with the Catholic Church has proven a great service to England. My name should offer my wife protection."

"It does and does not."

He raised an eyebrow in question. How did Blanche Parry know of the highly secret mission? *That answer was easy—she knew everything.*

"Very few know of your service so will simply see Frances as a country mouse, a Papist one at that. Those that do know will not speak of it. And then there are those who know too much because they were on the wrong side of the last plot—but to say anything would implicate themselves. Still, there may be a price on your head."

The recent Ridolfi plot to marry the Duke of Norfolk to Mary, the Scots' Queen and overthrow Queen Elizabeth had been thwarted, resulting in extra work for the Tower guards and headsman. Francis Walsingham, the Queen's spymaster, made use of Henry, a known Roman Catholic. He inserted himself into the conspiracy and proved integral in unmasking the traitors. Families of those executed or imprisoned still held him accountable for their fates. Looking around the courtyard, he spied at least three who may wish him ill will.

"You think this poses a threat to my wife?"

"I know I have heard your name spoken in unkind whispers, and I think she needs to be informed about the risks involved in being at court. Those involved may assume she is aware of your antics and support your seeming betrayal of what they consider the "one true church." Her very presence, especially as naive as she is, may renew attention to you. Some think you a hero, some a heretic. Frances may be burdened with guilt by association, and those driven by faith are capable of more than I could imagine, all in the name of God. And then there are those who hold all Catholics accountable for the behavior of a few. I would not intervene, but speculation about the St. Bartholomew's day massacre is already whipping up a fervor of anti-Catholic sentiment. She needs to be aware. It is not my place to tell her all."

"Devil take it," he cursed. "If she had stayed at Holme LeSieur, none of this would ever touch her."

Mistress Parry laid a hand over his glove. "But she is here now. I can help her integrate into Queen Elizabeth's ladies, but you owe her an explanation. It's possible that understanding the reasons for your regular absences will help resolve whatever the conflict is between you two."

The clock chimed four and the few remaining courtiers cleared from the courtyard. Devil take it! Mistress Parry knew of his service to the Crown, so why could he not tell his own wife? Would that mend the rift between them? Not that there was ever a sense of connection to begin with. He sighed to himself and looked up to the heavens, finding no answer. He didn't even know Frances well enough to predict how she would react to the information. Was she a zealous adherent to the Roman Catholic faith? If so, she may find his work to undermine the Catholic plot against Queen Elizabeth abhorrent. That would make *her* the traitor, and that was something he didn't wish to know.

No, better not to tell her. Let her believe he was always away in London playing the courtier and filling his role in Parliament.

"Time to dress for dinner. I will be meeting with Frances and her ladies anon." Mistress Parry released his arm, and he gave her a reverance.

"I thank you for your concerns."

"Of course you do," she responded, raising a sarcastic brow. "Your wife may find herself up to her neck in the muck here. I can only do so much. Your help is not only a courtesy—it is the only honorable thing to do."

"As you say." He nodded, and Mistress Parry turned to leave.

Dropping down onto a stone bench, Henry crushed his hat in his hands. Character, honor, respect, duty—these were the things that mattered more than anything, and the simple appearance of his wife in London put every single one to the test.

God help him.

Chapter Four

Rule Eleven: A lover should not love anyone who would be an embarrassing marriage choice.

Frances had, naturally, been concerned about the possible ill effects of taking a bath—everyone knew that body oils helped protect a person against disease. But now, as she ran her fingers through her newly cleaned hair, she considered that perhaps that health measure was simply superstition. Her skin still held the rosy glow from aggressive toweling, her hair felt soft as a babe's, and Frances thought she looked healthier already. Not only did she enjoy the decadence of bathing, she definitely felt better, even if Mary and Jane thought three baths in one week excessive. She didn't even feel guilty about asking this of the servants, something she never would have done at Holme LeSieur. Then again, the Holme boasted, at most, fifteen full-time servants, and all of them had regular schedules she wouldn't dream of interrupting. The servants at Hampton Court Palace outnumbered them exponentially, and many of them were dedicated to see to the varied and sometimes ostentatious needs of the courtiers. Providing warm water was nothing compared to the rest.

Mistress Parry joined Frances in her room and spent the day chattering constantly as Mary saw to Frances's grooming. Frances listened dutifully to the discourse on courtly manners and expectations, whereas Mary seemed obviously uncomfortable and occupied herself by vigorously brushing out Frances's long dark-amber locks. Mistress Parry took her leave after instructing the two women to meet her in an hour in the garden outside the

Queen's privy chamber. Frances promised she would and struggled to figure out how to dress for the occasion.

"It is hard to believe that Queen Catherine of France would instigate such horrors!" began Mary, obviously still very upset about the news of the massacre in Paris. "The Huguenots were French subjects—even though they were heretics."

"No more heretical than our own Queen, so have a mind for your tongue," stated Frances, looking around quickly. It wouldn't do to be heard calling your Queen a heretic. Growing up, Frances's family had changed between Roman Catholic and Church of England with each change of regime. Church of England for King Henry VIII and King Edward VI, Roman Catholic for Queen Mary. Her marriage to Henry finalized her official religion as Roman Catholic, unless *he* chose to change. Although her mother switched back to Church of England with Queen Elizabeth. Frances had never suffered from the fact the LeSieurs were traditionally Roman Catholic—but then she'd lived her entire married life on her husband's lands. Being a Catholic at a Protestant court full of anti-Catholic sentiment in the aftermath of the St. Bartholomew massacre… Well, Frances would just to have to wait and see.

By the time the two ladies left their chambers to meet with Mistress Parry, Frances truly felt changed. Her brows tweezed into neat arcs and her hair clean, soft, and shining, framed Frances's face with a soft golden halo and accentuated the pale blue of her eyes. The apparent ease with which Mary had performed these miracles left Frances in awe. It seemed a shame to detract from her hair by wearing the muted surcoat, but court was in mourning, and the drab gown would be appropriate.

They found Mistress Parry sitting on a stone bench under the shade of a large myrtle topiary depicting something with wings. She gave them a quick once-over, then announced, "Gentlewomen, follow me." And, with that order, Blanche Parry was up and gliding down the central path of the courtyard garden, sweeping the two ladies in her wake. They crossed the cobblestone courtyard and through the arch into the great hall, skirting the tables and benches, and then through the south gate and the water stairs and a waiting ferry which took them downstream amidst a flutter of Tudor banners. From there, the three ladies were directed to an open carriage manned by four servants in Tudor livery. They were off with a jolt, and the next thing Frances knew, they were being navigated through the rutted and bustling streets of London.

• • •

Mary seemed to have an innate understanding of how court dress had evolved during her time at Holme LeSieur and had jumped back into the fray with gusto. And every word and deed from Blanche Parry gave Frances a sense of relief—it was evident both ladies were superior in the field of shopping and fashion. Her only agenda was to find a white dress with satin trim—she'd promised her six-year-old daughter, Elizabeth, before she'd left for London.

Frances stood like a statue upon a small raised dais in front of a multitude of mirrors while a heavyset, mustachioed man of Mediterranean descent carefully paired various fabrics in a variety of colors and wrapped them around her person. She wondered what her husband had expected when he told her to buy clothes for court. She felt an odd sense of vindication as they entered the next shop. She would be resplendent the next time he saw her; he may well fall on his knees in worship. Wait, did she want that? She shook her head, telling herself no.

From the draper and tailor shops along Threadneedle Street, the trio headed directly to the Royal Exchange. The Exchange was an enormous brick building that would have appeared palatial if not for the hoards of people flowing in and out of every entrance. The proprietor's attempts to overshadow the stench with the overpowering perfume of lavender and roses only worsened the mixture of strong odors made up from unwashed bodies in close confines, greasy smells of cooking meat from the kitchens, and the eye-burning residue from the dye vats that clung to the vast array of fabrics. Inside there were hundreds of merchants with permanent stalls displaying their wares. The Exchange was designed to be a year-round, indoor market fair where the ladies of court could shop from a variety of quality merchants at one stop.

The constant bustle and noise of the exchange gave Frances a new burst of energy. The patrons were both high-ranking nobles and their servants. The sounds of haggling mixed with laughter and shrieks of delight as happy, if frantic, shoppers made their way from stall to stall. The three ladies merged into the flow of the crowd to make purchases at various cobblers, milliners, goldsmiths, and jewelers.

By the time they finished their shopping extravaganza, Frances and Mary were eager to collapse onto the benches flanking the outer wall and excitedly reflect on their purchases with all the polish and restraint of schoolgirls. Mary, aside from what was set to be delivered, had procured two new pairs of ivory kid gloves and an enormous pearl brooch. Frances was not even sure of everything she had bought since most of it was to be delivered to her rooms at Hampton Court. She was so in love with her new royal blue ostrich feather fan that she chose to carry it with her for the rest of the trip and had only stopped toying with the ornate pewter handle and the mass of overlapping fine feathers when Mistress Parry handed her a steaming savory beef pie.

Once more the current swept Frances away, depositing her back to her apartment at the palace. Frances walked into her room and made to throw herself on the bed, but the merchants had been ridiculously efficient and there were already boxes stacked on every horizontal surface of the room. At the sound of Frances's borderline obscene exclamation, Mary came running in from the connecting gallery. With a corresponding exclamation of surprise, Mary joined Frances in sorting through boxes. Frances began trying to arrange the new acquisitions into her wardrobe while Mary gathered up what she could carry and made her way to the door that connected Frances's room to the room she shared with Jane.

"Oh, Frances!" Mary shrieked behind her, almost pitching Frances headfirst into her trunk. "You must see Jane. So much for being discreet…" Mary's words tapered off into a series of giggles as she grabbed for Frances's hand and dragged her across the floor to the door between their apartments.

Frances, caught up in Mary's unexplained silly excitement, started to ask, "What on earth…"

Her hand firmly over Frances's mouth, Mary hissed, "Shhhh! Look." She gestured to a sliver of light shining through the gap at the open door.

Against the warning of the mature voice of her conscience, she placed her eye beside the opening. At first she didn't know what she was seeing, but, as her vision focused, she made out an abundance of exposed flesh and limbs writhing on the window seat. Frances jumped back, straightened, and looked to Mary with what was supposed to be censure but probably came across more as confusion. Mary took her turn at the gap. It was obvious that Mary saw this as potential ammunition for future teasing. She gestured to the door again, and Frances stepped forward.

Jane sat entirely naked, reclined against the sill of an open window with an equally naked young, well-formed man kneeling before her. Frances guessed from the taut muscles of his backside and thighs that he must be an accomplished equestrian. She could not see his face clearly enough to identify him as he ran his lips over every inch of Jane's torso. His chestnut curls skimmed Jane's skin as he paid homage to her with his lips.

Frances was not terribly surprised Jane had taken a lover. She was, however, surprised at how the man's hands roamed over Jane's soft skin worshipfully and how Jane had thrown her head back in abandon as she sighed her pleasure at her lover's attentions to her exposed bosom.

Was this what other women experienced in the act of love?

Frances's skin tingled with imagined sensation as she watched the mystery man run his large rough hands up from Jane's ankles, over her knees, up her thighs and across her hips, to settle over her pubis and sink in between her legs, spreading them wide. Jane's every panting gasp echoed within Frances's own chest. The man knelt in adoration in front of Jane and lowered his head from kissing her breasts, to her belly, down to her abdomen, then disappeared between her thighs. Jane's small fingers snaked through his tousled hair, urging him on.

Frances could not believe what she was seeing, had no frame of reference to interpret their acts. She knew she should give them privacy but couldn't look away. The only lover's attention she had ever had was that of her husband mounting her prone body and uncomfortably, sometimes even painfully, spilling his seed inside her then bidding her goodnight. Unless she was already pregnant, she knew to expect the interaction every night he was home during his quarterly visits.

Jane, with a man she must hardly know, was worshiped as some sort of goddess. Frances heard Jane's gasping becoming more frequent until it seemed like the pleasure was too much. Frances felt a knot in her stomach and her face bloomed with heat while she watched Jane's expression go from agonized to beatific in a cry of unadulterated joy.

"What a fine man. Do you know who he is? No? Hung like a stallion. It isn't a wonder she was nowhere to be found when we were leaving to meet Mistress Parry." Mary continued, "I wonder if it is serious or just a dalliance? Knowing Jane, she will not regret a moment. At least someone is having fun." Mary did not appear abashed in the slightest over witnessing her friend's intimate encounter. "So much for being discreet—in the middle of the day, in front of an open window, and in our shared room!" Mary continued to babble, obviously excited by the prospect of torturing her friend. Frances saw the humor but had a hard time keeping up the mischief with that warm, wanting sensation in her belly. She couldn't help but wonder if his hands had been hot against Jane's skin or what it would feel like to be kissed *down there.*

• • •

It was only an hour or so after Frances and Mary had spied on their companion, but it seemed like a lifetime. Frances was questioning so much, feeling bereft, denied something she'd never known existed. Although common sense told her that she, married and established, was in a more enviable position, today she felt downright jealous of Jane.

Frances sat toward the back of the great hall while half of London crowded into the upper galleries to watch the Queen and Her court feast. Across the board from her sat a lonely looking woman introduced as Baroness Ludlow. Beside the Baroness sat a lovely young newlywed, Lady Howard of Effingham. Lady Howard emanated the essence of springtime, being all things sweet, delicate, and budding with life. Baroness Ludlow, however, reminded Frances of herself, if only slightly older and hardened. She was a no-nonsense woman who did not engage in the games of court. Frances felt a kinship with the baroness and hoped to meet with her on another occasion—she was simply too distracted this evening.

Mary, with a permanent smirk etched on her face, sat beside Frances and opposite Jane, delicately picking at her meal between sly knowing looks across the table. Frances glanced at Jane surreptitiously. Jane was enjoying her meal with a gusto to rival the

Queen Herself. She positively glowed. Frances noted the way her eyes sparkled with mischief, but mostly how relaxed she appeared, as if there was nothing to worry about in the world. Frances turned back to studying her plate. Tonight's meal, a sumptuous feast of roast swan stuffed with figs and drowned in a savory cream sauce, should have impressed her, but all Frances could do was push the food around her trencher with her knife. She wasn't upset, only bewildered at what she'd seen through the gap in the door. More than that, her own body's response to the imagery confused her.

Frances shook her head as if to wake herself up fully and tried, again, to stop thinking about it. Could there be pleasure between a man and woman? Was Jane the aberration, or was she?

She looked down at her plate with the intention of taking a bite when she noticed that her savory course had been replaced with sweetmeats. She had been so distracted by her reminiscing she hadn't paid any heed to the meal's progression—or, it seemed, to the conversation around her.

"…and the look on Lord Leicester's face when I mentioned casually that Baroness Sheffield's corset seemed to be straining at the lacings…" Lady Howard's cheery voice continued on a story she had been telling.

"You did not!" interjected a finely dressed lady who must have joined their table after Frances had disappeared into her own thoughts.

"Yes, I did. And then I said that it was a blessing Lord Sheffield had passed before he could see how fat his wife had become." Gasps and stifled laughter ensued all around the table. "But then my Lord Sussex called me away. I don't know why; everyone knows he doesn't care for Lord Leicester."

"But he does care for his retainers, and your husband is in Lord Sussex's service." interrupted Baroness Ludlow. "Any perceived slight from you could reflect on Sussex's consequence and good name." Frances looked at Baroness Ludlow and, again, decided that she was someone she should like to know better. In response to her advice, Frances nodded her approval.

The conversation continued while Frances looked up the length of the great hall and saw the Queen and her selected table guests. If the scene was translated into a painting by one of the modern artists, all points of perspective would focus on the Queen at the glowing center of the work.

Earlier today the court had been in mourning, but they donned their finest for the evening's festivities. Queen Elizabeth, resplendent in white glossy satin, was a beam of light in her own right. Her gown was covered all over in puffs of aqua silk organza, forming repeating diamond patterns over her bodice. Each juncture fastened to the satin skirting with starbursts of rubies and jet beads set in gold filigree. Frances could not wait for the Queen to stand up from behind the table so she could see how Her skirt was fashioned.

Amazing.

Frances thanked God she had gone shopping and prayed that at least one of the gowns would be delivered tomorrow. It was funny to think that, prior to today, she would not have paid attention to design or color contrast.

Frances glanced at the occupants of her own table. Mary whispered something to Jane, and Jane's face, still sparkling with life, blanched, then flooded with a rosy glow. She turned sharply to look at Frances.

Frances laughed at the whole farcical situation. Jane sat still, her wide eyes unblinking, for a moment or two before responding to Frances's laugh with an embarrassed smile.

"If that shocked you…" Jane pressed her hands to her cheeks to calm her features. "I have a book you should see."

There was a lot about life that Frances intended to learn.

Chapter Five

Rule Twenty-Three: Eating and sleeping diminish greatly when one is aggravated by love.

Henry LeSieur sat supping amicably with Lord Howard of Effingham and the Earl of Sussex's retainers when Lord Howard drew his attention over to the new Lady Howard. Glad to distract himself from the feeling of unease that consumed him since his arrival at the palace, Henry began making the appropriate congratulatory comments. There was no real reason for Henry to worry, no more assignments from Walsingham. It must be only his worry over his wife.

Discounting his sense of foreboding, he joined in the manly banter with the gentlemen as they speculated about the three country ladies sharing Lady Howard's table. Sure enough, there were three handsome women laughing over some shared jest—two blondes and a brunette, all obviously fresh from the country. Good, his wife would have some less sophisticated and lovely ladies to befriend.

The other gentlemen at Henry's table were not as nonchalant about the prospect of new quarry among the stale ladies of the court. One man brought up the wager making the rounds marking the taller blond woman as the challenge. Ten pounds.

His head shot up, his gaze locked on his wife.

Although on an academic level he knew she must be twenty-four or twenty-five by now, in his mind she remained a pretty fourteen-year-old. Seeing her this past week hadn't changed that perception much. Yes, he'd been surprised by her seeming change in personality, but not her beauty. Yet there she was, her eyes sparkling with laughter and her hair glowing in a halo with nothing childish about her. In stunned silence, he took in her smile, the rosy glow of her cheeks. There was a familiarity to her features, and he could see the child bride she'd been so long ago, but now she was someone else. A woman. Logically, he'd known she had grown. They both had. But he'd never considered what that meant. The changes that had been happening before his eyes with each visit suddenly merged into one beautiful whole. Frances was breathtaking.

Literally.

He could barely breathe past the knot in his throat at the thought that this was the woman he'd felt obligated to bed at regular intervals to beget an heir.

Astounding.

Without thinking out his next action, he stood up.

"Henry?" Lord Howard broke through his reverie insistently. "Henry! Is all well?"

"Oh aye, forgive me. I was lost in my thoughts." He never should have approved her time at court. This was not a safe place for someone as sheltered as she, someone with ten pounds on her head. An angel who had no use for him.

Damnation.

Lord Howard clapped him on the back soundly. "About time you took interest in something other than your estate and Parliament. You're far too serious. There's nothing better than having a woman warming your bed to help put perspective on things. She is obviously from the country—a soft word or two from you, and she'll be on her back in a nonce!"

Ha! The man thought Henry wanted to pursue his own wife. The potential humor of the thought was muted by the worry that perhaps Frances would be an easy target for a practiced seducer. Again he was hit by the urge to publicly claim her as his wife. It was clear no one present knew she was anything other than a tasty bit of fresh country meat. Henry started to rise once more, then sat down abruptly.

What if she rebutted his attentions before the whole court? Both their standings would be damaged. Stupid Hatton.

Lord Howard looked at him inquiringly. "Well, man? Are you going to do it? Better be quick before these other young bucks take up the chase."

Henry was beginning to find the ridiculousness of the situation funny. "Did you know I am married, my Lord?"

"You have a wife?" Lord Howard raised his eyebrows incredulously. "Poor woman. What, do you keep her locked away in the country? Is she slow-witted or so homely that you need to hide her? I take back my suggestion—you do not deserve that delightful creature over there." He gestured to Frances. "You need to hightail home and do your duty. In the meantime," Lord Howard rose and reveranced his farewell to the gentlemen at the table, "I will happily see to it that I do not shirk my own."

Henry forced a polite laugh. He stood up and then grimaced and dropped down once more. He laughed again, this time at himself, then sighed and took a bite of his pudding. Lord Howard's assumptions had been wrong—Henry had never done anything but his duty. He married the girl he was told to and got a child on her despite of how awkward the experience had been. He arranged for the LeSieur estate to be comfortable. He joined Parliament… He was so damned dutiful it made him sick. But in respect to Frances, that was all he had ever been. Honestly, he wouldn't know how to have an open conversation with her. She intimidated the hell out of him.

Lord Howard had been right on one point, though—he had kept her holed up in the country. He had never offered her the option to do anything else. She had her duties at home just as he had his duties at court. Why would he think of anything other than that? And she had never asked. Of course, finding out if that was something she wanted would have involved talking to her about more than household accounts and tenant farmers... The thought alone made him feel like he was still the ungainly fifteen-year-old boy who had been confronted with a pair of breasts attached to a wife.

Henry's thoughts were interrupted by the sensation that he was being watched. On alert, he scanned the hall. He could see no obvious threats—still, the unease persisted. More than that, he felt almost sick. He took a step forward and the feeling intensified. While not a superstitious man, Henry survived in Walsingham's service by trusting his instincts, and, at that moment, his instincts told him that he should leave the palace at Hampton Court for now. Frances would have to wait.

He prayed she would be able to take care of herself.

• • •

Dinner ended with all the pomp and ceremony afforded the Queen as She rose with her entourage of favored courtiers and exited to Her presence chamber. Frances remained at her table, waiting for the crowd to disperse before she made her way back to her rooms. The townspeople that had previously crowded the upper gallery hoping to catch a glimpse of the Queen in Her finery were jostling each other in attempt to exit the hall and get to the Queen's privy kitchen door in time for handouts of left-over delicacies. Frances was watching this borderline mob behavior from a safe distance when she was tapped lightly on the shoulder.

"Mistress LeSieur." A liveried footman reveranced before her and waited to be given leave to rise. Frances waved for him to stand, and he continued, "Mistress Parry sends summons. You are to attend her in the Queen's presence chamber."

"My thanks," Frances replied as he turned to leave.

Her breath caught in her chest, and she locked eyes with Mary. Her already pale skin blanched entirely, the dark arches of her brows the only color on her face. Mary looked as nervous as Frances felt. Jane squeaked something like a giggle and bounced in place. They were going to meet the Queen.

The three gentlewomen rose in a fluster of skirts and tried to make their way through the hall and across the cobbled courtyard without hefting up their hoops and running. They met Mistress Parry in the gallery outside the state rooms, her assessing gaze taking in every detail.

"I do wish at least one of the gowns had been ready today," she began, "but mayhap it's fortune's way of showing Her Majesty your true colors when she is surrounded by artifice disguised in satin."

Frances considered Mistress Parry's words as she allowed herself to be ushered through the crowded presence chamber. In her preoccupation with the newly intriguing world of bed sport, she forgot to care about her appearance. The insecurity came back in a nonce and in abundance. Here in the Queen's presence chamber every single courtier was dressed exquisitely, although she felt sure many fashion decisions were based more on ostentation than taste. Frances's mulberry kirtle with navy surcoat that she had embroidered with vining blue forget-me-nots was respectable but, aside from the simple needlepoint, was completely void of any adornment. That aside, it fit her body more like a tent than a dress. Mary and Jane, though obviously lower gentry, at least looked attractive in their gowns. Both had a fashionable silhouette. Still all three were sadly lacking, at odds with the court as much as a lump of coal compared to a cut emerald.

Frances had not yet reached the dais to be introduced to the Queen when it was announced that the Queen would retire to her privy chamber, good night to all. Oh, and would Mistress Parry and her party please attend to Her Majesty immediately?

Blanche Parry, stunning in a deep crimson and black velvet gown, took Frances's hand and led her to the chaise where the Queen sat surrounded by her favorite ladies and a few very attractive men. The Queen's privy chamber was only slightly smaller than Her presence chamber, but instead of being one large open space to hold court, it was arranged to allow for much more intimate conversation and interaction. At the center was a sizeable open section of inlaid parquet flooring that was currently being used by a handful of very young ladies who were working through the steps of the newest Italianate dance. There, by the bay window in the south corner of the room, was a display of a wide variety of very fine musical instruments. Frances immediately noted the magnificent spinet—she was proficient enough in playing to consider it an accomplishment, but she had never mastered the lute, lyre, or harp. A group of musicians played nearby providing the accompaniment for the dancers. Frances noted that they had their own instruments with them, leaving the ones on display untouched—they must be for the Queen's personal use.

Mistress Parry approached the Queen, sinking back on her left leg as she straightened the right so that the toe of her satin Turkish slipper was visible at the hem of her gown—a graceful reverance and an expected show of respect. Frances did the same.

"Your Majesty, allow me to present Mistress Frances LeSieur, formerly Chatsworth, daughter of Elizabeth Hartford, the Countess of Spencer."

Frances used the formality of Mistress Parry's introduction to inflate her confidence as she pulled back her shoulders and raised her chin proudly. Still in a low reverance, she waited respectfully for the Queen to raise her up.

Queen Elizabeth gestured with a beringed hand for Frances to rise and said, "Ah, Bess's girl. Come closer, child."

Frances rose and stepped forward until she was just beyond arm's length from the Queen. Frances was impressed with her own composure—she had never been this close to her monarch before.

The Queen gave her a searching once-over, raising a well-shaped eyebrow not evidencing any sign of disapproval. "I know your mother well and have heard much of you over the years. Your late stepfather, Sir William St. John, was a dear and loyal subject and turned to Us for advice in arranging your marriage some ten years past," continued Queen Elizabeth, reminiscing thoughtfully. "His death was a loss to England."

Frances allowed herself to swell a little more with the pride of her familial connections.

"And, of course, your mother's new husband, the Earl of Spencer, is one of Our most trusted peers of the realm." That had been made abundantly clear to all when the Queen chose Spencer to "host" the Scots' Queen, Mary Stuart, during her enforced stay in England.

"My mother has been most blessed in her marriages," agreed Frances, feeling like she should say something.

"Blessed indeed!" agreed the Queen with a barking laugh. "Let Us pray she has no need for any more husbands or her next marriage may well make her a Queen!" Elizabeth slapped her leg with a raucous laugh. "Your mother has requested that We take you into Our service until Christmastide," Queen Elizabeth continued with a soberer demeanor. "She has given Us some explanation, but We do wish to hear it for Ourselves." With the conclusion of Elizabeth's statement, the courtiers who had formed little gossip conclaves nearby lowered the decibel of their chatter and pretended that they were not listening.

Frances, obviously uncomfortable to have been asked to show her wounds in front of the Queen and Her entire court, hesitated before answering. "I thought it best for my health if I were to leave Holme LeSieur for a time." Frances gave her answer plainly and with no further explanation. She was not being false with the Queen, nor was she laying bare her soul for all of court to hear.

The Queen, after an assessing gaze at Frances's expression, nodded her acceptance and smiled, "We understand. We think We shall discuss this further in more private surrounds."

Relieved, Frances wondered if the Queen was ever truly private.

"You will join Our ladies starting tomorrow and be of service to Us, if it pleases you," declared Elizabeth. It was obvious to Frances that whether or not she was pleased was of no relevance. She should be pleased; she should be over the moon at the honor. What gentlewoman would not be thrilled to be asked to serve their anointed sovereign in the most fantastical court in Christendom? Frances wished she felt the joy she was supposed to.

She sank into another graceful reverance. "It would please me very much, Your Majesty."

"Excellent! I look forward to your fresh face alleviating Our monotony. Now, mistress, join Us in Our circle. We are discussing a masque to lift the spirits of the court in this sad time of loss." A few courtiers crossed themselves. "Your mother has told Us that you are a wit when you set your mind to it. So, madam, set your mind to it and help Lord Leicester here devise something spectacular for the Monday following St Luke's day. My lords and ladies, We give you Mistress LeSieur, wife of Master Henry whom I believe you all know. Treat her as Our special friend." With that, the Queen rose unexpectedly and started toward the spinet. The minute the Queen began to rise to Her feet, all of the court stood and saluted Her with formal reverance. Frances was amazed at how alert the courtiers were, especially since many were engaged deeply in conversation or in their cups. Still, it was evident every one had an eye on the Queen at all times. Frances made a note of this for future reference as she, and the rest of the court, were given leave to rise.

Mary and Jane had melted into the woodwork during Frances's audience with Queen Elizabeth. Frances looked hastily around and found them sitting on the rug in front of the hearth. Judging from Jane's unsteady sway, she'd had more than one goblet of mulled mead.

Frances looked back to her new companions. They'd already forgotten her existence and were sitting with their heads together over a parchment full of scribbles. Frances joined them and accepted a goblet from a server. The scent of nutmeg and cinnamon enveloped her senses as she allowed the warm spiced-honey wine to seep into her blood and give her a sense of belonging. For a moment or two Frances mentally girded herself, then jumped into the melee of creativity.

Kit Hatton, a handsome man with a clean-shaven face, argued with the woman across from him. "A masque about flowers does not fit, Lady Rich. It has passed Michaelmas, and we are entering autumn. It would be silly to portray a parade of posies…"

"And not terribly unique," inserted Lord Leicester with authority.

"I know we have done Greek and Roman gods too many times, but I can think of nothing else." Lady Howard sounded defeated. Frances noticed that Lady Howard was being a little less silly than she had been at supper earlier in the evening. She was glad that, in the presence of her husband, Lord Leicester, and Baroness Sheffield, Lady Howard could control herself.

Frances looked at Baroness Sheffield's tiny waistline as she heard her say, "Please no more gods or goddesses. What if we were pastoral? A masque about idyllic lovers…" Disgusted sighs greeted Baroness Sheffield's suggestion, but she didn't seem to notice. She was gazing lovingly at Lord Leicester.

Leicester either didn't notice or care when he replied, "We need something different. Something almost indecent. Something Our Queen will remember for years to come as one of the nights she laughed loudest and longest. Something that will fill the hall with music and dance and a little debauchery."

At this, the lords and ladies in Lord Leicester's company were silent, studying their cuticles. Frances glanced again at Baroness Sheffield running her pink tongue across the edge of her teeth in the direction of Lord Leicester. It seemed to Frances as if Baroness Sheffield wished to devour him whole. She turned away from the wanton woman and thought on Lord Leicester's challenge. Something different. Something indecent. Lord Leicester *would* call for debauchery…

She had it.

"Sin." Frances said the single word clearly and succinctly. The members of Lord Leicester's masque planning party looked at her dumbly. "Dante's seven sins—lust," she looked at Baroness Sheffield, "avarice, gluttony, wrath, sloth, envy, and pride." Frances was a little proud herself as she saw each of their faces light up with delight at the idea. Frances continued, "Couple the sins with virtues."

"Lust with Chastity," inserted Lady Howard, obviously pleased with herself.

"Generosity with avarice and moderation with gluttony…" Lord Howard of Effingham added, gazing proudly at his young wife.

"Diligence with sloth, patience with wrath, and kindness with envy…" contributed Frances. She felt something warm growing at her center as the zeal of creativity took over. How long had it been since she had been able to make references to literature and have anyone understand her? How long since she'd cared? Too long, apparently.

"And I think that only leaves…" Lord Leicester counted on his fingers. "Pride. Humility goes with pride," he finished. "Mistress LeSieur, you are a blessing to this sad group of jaded courtiers. I think Our Gracious Queen will not be the only one to benefit from your fresh face and ideas."

Lord Leicester was rumored to be charming, but Frances was surprised at how his words practically oozed out of his handsome mouth.

The mood being thus lightened, the lords and ladies had a newfound camaraderie in their discussion of Frances's idea. A smile on her face and a mind brimming with ideas, Frances asked, "What I can't decide on, my lords and ladies, is whether the men or the women should represent sin."

Chapter Six

Rule Twenty-One: Love is reinforced by jealousy.

All that night, armed with quill, ink, and plenty of parchment, Frances worked diligently. She needed to write down each aspect of the event so that nothing would be overlooked, and there was no point in trying to sleep before completing this integral step of the planning process: *Lists*. The first included all the parts of sin and virtue along with suggested courtiers and costume ideas. Another list included suggestions for dances along with ideas on how to modify the dances to fit the theme. Yet another list outlined all of the items needed to transform Henry VIII's great hall into paradise and the nine circles of hell. A list about different foods for paradise and hell. A list about costumes for the servers. A list of suggested lesser sins and virtues for the other revelers. A list of Dante-inspired rhyming words to aid the poet in composing his couplets. Frances even created one list to help categorize all the other lists. She hadn't even realized she'd fallen asleep until an excited Mary bearing several large packages woke her the next morning.

Frances felt like a child on the first night of Christ's mass as she opened each package in turn along with a missive explaining that the second and third deliveries would arrive in no more than three days. Frances had handled all the payments, but Mistress Parry must have slipped the drapers something extra to ensure such prompt service—why, the semptresses must be working around the clock to accommodate Frances's new wardrobe. Mary was just as giddy as her mistress as she handled the luxurious green damask, shaking out the folds in the dress to let the copper embroidery catch the early morning light that filtered in through the open window. The new elaborate gowns required that she have at least one attendant to help her dress.

All thoughts about the masque temporarily disappeared while Mary laid the gown and accessories on the bed. Frances, used to the sensible woolen stockings she wore at Holme LeSieur, luxuriated in the feel of the cool white silk molding seamlessly to her calves. She secured her stockings with red leather garters and slipped her feet into the new, custom-made, copper satin slippers. She pointed and flexed her feet, getting used to the inch-high heel. She tried walking, then decided to test her dancing, repeating the chorus of some random dance: *reprise, reprise,* two *traubuchetti* followed by a *spetzatto tour.* The delicate heels clicked in unison on the wood flooring of her room as she landed the final move gracefully—yes, these shoes would do nicely.

"Mistress, if you are finished dancing in your underpinnings, stand still a bit while I lace you in." Mary approached Frances holding a stiff French corset in her hands.

Frances was not prepared for the force with which Mary yanked on the lacings. Mary, thankfully, expected such an event and helped Frances right herself with no damage done. The corset was only two or so inches smaller than her natural dimensions but would take some getting used to.

"Almost done. Bend and lift," Mary instructed.

Frances remembered enough of the process to know to reach into the front of her corset and position her breasts so they would gently curve above the neckline of her dress and not be unnecessarily crushed by the corset. She thought it was a shame that the only looking glass in the room was just large enough to see her face. She would have to wait and see the full effect once she was in the Queen's presence chamber.

Jane wandered in just in time.

"Help me with the gown." Mary's words were muffled by yards of heavy fabric. Together they hoisted the bulky gown over Frances's head, having a care not to disturb the elegantly arrayed coils of hair. The emerald damask settled perfectly around Frances's corseted form, and Mary set to lacing up the center back with a matching satin ribbon.

Looking down past her expanse of bosom, she took a deep breath. Fashion aside, the solid structure of her corset and the weight of the elaborate gown made Frances feel safe. Protected. Thus armed, she joined hands with her ladies and stepped out to greet the new day.

$$\bullet\ \bullet\ \bullet$$

The small circle of Her Majesty's favorites blinked in surprise at the changes in their newfound country mouse. Frances beamed at them all, giving them a graceful reverance to show her respect, and waited to be recovered by the courtier of highest rank in the grouping—Baroness Sheffield.

Disdainfully, Baroness Sheffield waved an idle hand in acknowledgement, and Frances rose. At that, a playful Master Hatton got down on one knee.

"My Lady, you must bless me with your name lest I die upon this spot not having known an angel." Just meeting his smiling blue eyes made Frances's breath catch in her chest.

"Prettily said, Kit, but I worry that your glib tongue and the licentious twinkle in your eye may well send this heavenly creature fleeing to less debauched pastures," interjected Sir Harry Lee suavely. Frances thought that Sir Harry and Master Hatton might well be the two finest men she had ever laid eyes upon. Sir Harry was renowned for his prowess and was the Queen's champion. His tall stature and broad shoulders made Frances feel extremely small and a little intimidated. The fair-haired Master Hatton was not much taller than she and, compared to Sir Harry, of slender build, but from his movements she could see the underlying strength. He was, after all, the current captain of the Queen's Yeomen of the Guard, Her personal bodyguard.

Frances managed to do nothing more embarrassing than blush and smile shyly as she did her best to dismiss the flirtation and focus on the details of the masque. She inserted herself amongst the conclave of courtiers and produced the parchments containing the details she had worked out on her own the previous night. Sir Harry rose to offer his seat to Frances and removed himself from the grouping, conspicuously followed by Baroness Sheffield. Kit Hatton rose and circled the periphery of the seating arrangement, only to stop directly behind where Frances sat perched on the chaise. It was almost impossible for her to keep on task when she felt his breath on her ear. "You are glorious." It was simple enough, but the purr in his deep voice sent shivers up and down her spine. As she tried to refocus her thoughts on the masque, she could hear the smile in his voice as he whispered, "Do not let me distract you, mistress. Just pretend I am not here."

That was exactly what Frances proceeded to do. Composed as she could be under the circumstances, Frances began to discuss the layout of the courtyard event and asked for constructive commentary on her very detailed plans. She scratched her quill across a fresh sheet of parchment, drawing the projected layout. "This half will be paradise and this half hell." She was ignoring Kit Hatton. She could feel his breath tickling the loose tendrils on her neck.

Ignoring him.

It had been so long since any man had shown interest, and none had ever desired her. Kit Hatton wanted *her*—and not as a dutiful wife. It was wicked. It was exciting.

And it would be very wrong to even wonder…

Ignore him and focus on the masque. The masque, think on the masque.

Frances forced her attention to everyone but Hatton.

"With purgatory in between?" suggested Lady Oxford, formerly Mistress Anne Cecil, with a considering glance. She appeared very young, but every inch the countess.

Frances did not show her relief at the fact that Queen Elizabeth's courtiers were following her tack. "Exactly. I think the food stuffs should be laid within purgatory with two different areas for dancing." Producing another list with the suggested decorations, Frances continued, "Paradise will be swathed in white and pale blue cloth, whereas Hell…"

Frances was interrupted by Kit Hatton who had switched his tone from seductive to playful. "Hell should be swathed in royal blue with gold *fleur de lis*, in honor of the French court."

"A pox on them all," Sir Harry Lee spat, any attempt at joking ruined by the venom in his tone.

Frances met Sir Harry's gaze over the edge of her parchment. Was that scorn aimed at her? No. Hatton laid a hand on her shoulder, and Frances stiffened. Flirtation was one thing, but she would not be any man's prize. She stood and crossed to sit beside Lady Oxford.

Sir Harry's look, still burning but no longer threatening, followed her.

"Now then," the Earl of Leicester tossed his elaborate printing of Dante onto the central table, "what are our roles? Lady Essex informed me she wishes to play Generosity, and I thought to match her as Avarice."

"Are you sure she would not be better suited to Chastity?" remarked Baroness Sheffield with what seemed to be her usual catty tone.

"Fie! I think we shall be hard pressed to find any lady at court willing to play the part of Chastity!" laughed Sir Harry, his eyes now buried in Baroness Sheffield's powdered cleavage.

"I shall, and happily," responded Frances in a small voice. Chastity would be a dream come true.

"You are setting yourself up as a challenge. What does Castiglione say about it? That love is nothing without the chase?"

Lord Leicester harrumphed in disdain, "Surely you're not quoting that ridiculous *Book of the Courtier* again?"

"I think the rules of courtly love are wonderful. Without them, how would we know how to recognize love?" Lady Howard's honest statement echoed Frances's thoughts.

Laughter followed, derisive, sarcastic, *mean* laughter. Poor Lady Howard. For a moment, Frances regretted her decision to come to court. Her new *friends*—they would think her a fool if they knew how, as a naive girl, she'd pored over those rules, fantasizing about romantic love.

"I enjoy the art of courtly love." Hatton's warm gaze poured over Frances as he continued, "I think the rules are not so much about love as about the sport…the chase, the challenge. It's always nice to understand the rules when one plays such a dangerous game."

Sport? Is that what this is? Does that make me the prey? The thought sent a shiver down her spine.

Lifting her chin with just a hint of a smile, she added, "The easy attainment of love makes it of little value—difficulty of attainment makes it prized. That is rule fourteen." The husky tone of her voice surprised her. It appeared the game was on. "I have never considered myself 'sport' before, but there is a first time for everything, is there not? Do believe me when I say that failure is assured, but you are welcome to try."

Was she flirting? Was that appropriate for a married woman? *I don't care.*

"So we have our cast! Mistress LeSieur is Chastity coupled with, you will all agree, Master Hatton as Lust." Again, the group chattered over each other merrily at Lord Leicester's words. "I would put Lord and Lady Oxford as Gluttony and Moderation…"

"Perfect!" proclaimed Lord Howard of Effingham with a bark of a laugh while Lady Oxford bowed her head in serene acceptance.

"Effingham, you and your lady wife shall be Sloth and Diligence," Lord Leicester continued, greeted by a sigh of resignation and agreement.

"That brings us to Envy and Pride. Sir Harry, at the look upon your face, you fit the role of Envy admirably." The Earl of Leicester clapped the menacing looking Sir Harry firmly on the back. At Sir Harry's less than jovial response, Leicester continued, "Here now, sir, it is not all bad. I will give you a gift… You can have your counterpart of Kindness. Baroness Sheffield, please console our Sir Harry."

Frances observed how Baroness Sheffield looked from Leicester to Sir Harry and back again in confusion, not quite knowing how to respond. Was she interested in Sir Harry or Leicester? This business of court intrigue was confusing to say the least. Well, she was sure there was a story there. And she was certain that Lady Howard was the lady to ask. Whatever it was, Baroness Sheffield should be more discreet.

"Sir Knight, I hope that my kindness will leave you no reason for Envy." At that, she focused on the object of Sir Harry's attention. "Really, Mistress LeSieur, you have blossomed over night. I have to admire your new gown. Simplicity suits you well. It's almost unbelievable that you were only a country mouse but yesterday." Baroness Sheffield reminded all present that Frances was still only minor gentry.

Frances felt the eyes of her newfound friends turn to see her response only to focus back on Baroness Sheffield. "The true worth of a person will shine through no matter her appearance." Baroness Sheffield puffed herself up as if to remind everyone that she was a baroness and cousin to the Queen. "It's a shame that Her Majesty has not bestowed a knighthood upon your husband and made you an actual Lady. Maybe he has yet to earn Her affection or admiration like he has with over a dozen of the ladies at court. He has most assuredly earned mine upon many occasions." It was a miracle the courtier's necks did not snap with the violence of their collective head turning.

Had Frances's husband bedded the strumpet? She shouldn't care, either way. Should she? Hurt she couldn't explain made her chest tight. The baroness was a bitch, but her husband…

Oooh.

"It is not a wonder, Baroness Sheffield," Frances calmed her face into the portrait of ladylike elegance, pushing her feelings deep and lowering her voice to a sweet sing-song, "that he has not yet been knighted. If *that* is how he should earn the knighthood, I am not at all surprised any woman would find him lacking. It is a good thing that you are not responsible for giving title else England would be overflowing with poorly qualified knights indeed!" Again, all heads turned in unison to gauge Baroness Sheffield's shocked response before looking back to see what more the surprising Mistress LeSieur would say. Frances continued in the same calm and pleasant voice, "And, Baroness Sheffield, worry not that anyone would ever doubt your true worth, regardless of how fine your attire."

Heads turned to look at Baroness Sheffield, then back to Mistress LeSieur. There was a moment of suspenseful silence while Frances and Baroness Sheffield's eyes remained locked.

Lord Howard spoke first. "Mistress LeSieur, with your biting wit, you should write the couplets for the masque!"

With that, all the courtiers present broke into animated chatter, completely dismissing the risk of offense to Baroness Sheffield.

Baroness Sheffield elegantly arose, reveranced those that outranked her, and walked from the room with stiff grace.

Sir Harry Lee crossed over to Frances, propping his hip against the arm of her chaise. "Mistress LeSieur, *Frances*," his use of her Christian name made her feel dirty, "do you know if your husband is wont to carry coin on his person?"

"Sir Harry, I do not understand the reason for your question." Frances shook her head, still dazed from her duel with Baroness Sheffield. "I do not know his habits in town."

"Of course you do not." He took her gloved hand in his and placed a warm kiss on her knuckles. "I only asked because I expect I shall need to collect on a debt shortly."

"The hell you will," Hatton interrupted as Frances withdrew her hand and wiped the wet leather in the folds of her skirt.

Lord Leicester stood and shook his head. "Lads, stand down. Mistress LeSieur only just arrived in London. We do not wish to frighten her away."

Hatton's posture shifted, all trace of menace gone. "My apologies, Mistress LeSieur. You are a breath of fresh spring air into a catacomb of rot. I cannot thank you enough for the hours of entertainment the retelling of this tale will afford me." Kit Hatton gave an elaborate reverance.

Telling the tale... By the saints, what would her husband say when he heard?

Chapter Seven

Rule Thirty-One: Two men may love one woman or two women one man.

By the time the group of courtiers finished with their input and began to disperse, Frances was torn between an obsessive need to complete her plans and an empty stomach. Immersed in her notes, she eventually looked up and found herself alone with young Lady Howard. "Lady Howard, are you heading to the hall for dinner?"

"Yes, although I am supposed to meet with my lord husband in the library first." Lady Howard was perfectly serious in her statement, but Frances could not imagine what Lady Howard would want with a library.

"Why don't you accompany me to meet with him? Then we can sup together, and I can tell you everything you need to know."

Only one week at court and the thought of more gossip made her gag. At least she wouldn't get lost in the palace. She smiled. "That sounds wonderful. Lead on, my lady."

Arm in arm, Lady Howard and Frances made their way through long galleries flanked with tall gothic windows to one side and dark alcoves and doors leading to unknown chambers on the other. All around them hung portraits and tapestries. Frances had never liked portraits of ancestors—she always felt like the long dead subjects were watching her. Still, the wall hangings helped muffle the echo in the long corridor. She would never get used to the cold grandeur of the palace.

Glancing at Lady Howard, Frances realized she'd missed half of a conversation.

"…and then Leicester just handed her to Sir Harry like a discarded baggage. I am amazed she did not explode right on the spot. After what he did to her…"

Frances stifled a moan as the young lady chattered on. She did not want to even think about Baroness Sheffield.

"I am surprised that Queen Elizabeth allows the light skirt into the palace. No woman in her right mind would set her sights so publicly on Lord Leicester." Lady Howard paused, as if taking a moment, for the first time in her life, to consider her words *before* they left her mouth. "Actually, my husband made me swear not to speak of my theories about the relationship between the Earl of Leicester and Queen Elizabeth under any circumstances." Her eyes looked genuinely sad as she offered a soft smile and said, "It's a shame really, but he said it would be slanderous gossip since I cannot prove the truthfulness of the tale."

With that, Lady Howard all but skipped up to the doors and gave a mighty shove.

The library. And Lord Howard in his shirtsleeves holding two goblets.

Lady Howard, sweet as she was, had no idea her husband had wanted her to join him in the library for a dalliance. Of course, Lord Howard didn't say it in so many words, but his meaning was perfectly clear along with his polite dismissal to Frances. It was inconceivable that anyone would wish to tryst in a library—especially when they had a completely serviceable bed chamber in the palace. Lord Howard must have to be some crazed deviant. Poor Lady Howard. Of course, Lady Howard just seemed pleasantly surprised when Frances left her with her husband in a corner lined with laden shelves.

Frances made her way back to the oak doors leading out, but instead of the gallery, she'd discovered a chapel of sorts. This was not the same one they used to hear services with the Queen, but it appeared to be still in use. She stepped farther into the dim light, allowing her eyes to adjust, and then heard a different door shut. Someone else entered the room, and, judging by the increased glow of light from behind the nave, they were lighting candles. She turned to leave this person to their privacy.

"It is the will of God." A harsh whisper broke through the gloom and stopped Frances in her tracks. Was the person talking to her?

"She brought it on herself, and she deserves whatever pain comes with it." Another voice, or was it the same?

Without a doubt, Frances knew she should not be hearing this conversation, but she also knew she did not wish to be discovered.

"I need more strength. I am too weak and swayed by mercy." The whispered rasp was softer.

"No, there is no room for mercy. Be swift. Your vengeance is an instrument of the Divine. It is for the good of all." This was harsh, cutting.

Frances tried not to shiver as the small hairs on her arms and neck stood on end. Something here was evil. Who was in danger? At this moment, Frances couldn't help but feel it was she. She had to get out of this room.

"*In nomine Patris…*"

Leave. Leave now.

The clamor from her heels against the marble flooring echoed throughout the library as she searched for an exit, any exit. Whoever it was in the chapel had to have heard her, and she prayed the distance between them would be enough so the person might, at least, not know who she was. Running, Frances spied another set of oak doors and threw them open to find the long gallery. Hefting her skirts, she sprinted as quickly as she was able until she reached the large double doors leading into some other public room.

Frances did her best to compose herself as she entered the room, shaking her skirts into place and pasting on her usual pleasant mask.

"There you are, mistress," Blanche Parry's warm voice soothed her ruffled nerves. "I was just about to send someone to seek you out. I was afraid you had gotten lost in your plans." Blanche's merry smile drooped. "What is the matter with you, child?"

Her query was interrupted by the newest arrival to the hall, and Frances had no time to answer.

An excited Lady Rich burst into the room and declared, "I just saw the ghost of Kitty Howard running in this very gallery!" The buzz in the room roared in response. Kitty Howard, the third wife of Henry VIII, was said to roam these halls, trying to find the king to plead for her life. Lady Rich must have seen Frances and, either fancifully or stupidly, took her for the ghost.

Better that than have to explain why she was running with her skirts around her thighs.

Mistress Parry raised an assessing eye toward Frances and said, "Let us make way to the great hall for dinner. I am famished."

The overheard conversation in the chapel had Frances on edge. *Afraid.* She was being silly—if the person had seen her, she would know by now. She had no time for this complication and no energy to deal rationally with the fear. Already completely exhausted by the mental exertion both in the planning of the masque and dealing with flirtation, Frances could not handle more.

Thankfully, Mistress Parry did not question her further as they seated themselves at the board and accepted the first course, a soup of creamed duckling.

Mary asked, "What more do you have left to finish for the masque?"

"Too much to detail." Absolute truth. "And, on top of the remaining planning, I am to be partnered with Kit Hatton. He seems to be an accomplished flirt—I'm unaccustomed to such attentions." Frances's skin puckered into goose pimples at the recollection of Kit's nearness in the Queen's presence chamber. His gaze. The way his words caressed her. "I hope I will not make a fool of myself."

Blanche Parry said nothing and focused on her soup. Frances shouldn't have been shocked at Baroness Sheffield's implication that Henry had not remained faithful. She should have expected it—in fact, she should welcome it. Why should she care one way or another?

But she did. A sense of her own inadequacy stung far more than any betrayal. From what she'd seen between Jane and her lover, she knew Henry took no great care for her during their marital relations, and therein laid the sting. What was wrong with her? Well, based on the suggestions and blatant offers she had received since her debut in the Queen's privy chamber, she would have to say the problem must be with him.

It seemed fairly commonplace for married women to take on lovers so long as they had already provided their husbands with a legitimate heir. Even her gentlewomen thought that was the motivation behind her stay at court. Maybe with a lover she might find the tender caresses she had witnessed between Jane and her gentleman with the firm backside. A memory of her marriage bed snuffed that thought, and Frances frowned, taking a healthy bite of her honey and walnut pudding before turning toward Mistress Parry.

"What do you think of the masque thus far, Mistress Parry?"

"I think that there will be those who find it offensive," Mistress Parry replied smartly. "This is to say, it will be an excellent entertainment and diversion for the rest of us."

"Offensive?" replied Frances. She hadn't considered that. She celebrated the works of Dante, not actual theology.

Mary piped in, "Of course some people may be offended—you are glorifying sin and portraying hell. Personally, I think it will be fun." Nodding her head firmly, Mary took another spoonful of her sweet pudding.

Frances considered a moment and said, "But we are also glorifying virtue. I, myself, am Chastity." At this, Mary choked on her pudding and had to be thumped soundly on the back by a sniggering Jane.

"Not for long, I wager," sputtered Mary between hacking coughs. Jane laughed in full force.

Blanche Parry smiled knowingly at the younger women. "Do what you will, but a warning—your husband is at court. Have a care for his consequence. Whatever may be between the two of you, do not make a public cuckold of him."

"Cuckold?" She choked on the word. "I do not wish for my own husband to touch me—why would I let another man do so?" She shuddered, wiping at imagined dirt on her sleeves. "Besides taking no pleasure in the act, taking the risk of having another man's child would be foolish. No, he has naught to worry from me—although, perhaps it would do him some good."

"Though God has blessed us with a woman as head of our country and His church, His word and England's law still holds that a wife is beholden to her husband. Again, do what you will but always *publicly* do your duty by him. That includes not insulting him behind his back." Blanche Parry stared Frances straight in the eye as she finished with her brief lecture on behavior. Frances could not fault any part of the argument—it was all part of the social mores she had known since birth. Still, she could not help a natural urge to rebel against the standards that had stifled her spirit.

"I have done nothing but my duty since my natal day. I am bone weary of being only a dutiful daughter, dutiful wife, and dutiful mother. What about my duty to myself?" Frances, like last night when she got caught in a creative surge, felt a pull of real feeling as the words poured out of her. "Oh, worry not—I am not so uncouth as to cause any person injury, but please, I am just starting to see myself for who I am rather than who I should be. It is difficult enough for me to accept this without added pressure." Frances nodded toward Mistress Parry. "And more than your admonishments, I need your support that I am doing the right thing in being here at all."

The four ladies at the table stayed silent. A liveried server removed the remnants of their puddings while a butler refilled their goblets with a fine burgundy. Frances was shocked when Jane, obviously moved by impulse rather than social etiquette, leaned across the board and smothered Frances in a bone-crushing hug. For such a small person, Jane was extremely strong. Of all the responses that may have followed Frances's declaration, she had not expected this. Tears welled up in her eyes as Mary joined in.

"So, Frances, what role have you left for me in your masque?" Frances was surprised by Blanche Parry's casual change of subject.

"Leicester, at least, has taken it upon himself to cast the remaining parts...but I think that Patience and Humility are still available," replied Frances, still wrapped in the collective arms of her gentlewomen.

"I think," Mistress Parry paused to sip her wine, "that Humility would serve me best at this moment."

Chapter Eight

Rule Sixteen: The sight of one's beloved causes palpitation of the heart.

The last beams of the early autumn sunset filtered through the leaded paned windows and gave the room a golden glow. Frances smiled as she took a deep breath, enjoying the scents of fresh baking that wafted up from the kitchens and through her open window. With the knowledge that the kitchens were working at full capacity in preparation for that evening's masque, she forced herself to relax as she lounged in a copper basin full of steaming water scattered with rose petals. This was her eighth bath in three weeks; even Queen Elizabeth took no more than one bath a month. Frances, eyes closed and her soapy hair piled high on her head, luxuriated in the heat of the scented water against her skin. She sank down to rinse and allowed the excitement about the masque to replace all anxiety. She had done everything she could, and all that remained was for her to enjoy herself. She breathed out in a flurry of bubbles and rose out of the water, stretched languorously, and reclined against the side of the tub.

Tonight truly signaled the start of a new Frances. A Frances that was desired. A Frances that mattered. She was no longer just some womb waiting to ripen. No, she was an intelligent and attractive woman, and other intelligent and attractive people sought out her company. She should not care whether or not her husband saw her for what she was.

Reaching over the side of the basin, she found a towel, wrapped her hair in a turban, and stood up. Was it her imagination, or did she hear cheering from somewhere outside? No matter. Stepping onto a thick bathmat, Frances toweled off her body and moved to sit by the fire for warmth.

Lying on her chair, wrapped in fine linen and silk ribbon, was a bunch of jasmine. Had someone come in while she was bathing? Her languor was immediately replaced by tension as she grasped a towel to cover her body.

Frances jumped with a shriek as her door opened to admit Jane and Mary.

"Mistress, calm your nerves. It is just us." Jane smiled sweetly and patted Frances on the arm as she bounced over toward the dressing table.

"Jasmine!" Mary declared, picking up the bouquet. "Lovely. We can make sachets out of the flowers for your trunks. Where did you get these?"

"They just appeared."

"Appeared? You mean you do not know?" Mary asked, incredulous.

"No. I do not know, and I do not like it."

"Flowers are hardly sinister, my lady," Jane contributed, moving to untie the ribbon. "And these were well-cut, the ribbon is silk—a lovely gift."

"Maybe you have an admirer?"

An admirer. Why hadn't she thought of that? Of course, she was so morbid that she only considered the villain from the deserted chapel. But an admirer... That made much more sense. "An admirer. Of course." She walked over to inhale the heady fragrance. Jasmine oil was supposed to inspire uncontrollable lust, and the flower represented sensuality. "But I cannot wear them tonight—I am Chastity!"

Jane teased Frances for her concern and volunteered to wear them in her stead. "Don't worry, I have no one to impress with my supposed innocence. Any who notice the jasmine will have a laugh. Speaking of sensuality," Jane pulled a bundle from her basket, "this is the book I mentioned. It's from the Orient and very exotic."

Frances removed the linen wrapping and opened to a middle portion of the book. With a gasp, she snapped it shut and immediately wrapped it once more. "That man was naked!" *And had a member the size of a canon.*

Jane eased it out of Frances's death grip and opened it. "This was written by a courtesan and describes the acts of love. This one," she held up the page with an image of a man kneeling between a woman's legs, "is what Jean, the fellow you caught me with, did—though he had to show me the book first too in order for me to believe that people actually did that." Frances stared at the line drawing, feeling her face slowly catch fire. When no one said anything, Jane added, "He is very French. He said men love to kiss a woman there because it brings her pleasure."

"And does it?" Mary asked, breathless.

Frances watched Jane's eyes soften as she smiled. "Oh, yes." She nodded. "*Mais oui!*"

Frances took the book, closed it, then placed it on her bed. "It is unseemly for my unmarried ladies to have such a book. Leave it here for now, not that I seek to school myself in the way of the courtesan." She tried to look stern, but she could tell from both Mary's and Jane's smirks that they knew full well Frances would be looking at the book later. She cleared her throat and willed her blush to subside. Catching view of the bunch of jasmine, she grasped that subject like a lifeline. "The jasmine. Do you think whoever gave me this expects a dalliance?"

Jane, with a merry laugh, commented, "If you do not wish to have a dalliance, you had best put on your clothes afore another mysterious stranger bearing gifts finds his way to your chamber."

Jane started on Frances's tangles while Mary laid out her gown. Immersed in preparations for the masque, Frances still felt a creeping unease. If an admirer could so easily come and go from her chambers, who else might? There was no reason to believe the sinister voice from the chapel knew who she was or what she had heard. Still, perhaps she should get a lock for her door.

•••

The cast of sins and virtues waited in the courtyard for the trumpet salute announcing the entrance of the Queen. Frances watched the masked courtiers arriving, each outfitted as a lesser sin or virtue, and wondered if her husband would attend. She couldn't imagine him engaging in revelry—that would be fun, and Henry and fun did not mix.

She took her place at the head of the line beside Kit Hatton, costumed as rampant Lust. His new clean-shaven appearance did nothing to lessen the feeling of understated strength he exuded—there was nothing boyish about him. He took her hand gently, turning it over to place a delicate kiss on the inside of her wrist. Frances's skin tingled, and he smiled knowingly into her surprised eyes as his caress caused goose pimples.

"You are the loveliest vision in all of God's creation tonight, sweet Lady Chastity. Pray do not let my lust frighten you."

Frances searched her brain for some witty response and found nothing. Opening her mouth to try to stammer something, she heard the trumpet and the music began for their entrance in a *Pavane*. Hatton led her into the hall.

Left, together, right, together, left, right, left, together… Frances mentally repeated the steps in her head. She had known this dance since she could walk but was so distracted by her partner and the vision surrounding her that she had to concentrate to keep on step. The group of players in this masque entered a transformed great hall. The east end was swathed in white and sky blue diaphanous fabrics creating an ethereal domain. Tall pillars bearing sconces lit the heavenly half of the room to a spectacular brightness that was reflected in the crystals dangling on ribbons from the gilded timbered ceiling. The plush chairs and pillows scattered in both corners of the heavenly hall were already occupied with merry courtiers bearing full goblets of chilled Canary wine provided by servers wearing white robes.

The *Pavane* promenade continued in a serpentine pattern throughout the hall led, in turns, by Lust and Chastity at the front and Pride and Humility at the rear. They continued through purgatory and into hell, the walls draped in shimmering red and gold silks reflecting the light of the few scattered candelabras in a fiery glow. There were cushions and chairs scattered to provide for the sinners' comfort even though more than half of the courtiers planning the event had thought that hell should be themed as a place of punishment. Lord Leicester had overruled them all, correctly it seemed, and stated that their version of hell would allow for idleness and debauchery. Frances noted that the subtle lighting created a more intimate mood, and that this end of the hall had several arched alcoves, now completely obscured by the silken swaths. More courtiers grouped here than in heaven.

Right, together, left, together, right, left, right—the *Pavane* continued to the cheers of the reveling courtiers. The seven couples ended in a line in front of the Queen's dais, turned so each of the sins and virtues were facing front, and sank onto one knee reverently with the rest of the courtly revelers following suit. Queen Elizabeth wore a high-standing ruff that framed her in a halo of gold and white. Her bodice and overskirt was a pale-yellow gold embroidered all over in sunbursts of golden thread. The skirt opened in front to show a forepart of midnight-blue silk studded with scattered cut crystals depicting stars in the night sky. Her eye mask glittered with the outline of the moon and sun halfway through an eclipse. *Glorious.*

With a grand gesture, Queen Elizabeth extended both arms and signaled Her court to recover. Once on his feet, the Earl of

Leicester stepped forth. "Your Majesty is the sun and the moon and the stars this night presiding over all poor sinners herein."

Queen Elizabeth smiled a sweet and simple smile that contrasted with the overt splendor of her costume, "I heard that not all were sinners but that Our ladies are good and virtuous."

Quick on the draw as ever, Leicester replied with a boyish grin, "Ah, but as the ladies are virtue embodied and men the sinners, it will only follow that sin shall try to lead virtue astray."

"Have a care with *my* virtue, Robin," laughed Queen Elizabeth with a coy flutter of Her lashes behind the mask.

Leicester shared a personal smile with the woman who was the Queen, then returned to his role as a courtier. "You are beyond all things virtuous, Your Majesty. You are our Sovereign, our ordained Prince. You are the sun, moon, and stars and need no masque to proclaim your rightful place," Lord Leicester finished splendidly. Turning to the players and the rest of the court, he shouted, "God Save the Queen!" to a resounding "God Save the Queen!" from every mouth and every heart in the hall.

• • •

Henry LeSieur had planned to strut his enormous codpiece with exaggerated arrogance for a humorous effect, but Frances left him dumbfounded. Speechless. Stupid.

Hand in hand with Mistress Parry, he went through the courtly motions, smiling when expected, walking, breathing…but it was Frances glowing in her white gown that drew him again and again. Once more it confirmed that he did not know his wife at all.

Frances, no surprise, had chosen Chastity. She had the face of an angel and a body to match, clad in a gown that seemed to be made of light. Could she be flirting with Hatton? He growled to himself as she blushed like a virgin whenever Kit Hatton smiled her way.

Ten pounds, my arse. The rumor mill already had them together. If not with Hatton, then with Sir Harry Lee. There was no way Henry was going to let his wife go to another man. Other courtiers may not care about fidelity, given their heir was already established, but Henry couldn't stomach the thought of another man even touching his wife.

"I see that you have noticed your wife, Master LeSieur." Blanche Parry voiced the impossible sentence quietly from the corner of her mouth with a sidelong glance at her partner. "Isn't she stunning?"

"Indeed she is, Madam," Henry responded through clenched teeth.

"If you want to gain her affection, you'd best act fast or you will lose her."

"Mistress Parry, I wonder now if I ever had her."

• • •

Frances began the next dance partnered with Hatton. Still very aware of the effect from his slight caress earlier that evening, she was surprised at the ease between them. Hand in hand they completed the four *spezatti* to the left as she tried to concentrate on the sensation of his hand surrounding hers. As they finished their turn together, Frances was surprised from her musing while Hatton tried to perform the chorus of *reprise* and *trabuchetti* as close to her as possible. Laughing aloud at his gall, Frances stayed at a safe distance thanks to his hilarious codpiece. Jane had pushed her to explore the possibilities there, but Frances couldn't think past harmless flirtation. What would it be like to take a lover? Probably just like being a wife, humiliating and painful. Then again, after what she saw with Jane...

The next stanza in the dance interrupted her thoughts.

Hatton moved away, passing her to Gluttony. The notoriously lascivious, and somewhat disgusting, Earl of Oxford also attempted to sidle close to Frances during the chorus, but was impeded by the enormous, padded belly of his peasecod doublet. Avarice, Sloth, and Wrath, at least, did not try anything improper. Finishing with Wrath, Frances completed a *spezzato cadenza* to the left and found herself partnered with Envy, Sir Harry.

Taking her hand for the series of *spezzati* and *passi presti* to the right, Sir Harry commented quietly, "I am truly envious of your partner this evening, Lady Chastity." Sir Harry managed to speak smoothly in spite of being in the sixth set of a rigorous dance.

"As you see, Sir Envy, I have had many partners tonight, including you. There is nothing to be envious of," Frances replied calmly, loath to touch him.

"Ah, but you are wrong. I envy every pair of eyes that has been blessed with your glorious visage."

Frances thought Sir Harry's words were prettily said, but all they accomplished was to give her a sense that he viewed her as his possession. If he had been the mystery admirer, he would not have left her undisturbed in her bath while he innocently delivered flowers. The thought alone made her shudder.

"I suggest you turn to your partner of Kindness to help alleviate your envy. She has not been able to keep her eyes off you all night." Frances gestured to Baroness Sheffield, two ladies to the right in the dancing circle, beautifully garbed in rose and butter yellow satin which, to her credit, did give her a softer appearance. Frances wanted to be polite despite the irrational urge to flee. At this, she completed the *spezzato cadenza* to her left and changed partners, followed by Sir Harry's scorching gaze. Still queasy with unease, she looked up and reveranced her final partner, Pride.

The tension in his jaw and taut cord of his neck framed by the courtly ruff gave the impression of a warrior pretending to be a courtier. It took her breath away.

"My lord, pray give me your name. I thought I knew all the players, but I am mistaken," Frances said with a confident smile.

As tall as Sir Harry, but more graceful and less brutish in his carriage, he was as dark as Kit Hatton was light. She had thought she was attracted to the idea that they matched, but the contrast flashed an erotic image to mind, her paleness pressed against him. *Damn that book.*

She bit her lip and swallowed against the warmth in her belly.

She found herself disappointed that he wore gloves. Still, heat pulsed through the supple leather against her hand, and he led her on the *spezzati* and *passi* to the right and met her eyes. "For tonight, my Lady Chastity, I am Pride. At this moment, I am proud indeed to have you upon my arm."

His voice, deep and familiar, washed over her skin like a caress. His mask obscured most of his face, but she could see his dark eyes and thick fringe of lashes behind the peacock feathers and his full mouth smiling below the black velvet of his half mask. He was clean shaven, but Frances could see the dark undergrowth working its way to the surface. She had never kissed a clean-shaven man—even her husband had had a silly little beard when they had kissed at their wedding. She wondered if Pride's lips would be as soft as they looked. Still strangely preoccupied with the idea of kissing, she found herself taking a larger step into him as they entered into the chorus where the partners faced each other in a circle around the other in a series of *reprise*. He shifted his body on the diagonal so that his cumbersome cod piece would not be a barrier and stepped so close that Frances's bosom pressed against his chest.

At the unexpected contact, Frances took a deep breath of surprise, causing her chest to heave even closer against the velvet of Pride's doublet. Being so close to him made it difficult to breathe, and her pulse raced setting an alternate tempo to the rhythm of the dance. She had never been so affected by a man. Still, not wishing to appear easily fazed, she finished her dance steps in this proximity—each up and down move of the *reprise* causing her breasts to shift against the silk of her corset. Doing her best to ignore the growing sensation, Frances met his eyes in an effort to continue the dance. Her breath caught in her throat as his gaze devoured her. He wanted her badly, and somewhere deep inside herself, she wanted him.

"Sweet Chastity, it would wound my pride to let you out of my arms without one chaste kiss. You can hardly deny me that."

Pride lowered his head.

Fear and desire fought within her, and Frances pulled away, shaking, no longer dancing. Too late she affected a playful laugh and found her place in the choreography. Her heart still pounding in her throat, she joined back with Hatton as all the partners reveranced each other and then turned as one to face the Queen upon her dais in heaven and dropped down on one knee in salute.

"Well danced, all!" the Queen declared with enthusiasm and gestured grandly for her dancers to recover. "Your dancing was so engaging that We wish to have a dance for Ourselves." With that, Queen Elizabeth rose, elegantly extending her right hand. Kit Hatton, being the closest to the dais, scampered quickly up to lead the Queen onto the dance floor. Queen Elizabeth called for a couples' dance, and the musicians struck up the tune.

Pride held out his hand, no longer gloved. Feigning courage, Frances joined him in the opening steps, circling around each other. The dance glorified love and courtship and was made up of a series of stanzas where the couple would dance together, show off their skills with a solo, get seductively close, then move away playfully. The dance was one of her favorites. She stepped, moving her left hip toward Pride in a *puntate,* then stepped back, turning left and then right in a swish of satin skirts and a hint of silk stocking.

He seemed so familiar, but she would surely remember such a handsome man. Then again, the past ten years had boasted a distinct lack of handsome men. Perhaps she should have let him kiss her during the dance and marked it up as playacting. Kissing fell within the realm of flirtation, and none could fault her for affecting courtly sensibilities, even her husband. Smiling up into his eyes, she wondered if she would see him without the mask later... Well, the night was young.

Chapter Nine

Rule One: Marriage should not be a deterrent to love.

Once Queen Elizabeth opened up the dance floor to all, the sounds of music and dancing became the pulse of Henry VIII's great hall. Revelers crowded into every corner of heaven, hell, and purgatory. Even though it was her own design, Frances felt guilty at the thought of reveling in hell. She had been impressed with her foresight in deciding to serve a chilled wine in the heavenly portion of the hall—the blazing candles created quite a bit of heat along with their divine light. With the heat from the candles and the exertion of the dancing, Frances found the refreshing libation more appealing than usual.

She handed her goblet to a passing footman as she was grabbed by two masked lady revelers and pulled onto the dance floor. As Mary, Jane, and Frances began their dance with a *balzetto*, they all began talking at once. Between Frances's flirtation with Pride and Mary's and Jane's questions, the three decided to continue their discussion privately once the dancing was finished. Dressed as the virtue of Humor, Mary wore a playful teal velvet gown with a forepart and sleeves in motley to match her mask and belled jester's crown. Jane costumed herself as the virtue of Innocence— or, rather, a satire of Innocence. She had not liked the mandate that the ladies were supposed to be virtuous and decided to be as provocatively virtuous as possible. She'd woven strands of flowering jasmine, from the bouquet left in Frances's room, into her mass of golden ringlets. Her gleaming white silk gown, scattered with cherry blossoms, had as low a neckline as possible without exposing her nipples.

When they finished the boisterous dance, the three costumed ladies escaped the confines of the hall, each grabbing a goblet of wine on their way. As they got farther away from the overwhelming noise of the masque and deeper into the darkness of the gardens, Frances could hear herself think once more.

Her attraction to Kit Hatton was minor compared to her immediate physical response to Pride. One man she barely knew and the other a complete stranger, and both wanted her. She took another sip from her pewter goblet and sat down on a stone bench under an arch of fragrant night blossoms. Mary and Jane joined her.

"Jane, I had no idea that you were on such good terms with Baroness Sheffield that she would lend you one of her gowns…" Mary's comment was cut short by a playful but effective swat from Jane's silk flowered fan. Frances took advantage of this distraction and laughed at her ladies' banter.

"Mary, you have no call to criticize Jane's costume. She looks lovely, although if she were to dress this way on a regular basis, I may have to dismiss her from my household."

Jane took Frances's teasing compliment with her usual good nature and responded with a low reverance, giving all present an eyeful of her ample bosom.

"Saints preserve us, Jane! Put them away! You are a wanton wench." Mary's response was playful, but she was clearly frustrated with her friend. Mary looked elegant as always and her costume choice showed her wit and character. Frances was not surprised that Jane had chosen to play the vixen. Since their arrival at court, Frances realized that Jane wielded her sexuality like a weapon— against what, Frances could not guess. She wondered if Jane behaved this way at Holme LeSieur and, if so, why hadn't she noticed?

"Mistress, what troubles you? We will be with your children soon enough, and tonight is a night for revelry, not guilt." Mary interrupted Frances's introspection.

"Nay, Mary, it's not guilt or missing my children." Frances tried not to think about that until she was alone in her rooms at night. "I am not troubled or upset... I'm more confused than anything else."

Mary and Jane waited while Frances finished the dregs of her goblet. "My husband is at court but has not sought me out. Did I anger him? Embarrass him? I have made myself respected among the Queen's elite, but he does not care." Frances continued, her words flowing faster and faster, "Now I know that men find me attractive, so why is it he finds me undesirable? And why do I care a whit about what he wants or does not want? Have I ever wanted his attentions? Certainly not! I have endured his touch for ten years, yet here am I worried about my marriage vows and *not* taking a lover even when I have at least one prime prospect and my husband has long since treated me and our vows with disregard..." Frances rambled on, not sure about her original point, but unable to stop. "And I blame him for my disgust at coupling. How dare any man touch a woman who does not want him? And why did I comply, knowing full well he did not want me? Duty. God's blood, how I hate the word. I will never again give my body out of *duty*." Frances had worked herself into wild pacing. She grabbed Mary's untouched goblet of wine and took a healthy swallow.

"But then, what is coupling all about if not the woman submitting to a man's desires? And, if that is so, how can it be at all pleasurable? So many women *choose* to engage in affairs. And they enjoy it! I saw you, Jane." Frances pointed. Jane jumped. "I saw you basking in the pleasure that man gave you. How so? I wish to never be touched again, but I want to know what you know. Kit Hatton is at my disposal, I know that. I am sure he'd be a considerate lover, but I do not want him and the risk of a babe is too great to even consider it. I do not know." Frances sat down, in a billow of skirts. "I mean, I should want him, if I were to want anyone—which I do not. No. But I do. And then there is that tall dark fellow with the massive hands and full mouth wanting to kiss me…but he may have just been playing a part. And my husband is somewhere at court and may have been lovers with Baroness Sheffield and God knows who else. And I cannot think why I am thinking so much on this." Frances would have slumped over and placed her forehead onto her knees, had she not been wearing a corset. She sat still for a moment, and then drained the remainder of Mary's goblet.

"So, let me get this correct." Jane held up her hands to count of the points of Frances's rambling argument. "You do not want a lover. Your husband is an arse. You *do* want a lover, but are afraid to be with child again. You cannot abide the thought of coupling." She had counted off four fingers. "You thought you wanted Kit Hatton, but now you are attracted to this other man. You do not want a lover, but you do want to know why some women like it." Jane had counted off a total of six fingers. She looked up at Frances quizzically. "Does that make sense to anyone here? It certainly makes no sense to me. I think, mistress, you may be drunk."

Ignoring Jane, Mary looked to Frances. "Mistress, do not do anything that you do not wish to do. If something is wrong, you will know. Do not think on it so much. Mayhap your heart will guide you and you'll be able to overcome your fear and memories." Mary handed Frances Jane's half-full goblet.

"When I want a man, I feel it like a fire in my belly," Jane explained. "I ache to feel his skin against mine. Even the touch of his hand is like a brand. It is like I want to drown in his kiss."

Like a brand—Pride's touch had branded her, sure enough. Maybe she should have let him kiss her…

"And when a lover has a care for you, he will wait upon your pleasure. He will read your responses and know how to please you.

It does not have to be an act of submission, but an act to fulfill your own desires," Mary added, her words honest and kind, not in the least bit arrogant. The words of a friend. "A true lover will find his pleasure in pleasing you. Remember, that which a lover takes against the will of his beloved has no relish. No man who loves you will cause you pain…"

"Unless you want him to," Jane finished with a giggle.

Frances, still uncertain about everything in general, smiled awkwardly and said, "You just quoted Castiglione. Was that rule five?"

Mary threw her hands up. "I think this night has gone on enough. I am off to bed."

Mary rose and Jane stood with her, saying, "Not me! It is early yet, and I have to meet the man I wish to tempt with my innocence." With that, Jane checked that her bosoms were still as contained by the dress as they could be and sauntered back to the festivities in the main hall.

Frances and Mary laughed together at the incorrigible Jane. Mary looked to Frances in seriousness and asked, "Are you finished for this evening as well? Or do you wish to find out if chastity is really what you want?" Mary gestured to Frances's costume. Frances looked down at herself, surprised by her appearance. She looked fabulous and, only for tonight, wasn't herself. Why not take a chance?

Before she could answer, a servant in angelic robes appeared before her bearing a silver slaver with a single folded piece of parchment upon it.

"Mistress LeSieur?" the man began with a reverance. Frances nodded, wondering how he knew who she was—she was wearing a mask, after all. "Mistress LeSieur, this missive is for you." He presented his tray, waited for her to retrieve the note, then bowed as he made his exit.

Frances opened the missive and peered at the script in the darkness of the garden.

I await your pleasure in the northern most alcove in hell.

• • •

Frances entered the great hall and into heaven, vaguely aware of others returning from the darkness of the garden. It seemed that the festivities were still going strong. Looking to the food, Frances realized she'd had at least five full goblets of wine on an empty stomach. She skirted the dancers as they ran with amazing energy in a snaking line around the hall. *Run, run, run, hop. Run, run, run, hop. Run, hop. Run, hop. Step back, step back. Kick-kick-kick, kick-kick-kick.* Frances did not know this dance and was relieved she had not been present at the start of it.

Finding the tables still piled high with delicacies, Frances chose a simple almond custard tartlet and prayed it would settle her stomach. She could not tell if the butterfly sensation was from the alcohol or the anticipation of her private meeting…but with whom? The mystery was part of the appeal. The probably very delicious tartlet was almost flavorless to Frances as she dutifully chewed and swallowed. Not sure if the dryness in her mouth was from nerves or the pastry, she signaled a footman bearing a tray. The wine was pleasingly wet, and, having thus fortified herself, she was ready to meet with her admirer.

She wove her way throughout the reveling sinners and stood considering the red satin draped wall. Which way was north? She took a moment to orient herself, thinking about where the sun had set when a strong hand took hers and guided her into an alcove.

Frances began an attempt at saying something witty when she was silenced by a warm, firm, kiss. Frances was too surprised to react. Of course her first instinct was to pull away, but then again, wasn't she here to test whether or not she could feel pleasure at a man's touch? Frances tried to follow her train of thought but found herself too distracted to think.

She closed her eyes and let herself just feel. The hot pressure of his lips against hers. The force of his large hands at her back. Wanting to be closer, closer. He teased at her lips, urging them to open enough to deepen the kiss. He tasted of honey and wine as his tongue entwined with hers. *This is a kiss, a real kiss.* The silk of his thick waves tickled her seeking hands as she laced her fingers through his hair.

Wait a moment… How did her hands get into his hair? And what was his tongue doing in her mouth? And why did she not want this kissing business to end? The pressure of his hands at her back pressed her up against the velvet of his doublet, the thick knap of the fabric a welcome friction against the sensitive skin of her heaving bosom. Sinking deeper into his arms, she marveled at the heat from his body. He was much taller than Frances had thought, she realized, angling her head back to match the slow onslaught of passion. His lips left hers, skirting with soft heat across her jaw, her ear lobe, down her neck. She could feel the smoothness of his shaved skin as his lips, teeth, and tongue created a riot of sensations on the base of her neck.

Head back and eyes closed, she sighed as she gave up on thought and let herself melt into the embrace. This was pleasure.

Without warning, she felt light pour into the alcove from a break in the satin draping and a sickening voice hissed, "Traitor!"

Frances felt the arms supporting her body loosen as she stood up straight with a sudden jerk and opened her eyes. The alcove was so dimly lit that she had to strain to make out the figure of the man she had just embraced so passionately as he moved to investigate the disturbing voice. It wasn't Kit Hatton. Was it Pride? Yes, but he seemed so familiar… As Frances's eyes focused in the gloom, she felt as if the world were spinning around her and that she was about to fall. She heartily regretted the last goblet of wine. Or the last few goblets. She bent over to clutch the bench under the slatted window in the alcove and, unexpectedly and violently, retched. *God's teeth, no. A lady does not vomit…* The man she'd just been kissing moved closer and, embarrassed, she tried to cover her mouth with her hand before everything went black.

• • •

This was not how Henry had imagined the night ending, but he was grateful that, at least, his wife had been with him when she collapsed. Shaking away the unpleasant thought of how vulnerable she may have been had she found herself in this situation with someone like Oxford, Henry lifted her limp form into his arms and escaped the revelry of the hall.

He had no trouble finding Frances's room off the gallery. He'd heard talk about how Frances had a penchant for sunlight, fresh air, and regular baths. She'd already taken more baths than the average courtier since her arrival, visible through her open window from the gallery across the courtyard. He shouldn't blame the gossiping men for trying to peek—hell, if he had spied her during her bath, he wouldn't have been able to take his eyes off of her. Still, she was his wife. *His.*

Reaching her chamber, he toed the door open and crossed the room to her bed. Laying her on the thick coverlet, he stood back and gazed down on her, still glowing like an angel despite the fact she had just vomited and passed out. She looked decidedly uncomfortable with her bumroll forcing her back into an unnatural angle, her corset cutting into her bosom, and her hoop skirts springing in all directions.

He should undress her for her own good, nothing to do with his less than noble thoughts. Henry truly believed himself to be acting in Frances's best interests as he rolled her onto her stomach so he could unlace the center back of her gown and her corset beneath. The hoops were tied to the corset, but he had to work his hands around to her abdomen in order to find the tapes securing the bumroll. Putting both hands under her shoulders, he lifted her free of her gown and underpinnings and noticed that she seemed smaller than he remembered. Of course, the last time he had seen her unclothed was immediately after she'd weaned the first babe that she'd lost. A girl, he couldn't remember the name. And here she was, having lost another.

She was like a rag doll as he shifted her in his arms, supporting her weight while he kicked the dress off the bed and onto the floor. Henry pulled back the coverlet and laid her down on the linen sheets. Tenderly, he removed her shoes and stockings and moved up to untie the silver mask and pick the small flowers out of the golden waves splayed on her pillow.

He tucked the coverlet around her once more and turned just as something heavy fell at his feet. A book. Picking it up, he stifled a surprised laugh. A pillow book? Where had she gotten it? And why? All the noble thoughts he'd clung to while undressing her dissolved immediately as he flipped through the explicit pages, pausing on the one marked with a ribbon, his erection becoming even more painful. He'd heard of this before. Something very French. He imagined Frances flushing as she pictured herself laid out for her lover to feast upon. He snapped the book shut and cursed. Perhaps the illicit knowledge from the book, the flirtations and regular trysts at court, had changed her mind about how it could be between a man and a woman. That kiss had certainly proved to him that she was capable of passion, even if she didn't think so. Had she even known the man she was kissing was him? Or did she hope for someone else? His chest tight, he exited her room, clutching a spray of baby's breath in one hand, the book in the other.

Chapter Ten

Rule Twenty-Two: Suspicion of the beloved generates jealousy and therefore intensifies love.

Sunlight flooded through the leaded pane glass windows of Frances's room. The lengthening fingers of the early morning sun caressed her closed lids, stirring her out of her deep sleep. She shifted in bed, moving her face out of the brightness in effort to hold on to the dream. She was still in his arms. He was kissing her mouth, her eyelids, her ear, her throat…and she reveled in his embrace, a sensual being. Her tongue twined with his, and she shifted against him, feeling his thigh press between her legs. The kiss intensified as pressure built against her pelvis, something deep within her winding tighter…

Despite her best efforts, Frances woke realizing she was in her bed, alone. Mulling over the ache in her belly, the sense of incompletion, she stared at the pleating on the canopy of her bed curtains. Last night's kiss… A shy smile played on her face as she stretched her body, enjoying the sensation of the cool sheets against her skin. Rubbing the sleep out of her eyes, she tried to sit up, only to fall back and bury her face in her pillow.

Was she dying? Had she been injured? Frances's head throbbed with such maddening pain that it was hard to think. Shielding herself with her pillow against the assault of light and sound, Frances tried to remember what happened the night before.

The masque. The wonderful kisses. Then what? How did she get here? She couldn't remember anything… No, wait—someone called her a traitor. Who? And why? Then what?

The memory struck her like a lightning bolt—vomiting all over the alcove. *God's teeth.* What must he think of her now? Grimacing in mortification, she realized she could not remember what happened next. And worse, she wasn't sure who he was.

Braving through the pain, Frances sat up again in bed, this time more slowly. Her rumpled gown lay on the floor and she was clad only in her waist-length fine lawn chemise. Had Mary helped her to her room? No, Frances remembered Mary leaving for bed. With a stab of worry, she realized it must have been the man she kissed.

Good. God. No.

Falling back and covering her face again with her pillow, she wondered exactly what transpired between herself and the man in the alcove. *I will assume it was Kit Hatton. Or Pride. Or someone else entirely?*

Her stomach grumbled.

Things could not be worse. She closed her eyes again as images from her dream came back. The sweet caresses, the way her body responded…to her husband.

• • •

Thick smoke curled along the low blackened beams of the guard house ceiling. Henry LeSieur watched Hatton fill his tankard, waiting out whatever hell was sure to come next.

Hatton placed the foaming mug on the sticky oak table, watching the puddle gather at the base instead of meeting Henry's eyes. "Mistress Jane Radclyffe, gentlewoman in service to your lady wife, was attacked last night during the masque."

"What?" Henry stood, jarring the table and ducking in time to avoid hitting his head on the ceiling. "How? Why? What of the guards?"

"The guards covered all points of access on the exterior and stood on duty within the hall. I expected some disturbances between the

Puritans and Papists at the court, but this sort of violence? Mistress Radclyffe, though she serves in a Roman Catholic household," he lifted his mug to Henry, "*your* household, is not an important person at court. You, on the other hand, may be."

Henry nodded, his jaw tight, and sat down once more. "Tell me about the attack."

"She was found just before sunrise in the privy gardens."

Too close to the Queen's rooms for comfort. "The attacker had access then."

"Hence the reason for my concern," Hatton confirmed. "She was beaten, that much is certain. She has bruises to the face and around her neck. The guardsman who found her said she was saying something about the jasmine in her hair."

Henry pictured merry little Jane Radclyffe, his wife's borderline wanton companion. She always had a smile for everyone. Why would someone do this to her? "Raped?"

"Not that we know of. She was, however, cut," Hatton paused and indicated the center of both his palms, "through the hands and positioned in the Christ pose." Hatton placed his arms out to either side.

"God's blood," Henry swore then winced at the words themselves. "This has religious significance then."

"Aye." Hatton nodded and took another swig of his ale. "Which brings me back to you."

Henry had known that a summons from Hatton the morning after the masque couldn't end well, but he'd figured it had something to do with his wife and the Godforsaken bet. This was worse.

Henry paced across the room and cracked a shutter, balancing out the pressure in the dark room. Smoke crawled along the ceiling and snaked out the window into the sunny morning. Whoever targeted Jane saw his role in stopping treason as betrayal of the Roman Catholic faith. Was anyone at court actually devout?

Remembering the drunken revelry from the night before, he doubted it. "Someone knows of my position with Walsingham. Who?"

"Well, Norfolk is now missing a head. Ludlow is in the Tower. It could be any of their retainers, but I know of none at court. If they have any wits at all, they'll be hiding in the country now."

Henry threw a leg over the bench and sat down. "Baroness Ludlow is at court." A small woman with a constant look as if she'd sniffed a chamber pot, he never liked her, but couldn't consider her a real threat. Still, her husband was in prison for treason—he couldn't discount her.

"She was at the masque and in costume," Hatton replied, fanning his hand in the smoke, "attending the Queen for most of the night."

"Do you have any suggestions?

"Mayhap Mistress Radclyffe was an easy target? What worries me more is that her gown was very similar to Mistress LeSieur's. White fabric with a generous display of..." Henry, his eyes burning from the smoke in the room, glared a warning at Hatton. "Beadwork."

Henry cocked a brow. Interesting thought. "You think my wife may have been the target?"

"It is possible." Hatton waved his hands in front of his face, ineffective against the thickening smoke. "Blasted chimney."

Henry coughed, the taste of ash thick on his tongue, and opened two more shutters as Hatton drenched the fire in the grate.

"We pulled rats from the flue two days ago. Before that there was a nest."

Henry grabbed a tankard and filled it at the barrel, taking a deep swallow before asking, "Nature or vandalism?"

Hatton worked a poker into the flue over the fizzling fire. A wet thud followed by hissing steam answered his question. "Sodden wool. Someone plugged the chimney. More of a nuisance than a hazard, unless it had gone unnoticed into the night." He ran a hand over his face, not easing the tension at all. "Damn it, this was done on purpose."

"Do you think it relates to Mistress Radclyffe?" Henry toed the smoldering mess. Plain, inexpensive wool. A blanket, perhaps?

"Either way," Hatton, also a smoldering mess, pounded his fist on the chimney breast, cracking the plaster, "something is afoot, and I will not stand for it."

"Someone has sabotaged the guardhouse, possibly three times, and attacked a courtier. These are very different crimes and may not be the same culprit."

"Wondrous. Multiple villains running amuck at Hampton Court—I look forward to informing Her Majesty, or worse, Baron Burghley."

"What are we telling to whom?" Blanche Parry eclipsed the light in the open door, filling the space with her skirts and plumage.

"Mistress Parry," Henry stated, dropping back in a reverance as Hatton did the same.

"Rise you up, gentlemen. And do have someone look into the chimney. A body could choke on the smoke in here."

"As you say, madam," Hatton offered, bowing over her outstretched hand. "Pray be at your ease here. I can offer you ale or wine, if you wish…"

"I wish," she interrupted, her sharp eyes darting between his face and Hatton's, "to see to Mistress Jane Radclyffe. I have been told we can find her here." *Of course Mistress Parry knew already.*

Hatton offered his hand, leading the way. "Aye, madam. She was found before dawn and brought here for succor and safety. I did not know her identity right away or who to inform of her whereabouts."

"Well I am here now, lad, and insist you show us to her at once."

Us? Henry looked up as Mistress Parry gusted past him and up the stairs followed by Mistress Montgomery. Frances remained in the doorway, her eyes wide.

He reveranced once more. "Good morrow, my lady wife. I trust you slept well."

The blood drained from her face, giving him warning he may need to catch her. She merely stepped sharply back and grabbed tight to the door frame as she steadied herself.

"My lord husband, you shaved your beard," she said weakly, her face almost green tinged. Apparently, not all the wine she'd consumed last night had been left on the floor of the alcove in the great hall.

"It is nice to see you this morn, as well, Frances."

• • •

Henry. She had kissed Henry last night. Her husband. Her husband was Pride. Henry, holding her now, his bare hand hot on her skin, saying her Christian name. Would he kiss her again? *God help me.* Frances swallowed against the bile that threatened and closed her eyes. The world around her spun, and she opened them once more.

"Frances," his voice poured over her again, his breath a soft caress against her cheek. "Is this the first time you have been hungover? I have never known you to over-imbibe."

She sat up, stiffening her shoulders within the circle of his arms. "You have never known me at all, my lord husband."

Henry. She wanted to say his name, feel it on her tongue. Would it be foreign, too personal? She couldn't remember if he had ever spoken her name before today. She was through being "my lady wife" and Mistress LeSieur, but to be Frances, her name on his lips, tempted in a way she couldn't define.

His jaw tensed, but he did not step away. She wanted him to, didn't she? Of course she did. How else would he see reason and grant her the separation? After all, that was the reason she had come to town, even though Jane had said she should…

"Jane!" The thought brought Frances into the present. She grabbed her husband's shoulders, using him to launch herself up. Telling her rumbling stomach to cease and desist, she followed Mistress Parry and Mary up the stairs, only remembering her manners by the time she reached the landing.

She turned to see Henry standing at the foot of the stairs, his brows steepled and a funny quirk to his lips. "God give you good den, husband." She muttered the nicety by rote as she gave a polite reverance. His gaze held hers, and she stumbled as she tried to rise. Had his eyes always been so dark? Had so many secrets hidden in them? Shaking her head, she turned and ran into Jane's room.

Mary knelt at the bedside, not quite touching Jane's bandaged hand. Jane lay there, bundled in woolen blankets, her fair hair slicked away from her face and fresh bruising rising along her jaw and cheeks. She looked so small, almost like a child, and Frances's heart ached for her.

Jane looked up from under blond-tipped lashes. "I look a fright."

"No, you do not," Frances spoke at the same time Mary said, "Indeed you do."

Jane smiled, then winced as the corner of her swollen lip cracked.

"Oh sweeting, what happened?" Mistress Parry asked.

"I do not remember the details. I was waiting for Jean Luc…"

"Who is Jean Luc?" Mary interrupted.

Jane sighed and closed her eyes. "The Frenchman I told you about, the one who gave me the book. You know," she lowered her voice to a whisper, "who did that thing with his tongue…"

Mary stifled a quick laugh, and Frances felt heat flush her face, then jumped as someone coughed directly behind her. She turned to see her husband propping up the door frame. He raised a brow and pulled something from a pocket in his breeches. A book. No, *the book*. Her face flushed with heat, and she turned back to Jane.

Frances turned back, her full attention on Jane, and prompted, "So, Jean Luc…"

"Never came, that I know of. At least, I am not sure. I remember a pain in my head and then I had a mouth full of grass and someone on my back." Jane partially sat up in bed, bringing her bandaged hands up to her chest. "I couldn't breathe, couldn't fight back. They smashed my face into the ground over and over, and then I woke up, freezing, a large man in the red of the Queen's Guard, lifting me as if I were thistledown."

Kit Hatton pushed himself into to the room. "One of my guardsmen found her unconscious around three in the morning. I do not know how long she had been there, but the blood on her hands was already caked."

"Have you investigated this Jean Luc?" Henry asked.

Hatton nodded. "He is with the French Ambassador's entourage and remained in the great hall all night waiting on Queen Elizabeth's ladies."

A soft snore drew Frances's attention back to Jane, small and pale, wrapped in quilts on a meager pallet.

"Will she be all right?" Mary asked. "Is it good for her to sleep right now?"

"She gave clear instructions that we were to wake her and check her eyes every half hour," Hatton answered, his voice lilting with amusement. "She may not remember the attack well, but she came to with her wits intact and no shortage of spirit. She prescribed herself a valerian-root tincture and instructed one of my men how to make an onion poultice for the wounds on her hand."

Frances nodded her approval. Jane knew her way around the herbs in a still room and always made herself available to those in need at Holme LeSieur. An onion poultice would pull out any infection. Valerian root would relax Jane enough to sleep through the worst of it without causing a bleed. The knot of dread that closed around her heart the moment Mistress Parry told her of the attack loosened, and Frances sagged in relief.

"Frances."

The spoken word, her name of all things, sent a shiver of pleasure along her skin. She turned to look up at her husband. A soft smile played on his face, and Frances could imagine the little boy he once was. In an instant, his jaw tensed, his lips firming into a harsh line as he glared at someone behind her. Looking back, she saw Hatton's broad grin. Frances felt helpless, caught between Henry's scowl and the laughter in Hatton's eyes.

"Mistress LeSieur," Kit Hatton broke the tension, tearing his gaze from her husband to smile at her. "We will move Jane back to your rooms as soon as she is strong enough."

"I thank you for your kindness, Master Hatton."

"Think nothing of it, Mistress LeSieur," Hatton responded, bowing low over her hand.

"She won't, I assure you," Henry interrupted, pulling her arm away from Hatton's grasp. "Frances, if I might have a word?"

"Of course, my lord husband," she said, inclining her head with a magnanimous bow. There was no reason for him to be rude. What did he think Hatton was going to do? Molest her hand?

Mary and Mistress Parry remained in Jane's sickroom as Frances followed Henry down the narrow stairs and out into the sunlight. She could almost keep time by the steady tick in his jaw.

"I trust this morning has found you well." Frances feigned a casual tone that she did not feel.

His mouth quirked in a half smile and, still holding her gloved hand, he leaned against the arched gatepost in the guardhouse kitchen garden. "I do very well and thank you for asking."

She heard the humor behind the banal pleasantry and wondered if he'd ever shown that trait before. "You are welcome," she murmured the expected reply.

Silence stretched, heavy with the weight of everything unsaid. Uncomfortable with the pleasant mask in place once more, Frances held her head high and did *not* wring her hands. Nor did she honestly smile or, well, anything. *Proper, always proper.*

The awkward holding pattern reminded her of that initial interview in his rooms at Westminster, both of them too proud and stubborn to allow the other to perceive weakness.

"My lord husband," Frances stiffened her spine and gathered her courage. Just like last night's wine, it was better out than in. "How did I come to be in my room last night?"

"Were you truly that far in your cups? I didn't know you had it in you."

"Answer my question, please." She held her ground, fists planted on the pleats springing from her hips. "And, yes," she admitted, "I have never been drunk before, and it does not sit well with my constitution. I remember very little."

A spark of an idea flared to life. Could she pretend she didn't remember the kiss? Frances looked up to see him watching her.

"So, Frances," why did her name sound so personal when he said it, "what do you think of court thus far?"

She watched his lips. "You shaved your beard." Hadn't she said that already?

"You changed your hair."

She raised a hand to her head and tucked a stray tendril behind her ear. She had known this man for ten years, laid with him, born his children—this should not be so painfully awkward. She turned away and walked to the bench at the far side of the garden, shooing a chicken out of her way so she could sit.

"Did you know it was me last night?" Henry's words broke the silence once more.

"At the masque? No, I did not recognize you." She resisted the urge to look back at him, to analyze the newly shaven curve of his chin for similarities to the husband she pictured.

"You flirted with me," he continued, sitting beside her on the bench, crushing her skirts.

"I flirted with everyone. I've learned that is the way of the court. It would be strange if I didn't." She tugged on the fabric to no avail. "It means nothing."

"You kissed me."

She raised her chin and met his warm gaze. "No, you kissed me. I cooperated."

His lips curved in a smile that hinted at a familiarity of years but seemed so new. "You liked it."

She looked down at her lap and cleared her throat. "As you pointed out, I was in my cups. I did not know myself. It could have been anyone kissing me." And that was the hard truth. She never saw, not really, the man she'd kissed. Given that, would anyone's kiss have roused her the way it had?

"That does you little credit, wife."

She snapped her eyes to his, his harsh tone snuffing out the building warmth in her belly. "Would it matter if I were to kiss another man? It was, after all, only a kiss. Those are traded about the court like sweetmeats."

"It could have become more than a kiss very easily."

"Really? You have me at a disadvantage in that, my lord husband. The first time I shared a kiss with you was on our wedding day. That kiss led only to breakfast. The other times were equally perfunctory, like we had a set of rules to follow. Kiss, couple, and good night. We never moved past the awkwardness of the wedding night. We were children then and never grew up. Not together." And all of it, every experience wrapped up together, was nothing, *nothing*, like what she remembered from last night. The past kisses, past coupling, had been obligatory and unpleasant. Last night's kiss *was* actually intimate.

Anger warred with wistful longing over what they could have had, at everything that their marriage was not. She wondered how the memories played out from his perspective. Had he been as nervous, as frightened, on their wedding night as she?

The only answer was the clucking of a hen as it worked its way around the garden at their feet.

"It matters."

"What?" her voice came out embarrassingly breathless.

"Whom you kiss."

Again, that blighted warmth blossomed in her center at the idea that he cared. She swallowed against it. "Why? Does it matter whom *you* kiss?"

"Me?" He laughed, actually laughed. "I do not go about court kissing ladies."

It was her turn to laugh, a bitter sound. "I agree on that point. Baroness Sheffield is no lady."

He raised a brow, that hint of mirth sparkling in his eye. "While I do not disagree, I wonder what makes you think I shared a kiss with Baroness Sheffield."

"Now that I think on it, it was not a kiss that she said you shared. My mistake."

"Upon my honor, I have had no relations, kissing or anything more, with Baroness Sheffield." His affront faded into a smile. "Frances, are you jealous?"

"Jealous? Me? That would be unseemly." She fanned herself. "I think that it is you who are jealous of whom I might kiss."

"But you kissed me."

"I had little say in the matter."

"You will not accuse me of forcing your hand. You kissed me back."

She nodded, unable to pretend she had not been a willing participant. Whatever happened next, she would hold dear that memory of strong arms, soft lips, and heat. In that moment, she'd known she was wanted, and no matter how drunk she'd been or what an arse her husband may be, God's teeth, even the thought made her chest tight and her mouth dry.

She looked up to find him staring at her. His lashes, too long to belong on a man, framed a gaze so dark she couldn't help but stare. "What?" She ran a hand over her coiled hair and straightened the pleated collar of her partlet. "Is aught amiss, my lord husband?"

"Henry."

Again, tingles ran across her skin at the sound of his voice. She couldn't tell if it was fear or, what? Anticipation? He leaned closer, and she bit her lip.

"Please, Frances, I would have you call me Henry."

"Henry," she whispered, her gaze shifting from his eyes to his lips. Was he going to kiss her? He was! Oh goodness, should she let him? Her jaw tightened as she leaned away, back stiff and eyes wide. Wait, no—why not? It went well last time, not counting the vomit. With a worried grimace, she squeezed her eyes shut, puckered her lips, and waited.

And waited.

Frances opened one eye to find him with his head cocked, regarding her with raised brows.

"What?" she asked, running a self-conscious hand over her bodice, her cheeks.

He smiled and asked, "Did you wish for me to kiss you?"

She straightened. Of course Henry wouldn't kiss her. That would be the behavior of a lover, not a husband. Damn his pride—hers stung more than ever. "I pray pardon, my lord husband. I forgot myself."

"Frances…"

"No, my lord. We have never been familiar with each other, and I see no reason to change the nature of our relationship." She stood and shook out her skirts. To think she'd wondered what he thought of her new gowns, her new role as a lady of the court. She would not care because he *could* not.

"Frances, I wish to discuss your request for a separation." He followed her up the garden path and braced his hands above her on the low lintel of the door. "I hoped you would reconsider after last night."

"Last night," her voice rang with a bitterness she hadn't felt since arriving at court. "The people last night were not us, husband. A masked man stole a kiss from a masked woman during a night of revelry. You and I are incapable of such..."

"Passion?" he asked, pulling the book from a hidden pocket in his breeches. "I disagree. Before last night, I would have thought so, but now..." He thumbed through the book, opening it to the page Frances had marked with a satin ribbon, one showing a man kneeling between his lover's thighs. The action itself had not called to her as much as the look of absolute joy on the woman's face, the sort of joy Jane described as coming from *la petite mort*.

"Something has changed between us. I want a chance to explore the possibilities with you before I agree to your request."

Part of her wanted the same thing, but a larger part clenched her legs together in a death grip at the thought. One very real fear reared and refused to be ignored. "I will not let you use me. I cannot survive losing another child." Her words rushed out garbled from tears she hadn't noticed streaming down her cheeks. When had she started crying? She hadn't thought there were any left, that she was too numb to waste the energy.

Gone was the polite stoicism, the mask that had become far too real over the past ten years. In its place pulsed a raw wound. She longed to hold her children, to be loved herself. Frances tried to soften her jaw and smooth her forehead but could not calm the sobs that wracked her body.

Hard arms wrapped around her, supporting her shaking shoulders. A warm hand drew lazy circles on the back of her neck, fingers speared through her hair, holding her head firmly against the heat of a worked velvet doublet.

This man was nothing like the husband she'd known, the man who would have politely bowed and left the room at the first hint she needed privacy. This man, *Henry*, held her despite the mess as everything poured out onto his fine London suit. Fear that she'd failed her children, the living and the dead. Fear for Jane's welfare, the niggling worry that there was more about the attack she didn't understand. Fear that she no longer knew herself. Who was this new Frances, so vulnerable and needy? She hadn't needed her husband these past ten years, so why was she crumbled and lost in his arms?

She looked up, tears blurring her vision but the concern still clear on his face. She closed her eyes in confused relief as he pressed a soft kiss to her forehead. Her shoulders sagged as she let herself, for the first time she could remember, be held.

Chapter Eleven

Rule Thirty: Thought of the beloved never leaves the true lover.

The masque for St. Luke's day in mid-October heralded the true end of summer. The deer park to the north of the palace changed from green to a stunning array of russet and gold as the days shortened, and the sunlight took on a softer quality as if it knew it was in short supply and didn't want to spend itself too soon. While October coursed its way toward November, Frances, Mary, and now-somber Jane learned routines at the palace only partly involving avoiding Henry LeSieur.

One warm November morning Frances waited upon Queen Elizabeth as she rose and dressed for the day. This routine was only different today because Frances and almost all of the women of the court were on their monthly courses and emotions ran higher than usual. Frances laced the center back of the Queen's heavy silk corset in silence while Lady Oxford presented various pairs of sleeves. Queen Elizabeth remained silent and selected the padded crimson silk. Even though two weeks had passed since Jane's attack, the air at court was thick with tension. All the ladies present, with exception of Lady Howard, knew better than to speak.

It was evident that Lady Oxford was stifling her irritation at Lady Howard's innocent but completely inappropriate comment about the comeliness of Lord Oxford's youthful retainers. Frances, lost in her own memories of soft lips trailing down her throat, of the way Henry had held her while she cried, tried to ignore the catty bickering that grew around her as she secured the tapes of Queen Elizabeth's farthingale and tied the bumroll, then moved out of the way while Lady Essex dropped the petticoat over the Queen's head.

Frances carried the heavy mahogany brown cut velvet overskirt for the ladies to drape over the Queen's petticoat of crimson silk. Lady Northampton, newly arrived to court after the death of her husband, commented uncharitably that Lady Howard should cease her prattling as it was giving her a headache. Lady Essex broke her silence and made the suggestion to Queen Elizabeth that perhaps Lady Northampton was unhappy at the English court and wished to return to Sweden. Lady Howard, prattling still in full force, fitted the Spanish Doublet style bodice over Queen Elizabeth's corset and fastened the covered buttons at the front closure. Lady Oxford, out of nowhere, mumbled some comment about the Howard family being best served by the axe as she pinned the front opening of Queen Elizabeth's overskirt in place to show the forepart to perfection.

Queen Elizabeth snapped. "God's wounds, ladies! Get you hence. Go sip some willow bark tea or whatever aids you, but cease your bickering and leave Us in peace!" Aside from Blanche Parry who remained where she was sitting, not one single woman questioned this directive as they each dropped what they were doing, reveranced the Queen, and then quietly exited the room.

"Frances, We would have you stay a moment more." Frances halted in the doorway and turned back into the chamber. The Queen held her arms out to either side while Frances and Blanche hurried to fit the sleeves over the fine lawn of the Queen's chemise and tied the points into the armscye of the bodice.

Both ladies worked in silence while Queen Elizabeth turned her head to address Frances. "Mistress, We do not like this melancholy. The world is a sad enough place without Our most beloved courtiers moping about. You had a most excellent conceit in the theme of Our last masque." Queen Elizabeth moved to sit down upon a small bench followed by Mistress Parry who automatically began styling Her hair. "Robin tells Us that you planned each aspect, from the designs of the banquet down to the costume of the servers. We are most impressed with your ingenuity and attention to detail. We charge you to invent for Us another wondrous evening of revelry to be held the Monday following St. Martin's day." Frances's jaw dropped at both the honor and the work involved, and she quickly checked her expression as the Queen continued, "You will be in Robin…Lord Leicester's charge, but do not let him cow you. We wish to be surprised by your thoughtfulness." Queen Elizabeth admired herself in the glass and smoothed her hands down the rich cut velvet of her doublet. Turning to Frances, she smiled and made a shooing gesture with one hand. "Go to and create for Our court a happy diversion."

A second masque. So soon after the last. A second request, and from the Queen Herself, was high praise—if she'd ever doubted her place at court, this confirmed it. Frances was absolutely up to the task and had so many ideas…

St Martin's day was but one week away. Frances untied the collar of her partlet as she exited the Queen's rooms, through the presence chamber, and out into the gardens. Inspiration and worry in equal measure warred with pride as she calmed herself with enormous gulps of fresh air. The only thing Frances knew for certain was that she did not wish to create another sweltering inferno. If the weather held, a true St. Martin's summer, perhaps the event could be held outside. She crossed the courtyard and out through the arched gate, smiling lightly at the guardsman who fell into step behind her as soon as she stepped from the protection of the palace perimeter. Sunlight glinted off the Thames, casting the river in a cloak of diamonds. The sight took her breath away, and she knew that whatever the theme, the masque would be upon the water.

Relief coursed through her as she smiled at the guardsman on duty and entered the palace once more. By the time she reached her room, she had composed lists in her head and merely needed to transfer them onto parchment for preparations to begin. She kicked off her slippers, and untied her farthingale and bumroll, letting them drop to the floor in a soft whoosh. Sitting on the bed she grabbed her lap desk and got to work, not worrying about crumpling her pale sea foam green silk taffeta skirts. By the time she was finished with the preliminary details, the oblong squares of sunlight had worked their way across her wall. Planning a new masque was an excellent distraction from worrying about Henry and his promise, or threat, to woo her.

All thought ground to a halt when she noticed a canvas-wrapped parcel sitting on her dressing table. Was this from Henry? A gift? Frances crossed the room and loosened the twine. She released her breath, not wanting to admit disappointment when it was only her underskirt returned from the fuller. Had they been able to get the stains out? She didn't have high hopes. The vomit stains on the delicate silk had seemed pretty permanent. As she unwrapped the canvas and held the forepart up for inspection, something heavy thudded to the floor, but Frances paid it no mind; her attention was fixed on her destroyed garment. Her hands trembled as she tried to understand the slashed, unrecognizable silk. She dropped the skirt as if burned and stepped away, only to step on something squishy. Hopping back, she saw the item that had fallen out of the bundle—a rat. A dead rat wrapped in a rosary. Frances felt the bile rise in her throat as she struggled to her feet in search of her husband.

• • •

Frances felt the heat in Henry's gaze as she paced the small confines of his room at Westminster. He'd seemed glad to see her at first, but the joy in his eyes promptly turned into menace when she explained her fears. She pitied the man he called enemy.

The dead rat lay on the pile of shredded silk on his desk. The rosary, not notable on its own accord, wrapped the rodent so tightly it cut through the fur around its neck. She couldn't look at it without shuddering. Even worse, Henry seemed to think there was more to it than a sick joke.

She faced him once more, her skirts twisting about her at the sudden movement. "You expect me to believe that Jane's attack was intended for me?"

"No, but I would like you to consider the possibility."

"It's ridiculous. I am no one at court, a country mouse with new clothes."

"Hardly that. Do not pretend otherwise."

"But I am still of no consequence. What would an attack on me accomplish?"

"It is hard to give reasons for the random violence I have seen in London. Sometimes there are no reasons for a madman's obsession. Do not discount yourself. This last masque made you something of a celebrity at the palace. You are important to the Queen, and She is at constant risk." He drew a hand over his face, suddenly appearing tired. "It is also possible..." He paused, true concern printed on his brow. "That an attack at you may be aimed at me."

"I am of less consequence to you than I am to the Queen. Harming me would do very little to you. Besides, why would someone wish you ill?" Frances found the idea ridiculous. "Does someone have it out for Nottinghamshire, then? They hate sheep?"

"Yes, Frances, they hate sheep," he said, his voice droll. "You think you are of no consequence to me? That I would not care if you were injured? You think so little of me, then?"

She stared at him, marveling at the guilt he manipulated from her. "The rat," she gestured to his desk, "was delivered to me. Now, not only do you wish to make it about you, but you seek to make me feel badly that I would not consider your feelings. My safety, the safety of my ladies, has been violated, and yet you wish me to worry that I may have hurt your sensitive disposition. Pardon me for being a harpy in this instance, but I refuse to bend to your whims." Henry LeSieur was, no doubt about it, a horse's arse. "Hence my wish for separation."

Fire flared over her cheeks, but she held her chin high, refusing to be embarrassed by her unladylike behavior. Unladylike? No, she was being a downright shrew and for no good reason.

Henry looked stunned for less than a second before smiling, straight, white teeth framed by his full lips. His smile made his eyes crinkle just so, made her want to smile too.

"If you stop looking at me like I'm a horse's arse," he said, "mayhap I can explain the rational thought behind my concerns."

Not only had he just read her mind, but it was very possible that he'd just called her irrational. It wouldn't have stung if it hadn't been true.

"Pray, my lord husband," she strove for serenity in her expression, "enlighten me."

• • •

Henry felt caught in a whirlwind as Frances jumped between anger and humor, the transitions as entertaining as they were endearing. "Was that fire always there in you?"

"What do you mean?"

"I mean the stubborn set to your mouth and the well-placed sarcasm. Your anger, amusement, and the lack of space in between the two. The light in your eyes and the courage to challenge me, to let me know you think I'm a horse's arse."

"I never actually said that aloud," she muttered past her hands. She almost achieved that bland look, that bored proper lady expression, then sighed and turned her face skyward.

"Are you imploring the heavens?"

"Something like that." She pressed her hands to her cheeks again, massaging her jaw. The stubborn pout faded, but her eyes still shot daggers. She raised her chin and straightened her shoulders, the smallest hint of neck visible above her pleated ruff made his fingers itch to touch her. Instead he watched her regain poise.

She was breathtaking.

"A lady is calm and pleasant in all things."

He cocked a brow and leaned closer. "So the horse's arse sentiment is unacceptable."

"Just so."

He prowled around her, his boots brushing the hem of her skirts. "You should be docile and pleasing toward your husband."

She nodded, hands held loosely before her, back straight, and head high—every inch the lady—as if her randy husband were not thinking about the easiest way to dissemble her layers of clothing. She probably didn't even know. She may have birthed five children, but she was almost as innocent as a virgin.

He tossed his gloves onto the desk and traced a soft line along the back of her neck, teasing the loose hairs there.

She shuddered as he completed his circle, stopping to face her once more.

"And," he continued, "a lady should never ask for a separation, drink herself sick, or kiss random men."

Outrage played across her face as her jaw dropped. He held up a staying hand before she could speak.

"Nay, Frances, I prefer this version to the proper lady of the past ten years. I do not know what to expect and that makes everything," no exaggeration, everything, from the flavor of food to the scent on the night air, all spiced by the constant anticipation knotted in his chest, "*everything* better."

Better was too weak a word, but that was the best he could do.

Sunlight caught and held on to the copper tips of her lashes. He'd never noticed them before. So much about her had changed, but he couldn't help but wonder if something in him had changed too.

"What do you think of the new you?"

She raised her eyes to his. "I don't know that I really changed. It is more like I've shed my masks. Everything I should be, every virtue I have stood for, been taught to value, my whole life. Take that away and, it seems, I do not know the woman who lies beneath."

"That is the woman who has charmed the court." He picked up her hand and placed a kiss on her gloved knuckles. "Has charmed me."

She pulled her hand away. "Do not patronize me. It does your character no credit."

"You think I play you false?"

"I think you seek to salvage your pride."

"And that I have no esteem for you?"

"As you say." She nodded, the stubborn set of her lips begging for a kiss.

"Can I do nothing to convince you otherwise?"

She shook her head. "There is too much past between us for me to trust."

"And yet you fell into my arms…"

"That man was not you. To kiss you, abandon all thought and give in to the moment, would be impossible. There is just too much," she gestured to her head, her heart, her stomach, "for me to let that happen."

"But it was me."

"And yet he was not. He was a moment of romance at a masked ball. That man had no expectations, no history. It was all new with me, the not-always-pleasant woman behind the mask."

He bit the inside of his cheek. If he wanted to start fresh with his wife—no, with Frances—he must truly start at the beginning.

"The man and woman who shared a passion at the masque were strangers then. Perhaps they shall meet again." He let his words hover and watched the suggestion take hold.

"Yes," she agreed, color flooding her cheeks again as she bit her lip. "The next masque is in three days' time. Mayhap they will find each other again then."

He smiled like an idiot. "Anything is possible."

Chapter Twelve

Rule Four: Love constantly waxes and wanes.

Frances had been fully awake since the clock chimed four but had not wished to rise and ready for the day. Not yet. So much had to be done for the masque—but first she had to let inspiration strike and give her a viable theme. *Any theme.* Please God, let inspiration strike…and let her stop thinking about what might happen there with her husband. The masque of sin and virtue had been her brainchild but, ultimately, was a group endeavor. This was all on her, even "Robin," the Earl of Leicester, had told her so despite the fact that it came out of his purse. But what to do? She needed a plan more cohesive than simply something on the river. Frustrated, but full of partial plans, Frances rose and rang for her ladies to assist in her dressing.

Good Lord! Frances stopped dead in her tracks, her eyes fixed on the wall sconce beside her bed. There, hanging in righteous splendor, was the rosary. Surely it was not the same one? A cold that had nothing to do with the November morning seeped into Frances's bones, and she sat down on her bed, her stomach a knot in her throat. Someone was mocking her—or threatening her. She had watched Henry throw it in the fire, watched it smolder and burn. This could not be the same one, but it was an exact duplicate. Henry may be right after all.

She still did not understand what would make him a target, and through him, her, but she had heard enough about some of the goings on at court to know that people did not need reasons for bad behavior. She pulled the rosary from the wall and tossed it in the grate, shivering in revulsion at the thought that someone had hung it in her room. It hadn't been there when she'd gone to bed, which meant someone came into her room while she slept.

Fighting panic, Frances closed and secured her windows and pulled the heavy damask draperies shut. The worries following the attack on Jane had been assuaged by the Queen's Guard, but she'd been foolish to let herself feel safe. Henry had warned her that she might be the subject of some foul intrigue, but that was so outside her understanding, she'd mocked him for it. She had gloried in the fresh breeze from the river and the natural light of the sun as it filtered through her open window. No more… No longer could she force a false sense of security. Henry was right—she was not safe here. It was as if she could not trust the palace itself.

Frances moved around the room, lighting candles in their sconces to illuminate the dark room. The bustle of activity made her feel proactive in the cause of her own protection but did nothing to ease her growing tension. How could she concentrate on festivities with this fear dangling over her? She had no choice.

Frances took a deep breath of the increasingly stuffy air of her shut up chamber, and began to ready herself to face the day and her responsibilities to the Queen.

•••

"How now, Mistress?" Kit Hatton gave a courtly reverance with a flourish of his feathered flat cap and gracefully lowered himself to the ground at Frances's feet. Frances's farthingale took up the whole bench, and Hatton, wearing his riding leathers, seemed to have no qualm reclining on the sod. "I am glad to hear Mistress Radclyffe has recovered well. She won over the hearts of half my guards in the hours of her stay." He had a boyish smile that would melt any woman's reserves, but Frances didn't feel it. Certainly, his admiration was flattering, but his flirtations would lead nowhere.

She hoped he knew it. When they first met, she'd been in awe that a man wanted her and wondered if she could respond. Since then, the feeling of being desired had become disturbing—Kit Hatton, at least, was playful. Sir Harry Lee made her skin crawl, his flirtation more like bullying. And Oxford… She threw up a little in her mouth at the very thought. He didn't flirt; he outright told her how he wished to use her body and expected her to be honored. She shook her head against the memory. No, despite the norm that seemed to apply to married ladies, she definitely was *not* going to take a lover at court and did not want to be accused of teasing. She thought she'd been clear in her refusals, but still Sir Harry and Kit Hatton persisted as if there were a price on her head. Sir Harry she had no problem slapping if need be, but she hoped it wouldn't come to that with Kit—he had the makings of a good friend.

"Yes indeed, Jane is much recovered. She is not entirely herself, but such a thing must be difficult to put from your mind." Frances remembered the rosary and the rat, and shuddered. She had not even been attacked—Jane must be struggling through fear every minute of every day.

Hatton's expression softened. "Mistress Radclyffe should be glad it was not worse. She will recover, but do not be surprised if little things upset her. I've seen the strongest men reduced to tears by a sound or smell that reminds them of violence from their past." He rubbed his hand over his face and stifled a yawn. "'Struth, I am tired. I have had the honor to spend every waking minute in audience with our Queen, and I am drained. I hope I can sleep before the morrow's festivities, although I delight in the prospect of a masque where I may simply be a man and not Kit Hatton, the Queen's favorite." He reclined back onto his elbows and lifted his clean-shaven face to enjoy the early November sunlight as if he was relaxing for the first time in weeks.

Though it was an elite position with potential for great political advancement, Frances knew that being the Queen's favorite had to be a huge responsibility. Frances changed the subject. "Well, I have made plans with the kitchens and the buttery for the details of the *al fresco* banquet and coordinated wines. The masque is well on the way to being an evening garden party along the riverfront— not entirely what I had in mind."

"Those of us in the know expect something brilliant from you. May I be of any help? Perhaps, be your muse?"

Frances appreciated his lighthearted charm. Still, she was no nearer to deciding on a solid theme. She had been so distracted by her own fears she could not concentrate on much else.

"And how would you inspire me, Master Hatton?"

He rolled onto one side and propped himself up on an elbow, "I can think of many ways I might give you inspiration. Unfortunately, I cannot provide my services in that department here, though it saddens me." He spoke with such mock sincerity that Frances could not help but smile.

"Worry not, Master Hatton," Frances struck a sober face. "I would not have you in poor favor with Her Majesty on my account. Besides, I have just learned that you are friend to my husband. I would be surprised if that would weather any attempt to *inspire* me too much." Frances stated these obvious facts with a completely stoic face, as if she were doing him a great service. It still seemed illogical that courtiers would dally with each other without respect to their spouses, let alone respect to the concept of fidelity. Flirtation was harmless, but this was too much.

Stifling a smile, he replied as seriously as he could, "Ah, but the threat of discovery is half the fun. I think that I would survive without Henry's friendship."

Unlike her husband, Hatton played by the rules of courtly love. He had the words, the actions; everything he did and said matched her ideas of courtship and affection. Still, none of it seemed real. For all of Henry's dark glares and claims to her person, something about him rang true and made her body ache to respond. None of that followed the course of a courtly affair and made no sense.

Frances attempted to shift the topic of conversation before she made a fool of herself. "Enough of my troubles… I heard that you were financing an expedition to the New World?" Frances had toyed with the idea of celebrating the glory of England by including cultural representations from each section of the English empire. But, the Spanish and French ambassadors would be present and, no doubt, would be a reminder that English imperialism was weak in comparison.

"I would not say it is an expedition. Drake, one of my men, is busy harassing the Spanish colonies of Hispaniola. I have not heard from him directly, but if the Spanish ambassador's complaints have any truth to them, Drake will have made more of a name for himself as a privateer than an explorer."

"Surely Queen Elizabeth does not endorse such acts?"

"What do you think? We all know She will gladly accept gifts from the bounty. I'm sure that Francis Drake will become one of our Queen's favorites if he continues to provide England with riches and embarrass the Spanish at the same time." Hatton was fully reclined on the grass, his hands behind his head and his eyes closed in the sunshine. "Besides, most of the court finds the idea of pirating exciting—scurvy and rape aside."

They both stayed there in a comfortable silence for a moment or so while Frances pondered Kit's words. Up until now, the Turks had dominated the African coast with their pirating. The idea of the Barbary pirate—the swarthy swashbuckler that conquered the waves with ships laden with jewels—was thrilling. Of course, Francis Drake had made English pirating somewhat more official with the idea of the privateer.

"That's it!" Frances jumped to her feet as the idea hit her square in the forehead.

Kit Hatton opened his eyes, lifting his head a fraction to look at her standing above him. "What is?"

"The masque. Pirates! I must make arrangements…" Frances, in an excited frenzy, leaned over the bench to pick up her notebook then righted herself and started toward the gravel path, having momentarily forgotten that Hatton was lying on the ground at her feet.

Her foot caught on Hatton's boot, and there was nothing Frances could do to stave off the inevitable—falling. In a fluster of skirts and loose parchments, Frances found herself sprawled directly on top of Kit Hatton. She struggled to support her weight with her hands only to find herself looking directly into a pair of merry blue eyes. While surprised, he did not appear to be injured.

"Pirates?" Hatton's voice had deepened into a husky whisper while he moved his hands from behind his head, to brush a stray tendril from her face. Frances could not move.

"Yes." Frances's mouth was suddenly very dry. She moistened her lips with her tongue. "It will be perfect." Frances's gaze moved from his eyes to his mouth, so close to hers. Would his kiss devastate her the way Henry's had?

"Perfect," was all he said as his hand slid behind her neck to cup the back of her head and draw her face down.

Their lips merged in a hard kiss. Frances knew without question that he wanted her—wanted her badly. Tentatively, she softened her lips and tried to melt into the sensation. At the first sign of invitation, he deepened the kiss, plundering her mouth. All Frances could do was to allow the onslaught—he was so dominant she could not even participate. It didn't feel right—there was no sweetness to it. The thought that she aroused his desire made her heart beat at double pace, but instead of feeling passion to match his, all she felt was panic. Kit's fingers splayed against the back of her scalp as she tried to lift her head from the kiss. She could not move.

"What's this then?" The deep male voice had a harshness that made Frances stiff with fear.

Hatton opened his eyes and looked up at the intruder upon their all but inaccessible lair. "Sir Harry!" He sounded as jovial as always. "I cannot imagine what you must think. Then again, maybe I can…"

"Mistress LeSieur, my Lady *Chastity*," he said with a sneer and a sarcastic reverance, "it is one thing for a proper lady to stay true to her husband, but another thing altogether for a wanton to look me over in favor of the Queen's plaything."

The malice in his voice sent chills down her spine. Sir Harry had made Frances uncomfortable with his obvious ogling, but she had never thought of him as threatening. She certainly did now. She struggled to get to her feet and brush the grass from her dress as she surreptitiously backed a little farther away from the irate Sir Harry.

"Calm down, Sir Harry! The lady stumbled upon me, and I took a kiss for my troubles. Do not blame Mistress LeSieur for anything other than being clumsy."

"Thank you, Master Hatton. I think." Frances nodded to Hatton as she picked up her scattered papers and secured them once again in her notebook. She could not bring herself to meet Sir Harry's angry stare as she made a quick reverance and continued off to adjust the details of the masque. She hurried toward the kitchens, trying to ignore awareness of Sir Harry's eyes boring into her back as she fled.

• • •

Henry LeSieur sat in a darkened corner of a reasonably reputable tavern. He sipped his small ale from a clean-enough tankard and waited for his companion to arrive. Most of the patrons were seated at the bar or in front of the fire. Henry already felt uncomfortably hot and, not knowing the reason for this meeting, did not want to be too visible. What was so important that Kit Hatton could not discuss it during their meetings at the House of Commons?

Henry had never had a real friendship with Hatton, more of a mutual respect tempered by a touch of competitiveness. Hatton was the Member of Parliament for Northamptonshire, more than a day's ride away from Holme LeSieur, so Henry considered him a neighbor. What could that prancing fool want of him? Not that he was a fool entirely—he was captain of the Queen's guard and, more importantly, an astute businessman and lawyer. Hatton was more of a financier than an estate manager and saw the idea of enclosing the common grounds traditionally used by tenant farmers as a financial opportunity for the gentry. Henry opposed enclosure on the basis that the gentry needed the tenant farmers to be well fed and happy in order to survive. Maybe his soft spot for the working class was a left over from the ideals of *noblesse oblige*: whatever it was, it was a constant battle, and Henry's side appeared to be losing. It wasn't too much of a surprise—most of the Members of Parliament in the House of Commons had higher aspirations and enclosure certainly put more shillings in their pockets.

"Master LeSieur." Henry looked up from his ale to see Hatton giving him respectful reverance. Henry stood up, removing his tall felt hat and reverencing in return. Without a word, he gestured to the seat across the board and sat down. Hatton followed suit.

Henry said nothing, preferring to allow him to show his hand without the advantage of reading his opponent. Were they opponents? Definitely, especially given the ten pounds Hatton put on Frances taking a lover.

Henry nursed his ale and waited patiently.

"I thought we should be forthright with each other," Hatton began. He seemed to be waiting for Henry to say something.

Henry did not oblige.

Hatton continued, with some awkwardness. "I kissed your wife today."

In his mind, Henry neatly inserted his fist into Kit Hatton's pretty face. In reality, he took stock of the situation in as calm of a manner he could. "And you thought that telling me would be a good idea…?" Henry let his words trail off in an unspoken threat.

"Well, not exactly. No." Hatton shifted uncomfortably. The merry sparkle was missing from his eye. He was serious about this. But why? Henry remained silent, willing Hatton to continue. He didn't know how much longer he could hold his temper in check.

"Look—she tripped and fell on me. I took advantage of the opportunity and kissed her. She was not particularly responsive, I should tell you." He took a deep quaff of his ale before continuing. Henry had never seen him so awkward. "The bigger problem here is that Sir Harry Lee happened upon us. He had marked Frances as his but accepted that she did not wish to dally outside her marriage…"

"And he was none too happy to find her dallying with you." Henry's patience was strained close to breaking.

"Precisely." He nodded.

What was he up to? Why would he tell a man that he had just been caught kissing his wife? Henry paused a moment before continuing. "Master Hatton, you have never struck me as a stupid man…"

"I thank you for the observation."

"So what, pray tell, could have possessed you to tell me about your attempt at cuckolding me? Do you want me to call you out?"

Hatton looked genuinely surprised. "You would? Over this?"

With a grimace to cover the feral urge to bare his teeth, Henry murmured, "Before I come to any decisions over what to do with you, perhaps you'd best explain yourself."

"Of course…" Henry was pleased to see Hatton so discomfited. "I wanted to tell you because Sir Harry is not an enemy I should wish for. But my concern is not for myself but for Frances…. I mean, Mistress LeSieur."

"I am moved to see you hold her so high in your esteem."

"Sir Harry now feels spurned. And he can no longer soothe his pride by writing it off to her being a virtuous woman."

Understanding dawned and Henry sighed. "And you worry he may take more aggressive action toward her." That was the last thing he needed—one more threat against his wife.

"Exactly. You understand my concern now." He had a hopeful expression. It was clear that he did not wish to cause offense—or maybe he simply did not wish to be killed. It appeared Hatton had a healthy fear of Henry. Perhaps he was smarter than Henry had previously credited.

"I think I'm beginning to." At least he would there to offer the protection of both his name and his fists at the masque. Perhaps it would be best for him to assert himself as a possessive husband publicly and end this charade about their separation. This had gone on too long. He'd done it to it himself by, through omission, never indicating to anyone that he had a wife and children at home. To him it had been immaterial, and his relationships with the other courtiers were hardly personal enough to share such intimacies. But now that she was here and not asserting herself as his wife, it made her open to any and all advances. It was part of the games at court, something she wouldn't have been prepared for. And he'd only fueled the fire.

She's my wife, damn it all, and she's going to acknowledge it even if I have to make her.

Then again, that would end any chance he had of actually winning her. Then again, if her idea of a separation involved kissing Hatton…but no, today's kiss had been foisted upon her and even Hatton agreed that she was not a willing participant.

"One more thing…" Hatton interrupted Henry's thoughts hesitantly, as if not sure if one more thing would prove too much.

Nodding magnanimously, Henry took a sip of his ale and encouraged his companion. "Yes?"

"Should Queen Elizabeth believe that Mistress LeSieur and I are lovers, it will put us both in poor favor."

"Master Hatton, if you and my wife are lovers, you will have more to fear than the Queen."

• • •

Pirates. The very word filled Frances with excitement. Well, this changed everything. There was still time enough to alert the bakers to make the bread trenchers shaped as small ships. Of course, fine wines would not do—no, the servers would provide ale and cider in tankards. The pavilions set around the southern flower gardens would be draped with yards of silks from the orient as if a pirate bounty had been unfurled at random. The plate and service ware would be fine but mismatched. Oh, it was all coming together. Frances only needed to tell a few of the courtiers to spread word so the lords and ladies could assemble their costumes.

This would provide the perfect venue for revelry and give the jaded courtiers the opportunity to lose inhibitions and fears as they danced under the stars and pretended that their masks made them truly incognito. Frances knew from the way her creativity sparked and the plans flowed through her that this was the right course—even if it was only a "masque" in the sense that the guests would be masked. Deviation, albeit unknowing, from the norm had served her well with the St. Luke's day masque, and she was sure it would again. In fact, Frances had such a strong feeling of rightness about the event that, as the plans progressed and time sped on toward the Monday masque, she never found herself questioning any of her decisions or consulting other courtiers.

The day before the masque passed in a blur. Frances felt as if she were constantly running to confirm or change plans with the head chefs, gardeners, butlers, and steward. She instructed the servants working on the decorations for the garden pavilions. She supervised the servants working on the barges. She arranged for some of the finer specimens in the Queen's guard to be costumed for the court's entertainment. She organized the sequence of dances to tell a story. She created the thematic menus. She was proud of herself. She was exhausted.

St. Martin's day arrived and, being Sunday, was a day of much needed rest. Everything was set in motion for tomorrow, and Frances could sit back and enjoy the fruits of her labors. Dressed in a lavender gray velvet gown, Frances left her rooms to join Queen Elizabeth and Her ladies at Mass. It was probably sacrilegious, but all throughout the sermon, Frances could think about nothing other than the possibility of what might happen with Henry, or rather, her masked mystery man.

She closed her eyes as if in prayer and, instead, remembered how he felt—the press of his hands at her back as he crushed her breasts against his chest. She drew as deep a breath as her corset allowed and imagined that the pressure of her gown straining against her nipples was the caress of his hand. His lips as they traced down her neck. Frances wondered what it would be like to feel that mouth press hot kisses on her…

Breaking out of her reverie, she chanted "And also with you" and stood with the congregation. Lately, she had successfully avoided succumbing to these fantasies by keeping her thoughts completely occupied with plans for the pirate masque but, from time to time, she would catch herself wondering about him. Did he think of her too? And how far was she willing to go? On the whole, she managed to keep her head on task and out of the clouds. Of course, it was difficult *not* to let her mind wander during the preacher's lecture on the many faces of Satan. How irreverent of her.

Frances maneuvered her farthingale as she exited the pew she shared with Lady Howard and Baroness Ludlow. She faced the apse and crossed herself before turning to leave the sanctuary. Her behavior in church was habit and hard to break even though the cross above the altar did not bear the body of Christ. She never advertised her family's Roman Catholic background, nor had she kept it a secret. Queen Elizabeth knew and did not seem to think less of her for it so long as she gave her allegiance to the Crown. In truth, Frances had not once made an effort to hear a Roman Catholic Mass since her arrival at court, feeling that the Church of England provided ample spiritual sustenance.

It was apparent that not everyone at court approached the controversy of Roman Catholic versus Church of England with the same blasé attitude. Some of the courtiers were so fervent in their opinion on the subject, that Frances found that she would rather not give anyone fodder for abuse as far as her beliefs were concerned. The only evidence that her family's religion had been noticed was that blasted rosary. She shook her head to clear away the unwelcome reminder.

"I am glad to see you still cross yourself, even if it is to a heretical symbol."

What? The unexpectedly harsh whisper came from over her shoulder as she exited the chapel. Turning, she came eye to eye with Baroness Ludlow, who was smiling despite the tone of her voice. Perhaps Frances had misread her intent.

Smiling to her friend, Frances replied congenially, "It is a habit. I hope I did not give offense."

"No, no. You mistake my meaning. I am much gladdened to see that you still hold the true faith in your heart," Baroness Ludlow said with a sincere smile. While never jovial, Baroness Ludlow was at least pleasant. Frances still hoped to call her a friend—it seemed sad that Baroness Ludlow seemed so very alone at court.

"The chapel at Holme LeSieur still has a Catholic priest, and we pay our fine to the Crown gladly. Still, I do not wish to make enemies at court given the suspicions stoked by the massacre in

Paris." Frances may not have felt, personally, very strong about the subject of religion, but she would not do any disservice to her family name.

"And yet you attend Church of England services?"

"As do you, Baroness Ludlow." Frances held on to her smile. What was Baroness Ludlow trying to prove? Weren't they both just leaving the same chapel?

"Oh, yes. I do what I must do to survive, but I do not pray so fervently to false gods."

Frances almost protested that she had not been praying at all during services, but that wasn't necessarily better. Besides, what right was it of Baroness Ludlow to know the innermost workings of her heart? *Goodness*. No wonder Baroness Ludlow was so alone.

At Frances's silence, Baroness Ludlow appeared to remember where she was and corrected herself, "Please forgive me. I am not myself. I did not mean to attack your faith. I'm sure you do only what you must in these difficult times." Even her apology dripped with judgment.

Frances smiled an acceptance and, in a gesture of friendship, took Baroness Ludlow's hand and laced it through the crook of her arm, pulling her to walk alongside her. "Come. Let us sit in the gardens afore dinner. I wish to hear about what you are wearing to the masque tomorrow."

"Since Queen Elizabeth commands my presence, I will be there." Baroness Ludlow's face was marred by a petulant pout. She did all but stamp her foot in childish defiance as she continued, "But I refuse to make merry."

Chapter Thirteen

Rule Twelve: True love excludes all from its embrace but the beloved.

Monday dawned with the promise of a fine day in keeping with St. Martin's summer. Tonight Frances would dance under the stars and lounge on the royal barges upon the Thames. The days were short and the nights were long—the perfect opportunity for dalliance. Frances ran her fingers through her tangled hair as she stretched herself awake. She could hardly wait for the day to melt into twilight.

Frances rose from the bed, walked over to her dressing table, and poured an ewer of tepid water into a basin. As she placed the jug down, she noticed a small parcel wrapped in fine linen and silk ribbon. Her chest tight, she struggled to take a breath and fought the fear and forced herself to be rational even as she backed away. Should she open it? Bring it to her husband? She held her head high. Whatever it was, she could face it. She would not let this evil ruin her night. Determined to be strong, she walked back to the package.

Summoning her courage, Frances pulled the ribbon loose and removed the folds of yellow linen. Inside lay a plain box containing a delicate item in a fine velvet pouch. Next to that lay a sprig of baby's breath tied with pink ribbon. Her breath caught in her chest as she realized Henry must have been in her room as she slept. Fear turned to joy as excitement pulsed through her veins. *I will see him tonight.* Her skin tingled in anticipation as she opened the velvet pouch. Inside was a beautifully wrought silver bodice dagger and sheath set with garnets and amber. It was glorious and, even better, would go perfectly with her costume.

This ensemble was as bold as her previous one had been innocent. The bodice and overskirt were luxurious black silk velvet. Her bodice closed with hidden hook and eyes at the center front, the seam disguised by a row of garnet cabochons bezel set in silver filigree ovals. Other than the glittering stripe of silver and garnet up the front of her bodice, the black was unadorned and offered a striking contrast against the exposed décolletage of Frances's pale skin. She did not wear elaborate oversleeves, instead choosing to expose the sleeves of her billowing white cotton lawn chemise which hinted at the state of undress. She smiled as she felt the weight of the jeweled hilt of the small dagger in her palm.

Frances called for Mary to help her as the sun sank lower behind the haze of smoke from wood fires that billowed above London city. Mary dressed Frances's hair in a looser and more rumpled looking version of the current fashion, allowing for clustered tendrils to flow down Frances's neck and frame her face. Frances put on her simple black leather eye mask and secured the ribbons behind her head. Mary placed a deep red rose into the mass of amber curls above her ear while Frances completed her ensemble with a pair of black fitted kid gloves with a broad gauntlet style cuff and placed the sheathed dagger in the busk channel of her corset, pleased with how the glittering bejeweled hilt sparkled like a suspended brooch against her breasts. The vision in the mirror was a little bit ladylike and a little bit wanton. Perfect.

• • •

Hundreds of glittering lanterns hung suspended from the boughs of the oaks that bordered the eastern edge of the flower gardens. Torches mounted on makeshift pillars of chunky driftwood and laden tables covered in fishing nets dotted the geometric flower garden. Pavilions of varying sizes draped in elaborate arrays of silks and satins from the Orient obscured the brick façade of the southern walls of Hampton Court Palace. A trio of gilded mermaids augmented the babbling song of the tiered fountain in the center of the gardens as they harmonized their vocals with melody from their lap harps. Cables of thick nautical rope dripping with orbs of light streamed in a fan shape from the ramparts of the palace down to the archways framing the entrance to the three river piers that moored the Queen's barges.

Frances arrived long before the other courtiers in order to finalize any last-minute questions with the servers. She smiled in triumph, her heart swelling with pride as she took in the vision of a Barbary pirate fantasy. Beautiful. The plethora of twinkling lights lit up the November night sky and reflected off of the urns of overflowing paste gems and pearls. The luxurious fabrics, apparently pillaged from a Spanish galleon, adorned the banquet tents with splendor fit for a pirate queen. Haunting music from the mermaids in the fountain drifted throughout the garden on the soft river breeze. Frances checked with the butlers that the three "dockside taverns" were stocked and ready to serve the noble pirate guests from their rough-hewn bar atop empty barrels. The St. Martin's summer night was pleasantly warm, and the pewter tankards were chilled and brimming with frothy ales and crisp ciders.

Frances stopped next to a dingy-turned-table full of treasure chests of sweetmeats. The open chests spilled heaps of tartlets bearing ruby cherries and amber glazed pears, flowing strands of candied figs, marzipan jewels, and almond jumbals painted with saffron to give the appearance of being gold medallions. She popped a fig into her mouth and willed herself to relax and shift her mindset from organizer to reveler.

The Earl of Leicester was the next courtier on the scene. His Turkish turban was laughably ostentatious.

"So the master of the revels has arrived! How now, my lord?'" Frances extended her arms out to the sides to better display her costume as she made her courtly reverance.

With an almost imperceptible gesture for Frances to recover and a very obvious appreciative appraisal of Frances's appearance, Leicester laughed. "I see you are in excellent spirits! And why not? This masque looks to be an excellent event. You have outdone yourself. What is worse, you have set the bar high! I shall be hard pressed to best you when I next have the honor to host Her Majesty's progress."

"Best me? My lord, you are an optimist. Have a care lest you fall into a melancholy over setting unattainable standards." Frances extended her leather gloved hand to the Earl of Leicester, and he dutifully led her to the pavilions at the mouth of the gardens to greet the revelers as they arrived.

The masque was designed to appear to be an open forum for revelry and making merry, but every minute was accounted for in Frances's plan. She had scheduled the first hour of the festivities to be an open time for the guests to socialize. Frances had to laugh at herself as she looked at her agenda for the event and saw that section of time blocked off as "unplanned." The first hour gave the courtiers ample time to be fashionably late and still not miss the section that was, in fact, planned. They arrived in a steady flow, availing themselves of delicacies all while they pretended anonymity protected them against any recrimination for bad behavior. It was going to be a memorable evening.

As the courtyard clock in the distance struck seven, a trumpet salute was heard from upriver. A few moments later a responding chorus of trumpets sounded, this time a little closer. The courtiers paused in their carousing and silently searched out the source of the musicians. Again, an even closer salute and the glorious barge became visible as it rounded the river bend and progressed toward the center mooring station. At its approach, the breeze carried a haunting harmony of harps and young voices to the courtiers as they waited in anticipation for something wonderful.

The barge neared, and the song from the river merged with the song from the mermaids in the fountain. The court, in their Oriental silks and nautical finery, edged closer to the river walk and the piers. The music was hypnotizing. The vessel pulled up to the post and four excellent specimens of manhood jumped lithely to the dock and secured it in place. A curtain shielded the occupants of the barge from view and shimmered like a thousand sparkling scales in the light of the lanterns as the debonair sea men slowly secured it open and hoisted the sedan chair at its center. Queen Elizabeth was raised, as if suspended in a crystal bubble, and carried onto the pier. Her skirts flowing around her like seaweed in strands of aqua, peridot, cerulean, and azure silk. Her bodice seemed to be constructed out of shards of mother of pearl and twinkled in the lamplight reflected off the river. Her hair trailed down over her shoulder in blue and silver waves. In Her right hand, She held a magnificent trident. She was the Queen of the Sea.

As one, the courtiers dropped reverently to one knee as the Earl of Leicester declared, "Three cheers for Elizabeth Gloriana! Hip-hip!" and the crowd boomed "Huzzah!" By the third "Huzzah!" the crowd was so focused on their sheer adoration for their Queen that the very implication that She might speak caused a hush.

"For tonight, I am the Queen of the sea and those who sail upon Our domain had best pray We are in goodly spirits." Queen Elizabeth's voice, as always, rang with authority, but tonight Frances could also hear the subtle warning to Her favorites.

"Madam, we will all do our utmost to keep you well pleased this evening. Are we agreed?" In response to Leicester's question, Kit Hatton and Sir Harry Lee both went down on their knees yet again and laid their hats over their hearts. Frances was surprised that Sir Harry was within the elite group—but then he *was* the

Queen's champion, regardless of how boorish and intimidating Frances considered him.

Leicester continued in his role as master of revels for the masque. "Your Gracious Majesty, is there naught that could be done to win your good graces?"

Queen Elizabeth had contributed to this portion of Frances's script herself. "Yes, Master Pirate. I would have you prove your worth to sail upon Our sea and win the treasures We hide within." *How scandalous.* "Musicians, the galliard!"

The drummer struck up the beat, and Leicester lost no time in hopping into the dance. Kit Hatton, notably the best dancer at court, jumped into the fray and turned a fine leg to the enjoyment of all. Frances scanned the male dancers, searching for Henry. He would be costumed—would she even recognize him? Disappointed, Frances hefted a pewter tankard of cider from one of the driftwood ale stands and meandered through the thickening crowd. All around her there was laughter and shrieks of surprise and delight as the courtiers drank and jested and danced and flirted under the protection of their face masks. Frances made her way to sit on the edge of the fountain and sip at her cider.

"Mistress, this is a most wondrous conceit and will long be remembered by many as the night their illegitimate child was conceived." An unusually merry Lady Oxford spread her skirts as she sat beside Frances. She was generally of a serious bent that belied her young age.

Frances let out an awkward laugh. "Really, Lady Oxford, I cannot tell if you jest or seek to censure the court's illicit delights."

Lady Oxford smiled sincerely. "No, no, Mistress LeSieur, it is exactly what the courtiers would wish for. Brilliant really. Tonight's theme is something that most can enjoy in whatever way they like. I will enjoy the dancing and the costumes and watching others make fools of themselves. You may enjoy a flirtation or two," Frances blushed, "and my husband will attempt to violate whatever creature under God that he can and all around will cherish the laughable memory of his antics for years to come." Anne Cecil was obviously in no humor to ignore her husband's publicly debauched behavior—but it was hard to tell if it was something that actually upset her. From everything Frances had heard, Anne Cecil had known what she was getting into when she married the Earl of Oxford.

Frances smiled in sympathy. "Well, Lady Oxford, I think he is due to be sorely disappointed and not a little embarrassed." With a nod of her head she gestured to where the Earl of Oxford stood on the wall of the fountain, oblivious to the crowd that gathered around him, improvising poetry in an effort to woo the gilded mermaid musicians at the center of the fountain. The players, probably used to this type of abuse, very ably continued their music even while they crooned rejoinders to the Earl's obscene suggestions.

The Earl of Oxford, either unaware or uncaring of his wife and Frances watching him from less than five feet away, removed his boots with great aplomb and stepped over the wall and into the bubbling fountain. The mermaids squealed in dramatic delight and continued their song. Frances could not tell if they would have fled Oxford's advances had they not been handicapped by their tails or allowed him to catch them anyway—they were hired players after all. The crowd surrounding the fountain cheered Oxford on as he hoisted one of the golden-haired beauties over his shoulder and made to carry her away. The mermaid feigned a swoon while her comrades hurled witty curses in couplets at the abductor.

Oxford dropped the mermaid into a pile of silken cushions at the entrance to one of the garden pavilions. Playing to his audience with grand gestures, he moved the golden tresses that artistically concealed the mermaid's apparently naked form only to reveal a disappointing lack of bosoms.

"This lass has the chest of a twelve-year-old boy!" Oxford exclaimed with a laugh of derision, moving the mass of hair aside further as he displayed the topless mermaid to the crowd.

With the earl's rough handling, the mermaid's blond wig tumbled to the floor to reveal closely cropped dark hair. Having been thus discovered, the hired actor, presumably deciding to play to the crowd rather than try to preserve the charade of being a mermaid, replied in a youthful but masculine voice, "No, my Lord, not twelve—I am a nineteen-year-old man!"

At this, the laughter of the crowd and the crush of bodies attempting to witness the Earl of Oxford's unfortunate behavior completely blocked Frances and Anne's view. "He should not have been surprised. Did he think Queen Elizabeth would allow such blatant immorality at Her masque?" Frances replied between laughs. What had started as an unaffected viewing of a man embarrassing himself and his family had evolved into a genuine comedy. He deserved any humiliation he got. Stupid man. It was common knowledge that women were not allowed on the stage in London. Though it was a private party and outside London, Frances had still chosen to err on the side of caution and hired a company of reputable players to play the mermaids and help add an element of drama to the surprise entertainment later.

"Worry not, mistress. My husband's amorous pursuit of the poor player will only be postponed for enough time to gather his wits and change his tactics." Anne's acerbic assessment of her husband was not wasted on Frances. While it may have been borderline acceptable for the earl to have dallied with a woman in public, he could not do so with a man without the very real potential for recrimination. Most courtiers were calloused to sexual exploits outside of the norm; nonetheless, sodomy was a crime. In regard to the Earl of Oxford, even though no one openly spoke of his varied interests and exploits, everyone knew—especially his wife. Frances felt sorry for her. It must have shown in her expression.

"Mistress, you are kind to worry over me." Lady Oxford raised an elegant hand in soft protest. Her husband may be ravaging a hired actor behind a bush somewhere, but she held her poise, ever the lady. "I had no illusions of fidelity when we wed. This does not change anything. I am still a countess. I am at court with Queen Elizabeth and have title, wealth, and leisure time. I am not to be pitied." For a split second, Lady Oxford's face hardened behind her smile.

Frances, feeling nothing but pity, could think of nothing good to say. As unhappy as she had been back at the Holme, she had never been disrespected so publically or embarrassed. She'd simply been ignored to a point where she wondered at her own value. She deserved happiness, as did Lady Oxford. Perhaps, eventually, they'd both figure out how to achieve it.

"Ladies, I think that the story of Oxford's debacle will rank upon the top ten memories in my lifetime."

Frances was saved from having to respond when a turbaned Kit Hatton seated himself between the two women, crushing their skirts. "At the last masque, my favorite story was of Baroness Sheffield and Sir Harry Lee's unsuccessful dalliance. I wish I had been able to see it! They say that Baroness Sheffield started screaming from an alcove off the hall. Nearby revelers rushed to help the lady, but instead found her on her knees in a pool of vomit!" Hatton's boisterous laughter began to attract attention. Frances had not heard this story yet. Vomit? *Oh dear*. Lady Oxford took this as her cue to leave. Rising, she dislodged her skirts, forcing Hatton to move closer to Frances.

"You must be a scoundrel indeed, for you have no regard for the care of my gown," Frances half joked.

"It is true, Lady Pirate. I hate that gown. Though you are truly ravishing in it, I would rather see it crumpled upon the floor of my chambers." Hatton leaned closer and took a deep sniff of the rose in her hair.

She remained still, but stiff. Was Henry here, watching? Would he be jealous? Jealousy, so the rules of courtly love said, was a sign of love. Silly nonsense. Henry had never shown any emotion of any kind, even at the death of his own children. He'd told her that these things happen, as if she had not already heard that a thousand times. If he could not bring himself to feel something over his own children, it was impossible that he was capable of romantic love, no matter how confusing his behavior had been of late.

Frances almost laughed as Hatton nuzzled his nose into her curls. He continued, "I was hoping to smuggle you onto to my ship and finish what we began earlier this week." Actually, it had been that clumsy kiss which told her for certain that, as handsome as he may be, flirtation would lead nowhere. The kiss at the masque, those stolen moments with Henry as a masked stranger, still curled her toes. Hatton's kiss just left her feeling awkward.

It seemed he hadn't gotten the message that she wasn't interested. Frances was saved from having to respond to Hatton's obvious suggestions by the arrival of the surprise portion of the entertainment.

The wonder of the entertainment, decorations, and feast had mellowed as the party progressed and, overall, the festivities were beginning to slow down. This was the perfect time for the courtiers to gain a new burst of energy, and Frances planned to give them just that. Two barges and three smaller vessels advanced upon the piers. Masked men in varying states of undress, some shirtless and some merely in their shirtsleeves, boots, and black breeches tied at the waist with exotic silk sashes, leapt onto the docks with a riot of shouting before the boats were even completely secured. More than twenty broad-shouldered and bronzed guardsmen in Eastern turbans rushed into the fray of astonished courtiers causing a melee of delight and surprise.

Hatton sighed and shrugged his shoulders before meeting her even gaze. "Mistress, I fear I will be missed at Her Majesty's side. Anon!" He pressed an ineffective kiss to her gloved hand.

Frances smiled as she heard the ladies of the court shrieking with mock outrage as England's cleanest and most attractive privateers carried them off. Of course, Frances gave instruction as to who should be targeted. She chuckled to herself as she imagined what stories Mary would tell in the morning. Perhaps it would provide enough merriment to make Jane sorry she had chosen not to attend. Standing, Frances took in the scenery with a pride of ownership and moved to mingle with the crowd. If Henry was here, let him find her now.

She had not stepped two paces when a large hand gripped her wrist, spun her around, hefted her over his shoulder, and began to weave through the laughing crowd. Frances, in her meticulous outlining of every aspect of this masque, was fairly certain she had not scheduled her own abduction. Still, it wouldn't do to be a spoilsport, so she protested with as much silly melodrama as she could muster as the masked pirate with a very firm behind ran with her to his ship.

• • •

It stood to reason that when a woman is flung over a man's shoulder, the woman would be hanging upside down. If the man in question runs, then the woman will be upside down *and* bouncing. Add to that the impact of the corset—this was very bad indeed. By the time the pirate plopped Frances down onto a pile of cushions, her hair was beyond repair and her stomach was in her throat. She had no one to blame but herself—this had been her scheme after all. Perhaps she should have had some of the guardsmen demonstrate exactly how they planned to abduct the women. Yes, then everyone would have known that carrying a woman like a sack of grain was not feasible if that woman was wearing a corset with an English oak busk at the center ending in a point just above the pelvis. Well, now she knew. Thank God that bodice dagger was sheathed.

"This was a horrible idea," Frances mused aloud to no one in particular. She adjusted her position on the pillows to better accommodate her bumroll and smoothed out her skirts into a more ladylike puddle as she felt the barge begin to move in the last step of the primary masque. Queen Elizabeth and a select few would escape on the barges only to moor them farther along river in the countryside. They would anchor the barges together and have a four-barge square platform for further revelry away from the general court and London. The barges themselves were outfitted with silk draped pavilions, plush floor cushions, and ample food and drink. On top of that, a wagon train waited at their docking site full of servants ready to meet any needs the revelers might have. Frances's only concern was that the court ladies might show favoritism to the previously not noticed guardsmen over the more regular male courtiers. She would just have to wait and see. As Frances did her best to recline into her pile of cushions, she realized, with some disappointment, that being with Queen Elizabeth's specific guests meant that her opportunity to meet with Henry was gone. Her presence on the river was not part of the plan. Right now, the Queen's guard, filling the role of Barbary pirates, would be presenting themselves to the Queen. The other abductees would have their comfort seen to by the servants while they witnessed some pretty poetry and exhibition of male prowess. Whoever had taken Frances had deposited her far from the show, and she was thankful, at least, for that. She hated that she was here at all.

She did not expect the tears that threatened. Steeling her nerves, she blinked the moisture away just as a young serving girl dressed in the Turkish style reveranced her. Frances gestured with a flick of the wrist as she said, "Rise up, mistress. What would you have of me?"

"It's my duty to assist you in removing your farthingale, my lady." Frances had forgotten about this accommodation—but then again, *she wasn't supposed to be here. Damn, damn, and damn.* "The barges are too small for all the ladies in their farthingale to move freely. So, my lady, if you would allow me to assist you…"

Frances offered the girl her hands and was raised out of her pile of cushions. The wench promptly dove under Frances's skirts and undid tapes securing the farthingale to the corset. As the young girl reemerged from the velvet, Frances felt her farthingale drop to the deck and stepped out of it. The girl retrieved it, thanked Frances for her cooperation, and then bore it away. Without the farthingale Frances could feel the weight of the skirts swishing around her legs. At least her skirts were not too long to walk in.

Frances moved through the curtains enclosing the pavilion to stand on the open deck of the barge. The short display before the Queen over, most of the other ladies waited outside already. The barge had a few torches on the deck but, as they sailed further away from the haze of the city, the moon and stars offered ample light.

"Mistress LeSieur, what is the meaning of this?" Two ladies rushed toward her, Lady Oxford and Baroness Ludlow, both without their farthingales. Frances smiled to herself as she wondered what Baroness Ludlow thought about being abducted. She didn't have to wait long.

"Mistress, I have never… That was simply scandalous! I am a virtuous married lady!" Baroness Ludlow was still in too much shock for Frances to tell if she were truly angry or not.

Frances decided to head her off before she could build up steam. "Baroness Ludlow! I am so glad you agreed to come! I hope it is clear after the performance that those men were from Her Majesty's guard. They would have released you if you had instructed them. Nothing will happen this night that you would be ashamed of…"

"Unless you want it to." Lady Rich had joined their circle and was obviously enjoying herself.

Frances laughed, "Aye. This is a private party hosted by Queen Elizabeth, and those herein are honored to be here." Frances spoke with merriment but silently prayed her words carried weight with Baroness Ludlow.

She sighed in relief the instant she noticed Baroness Ludlow's shoulders relax. Frances knew she was taking a chance by having her invited, but she felt that excitement and the opportunity for abandon was something the dour woman sorely needed—whether she knew it or not. Perhaps tonight would be a revelation.

"Mistress LeSieur, this was an amazing idea." Lady Oxford sounded sincere as she looked around at the furnishings on the barge. "My only concern is…"

Frances interrupted with the answer to the unspoken question. "I'm sure that your husband was discouraged from bringing the mermaid player along."

At this, Penelope Rich broke into hiccups of laughter. "Do you know us so well then, oh, self-proclaimed country mouse?"

Frances smiled and gave Lady Rich a playful reverance. "And, of course, Lady Rich, your husband is not here—which should be no surprise." Frances paused, giving time for Lady Rich to raise an eyebrow questioningly, as if testing her. With a wink, Frances continued, "Yes, Colonel Blount *is* here."

Clapping her hands softly in a flutter of wrist ruffs, Lady Rich declared, "Brava, mistress. You have proven yourself worthy."

"Who else is here?" By now Frances was surrounded by at least ten ladies.

"Ladies, please. We are all in disguise! You cannot know the identity of all the revelers. It would take away from the mystery. Remember, you are all anonymous yourselves!" With a playful wag of her finger, Frances mockingly reprimanded the costumed ladies of the court for their impatience.

Before anyone could respond, one of the men guiding the barge yelled something inaudible, and there was a heavy thud as their barge sidled against one of the others. The ladies sat down to wait out the process of the two barges anchoring to one another. Frances watched with appreciation as the sailors removed sections of the balustrade that enclosed the deck and laid down thick planks to make the gap between vessels as seamless as possible. It was expertly done, and before long, four separate vessels became one large venue for a riotous party of the Queen's favorites. Frances had planned the foodstuffs and beverages to be lighter fare than the decadently savory and sweet feast at the primary masque site. Servers from the wagon train on the riverbank carried small wood goblets of crisp golden Canary wine and trays laden with thin sliced manchet topped with smoked fish and soft cheese.

Frances found herself moving to the periphery of the festivities. She was proud of her accomplishments but was exhausted from the week of planning and still upset that she had lost her opportunity to explore the possibilities with Henry under the guise of a mystery man. She leaned against the railing as the selected courtiers mingled under the November sky. As much as she tried to feel excitement at being included at the Queen's private pirate party, she could not shake the bitter disappointment. It felt as though she had lost the chance to discover something very important— something that was a key part of her being. Coming to court helped her redefine who she was as a lady, but as a woman? She had just gotten a taste of her sensual nature at the last masque and it was enough to peak her curiosity. In fact, it was beyond mere curiosity—it was a desperate longing. She needed to explore that hint of passion that had been unearthed in the alcove by an incredible kiss.

Now she might never know.

Fighting the lump in her throat that threatened tears, Frances turned to face the breeze from the river, letting it lift her hair away from her face and sooth her senses. She took a sip of wine and closed her eyes in pleasure as chill sweetness tickled the roof of her mouth and the scent of apples merged with the fragrance from the newly mown fields of the late harvest.

"It is a beautiful night." A deep voice murmured against her ear. "The breeze is so sweet it feels like a lover's caress."

She couldn't move.

He stepped closer, and she could feel the press of his thighs against the back of her skirts. His large hand snaked around her waist to urge her to lean back against his broad chest. Frances felt the heat of his touch through the layers of her bodice and corset as his fingers splayed across her abdomen and ribs, his thumb resting just below the swell of her breast.

She whispered, "You're here."

"Who did you think abducted you?"

"That wasn't part of my plan," she chided.

He answered, "I made my own plans." Frances could hear the smile in his voice, his breath warm at her cheek as he spoke. "Your hair glows like copper silk in the moonlight." He burrowed his cheek into her tumbled curls. "And it smells like springtime."

Frances shivered at the soft heat of his lips as he whispered against the curve of her ear. His breath teased the small wisps of hair framing her face, and she shuddered.

His right hand still held her firmly against his body while the other slid up the length of her arm, then across her bosom and up her neck to cradle her jaw. Frances could not help allowing his hand to guide her as she turned her head to the side then up, her eyes still closed.

His lips closed on hers in an instant, and the world around her disappeared. This man, the man who sparked a wanting within her, a man she could not think of as Henry, he'd found her. He was hers for the night.

Chapter Fourteen

Rule Twenty-Seven: There is no such thing as too much of the pleasure of one's beloved.

Frances stepped onto the broad planks linking the four, no five, vessels. How had he accomplished this? She'd had a difficult time coordinating the royal barges, along with some privately owned, in order to complete one large floating platform. Henry had added a fifth, smaller, craft and moored it to the others. Somehow, he'd both discovered her plans for the night and modified them to his needs. Did he have such clout at the palace, then?

"Henry…" He silenced her with a soft kiss, walking her backward across the gangplank. As if under a spell, she pushed through the silk strewn canopy of Henry's barge and stepped onto the plush silk Oriental rug scattered generously with cushions. She steadied her balance as the craft pushed off into the open river, separating from the court's festivities. They were alone. A shiver ran down her spine. Was it fear or longing?

This is what I wanted, isn't it?

The magic began to evaporate as Frances helped herself to a goblet of wine—excellent, the same crisp white from the masque— and made the mistake of stopping to think.

"Does something trouble you?" The question was casual, but Frances could see the concern in his eyes. Who was this man, the man she'd married? Did she really want to know?

"No, I am not troubled so much as thoughtful."

"There is more going on in your head than I would have ever given credence to before. Is it true that this masque was entirely of your own creation? I knew you were competent, but this is so much more. You are exceptional, and I am humbled."

Frances blushed and nodded acceptance as he lowered himself to the cushions beside her. This conversation was nice, but too safe—safe and disappointing. This was a conversation between a married couple, not a seduction.

"Again, the look of worry—no, excuse me, thoughtfulness." His hair was wrapped in a dark scarf that merged with the black leather half mask and the moonlit darkness under the canopy. His full lips curved into a nervous smile. "You have naught to fear from me."

"I am not afraid of you."

"That is comforting." His smile made her smile with him. "Then what is it that concerns you?"

Frances paused a moment before deciding to be direct. "I keep thinking of you as Henry and of myself as your wife. Tonight, I wanted to simply be Frances, a woman with a man. But I cannot pretend. I keep thinking…"

"Therein lies the problem." He reached out and traced the line of her lip with the pad of his thumb, cupping her cheek in his warm hand. "Stop thinking."

She laughed, parting her lips, her own breath adding to the tingling left in the wake of his touch. "Easier said than done." His thumb continued the sweet torment, dipping into her open mouth just enough to bring to mind images from the book, she gasped and, on impulse turned to catch his thumb with her teeth.

He growled softly as she drew his thumb into her mouth, whirling her tongue around the rough pad. The desire in his eyes made her chest tight, her belly pool with warmth. He wanted her. *Her.* Frances, the woman.

With an oath, he pulled her to him, claiming her mouth, her breath, her thoughts. The heat of his kiss branded her, his hands held her firm and made any consideration of escape moot. She wanted this.

Frantic, hot, and needing more, she opened to him as he conquered her, their tongues dueling, both caught in each other, in the moment. Clutching through clothing, she pressed closer, not close enough. Everything ached with want, and Frances broke from the kiss, breathless.

Still holding her face with a gentle touch, Henry toyed with the escaped curls at her ears. His gaze bore into hers, his eyes almost black in the meager flickering light of the torches.

"You amaze me."

She laughed, suddenly shy, embarrassed at her own ardor. "I amaze myself. This is not me, I think."

"Wasn't that the point? Not to be ourselves?"

"Aye," she whispered, nodding, "but what comes next? I am afraid."

"I will not hurt you."

"Won't you?" Frances raised her eyes to his once more. "This desire between a man and a woman has a natural course. If I consent to lay with you," she broke off, uncertain. "Again, I am not ready to take that risk."

"If we lay together," he began, pressing his forehead to hers, "I want more than your consent. I want your participation. I want you to want me as much as I want you."

He words, soft and deep, washed over her in a wave of heat, and she groaned in response, her body clenching tight of its own volition.

"I want...wait." He pulled back, his hand reaching under a pillow on the rug to retrieve something. A book. *The* book.

God's blood.

He held the erotic book open to the page she had marked, the one with the woman opening herself for the man's intimate kiss. "I want to see this look on your face, to know that joy comes from me, my touch. Now that I know how you felt about my...your husband's attentions all this time," his voice cracked, emotion raw and pained clear in every word, "my only pleasure is to know that you feel it too, that you long for something only I can give you. It is as necessary to me as breath. You make me a beggar with lust, yet I only want to love you, to bring you pleasure."

Frances wrapped her arms around herself, the tight weight of her breasts painful against the confines of her corset. She pressed her legs together, closing her eyes at the promise of something unknown that she needed, that waited just out of reach.

He dropped the book between them, gently prying her hands loose and placing them on his chest. "Lead me, show me, let me pleasure you." His harsh whispered words flowed over her, melting her into him. With a sigh, she sagged forward, pressing her cheek over his heartbeat as her hands found the ties at the collar of his shirt, the buttons of his doublet. Her fingers slipped within, seeking out the smallest bit of heated skin. He growled low in his chest and grabbed his collar, wrenching open the velvet in a shower of buttons.

Hands splayed over his chest, her fingers traced the ridges of his collarbone and toyed with the dusting of dark hair. Heat heavy with the scent of cinnamon and cloves surrounded them, the sounds of the river lost against the rapid beat of her heart.

He laid his hands over hers, twining their fingers together. "Frances, I need to know that you want me, what you want of me."

"I want…" she started, chewing her lip. She darted in to place a shy kiss at the base of his throat. She lingered, kissing him again, this time her lips barely brushing the skin. "I want you to kiss me. To touch me." She closed her eyes and traced her nose along the taut tendons, breathing in his heat. More brazen now, she lowered her hands to his abdomen, feeling the muscles there tense and quiver. "Please, kiss me, touch me where I ache."

He swallowed. "I do not want to take liberties."

She pressed another kiss to his neck, his jaw, skirting her lips to his. His mouth opened under hers, and she paused, merely a breath away. "I want what you want," she whispered against his mouth. "I want what is in that picture."

He closed the difference with a growl deep in his throat, claiming her mouth once more. Frances whimpered against him as he pressed her back against the pillows, his weight a welcome relief to the tension building between them.

"Where do you ache?" he asked, his words humming against her throat as his hand slid down over her breasts, his fingers pressing under the hard ridge of her bodice and corset to tease her tight nipple. "Here?" His mouth followed, the heat of his kiss, sudden pain of his teeth on her sensitive skin driving all coherent thought from her mind. Frances moaned at the contact, her body arching toward him to increase the sensation.

Her head thrown back against the silk, she heard her own voice, one she hardly recognized, call out for more. "Skin to skin," she urged, raking her hands, her nails, over the corded muscle of his chest.

He raised his head, his eyes level with hers. They were so close that his thick lashes brushed against hers as she met his gaze, his unspoken question. Shaking, she guided his hand lower, to the hooks fastening her bodice, and undid the first one. He took over the task, and she closed her eyes, surrendering to his kiss once more. She moaned against his mouth as the heat of his body seeped through the heavy silk and boning of her corset.

It still wasn't enough. Before she could protest, he pulled away, sitting back on his heels studying her.

Words died on her lips as she took in the tension of his jaw, the strength in the set of his shoulders. This was a man fighting for control and on the verge of breaking. Over her. She sat up and shrugged out of her bodice, running her hand over the swell of her breast above the line of her corset. His breath hitched, and his hands tightened into fists but remained on his thighs. Tugging at the ties at her waist, she slowly unlaced her skirts and then stood.

The velvet and silk layers fell to the rug with soft puff of air, leaving her standing only in her corset, chemise, and stockings. Both vulnerable and powerful, Frances could almost feel the flickering torchlight touching her, outlining her body in gold and shadow. Henry's eyes burned dark behind his half mask, memorizing her. Reaching up, she loosed the few remaining hair pins and let her hair tumble down. With a toss of her head, she moved the dark gold waves over one shoulder and then turned around and knelt back on the pillows, presenting him with her back.

Anticipation caught in her chest as she waited. Reverently, his large hands moved onto her shoulders, the tips of his fingers just skimming her skin. Frances held in a quick breath as he softly caressed along her collarbone, then back to the nape of her neck and down her spine. Both hands moved down over the stiff black silk as if imagining the flesh that lay beneath it. She reminded herself to breathe as his hands worshiped her concealed body, moving down to the curve of her hips, barely covered by the fine linen of her chemise.

She had never felt so beautiful, so treasured. His desire left her heady with a sense of power that undid any pretense to modesty. Frances, as a wife and mother, could never have envisioned this moment—this moment when Frances, as a passionate woman, knew she was wanted, and, above all, free of all constraint and expectation.

A soft tug and hissing of silk ribbon, lacings plucked one at a time from their eyelets and then her corset fell onto her thighs in a stiff heap. She let out a breath on a sigh as the heat of his touch claimed her.

Fingers locked together, he stretched her arms high above her head then released her. She held her arms aloft, shivering as he skimmed his hands down, his touch leaving goose pimples in the wake. She melted back against him as his searching hands moved forward and cupped the weight of her aching breasts in the heat of his palms.

She was too in awe of her body's response to argue as he turned her and pressed her back into the silk cushions. She wanted so much and that scared her. After everything, his cold neglect in the past, could she trust him with her body like this?

Meeting his eyes behind the false anonymity of his mask she asked herself if she would trust a stranger, make herself open to his eyes and touch, like this and knew the answer was no. The way his hands and gaze worshipped her, the way he'd so carefully planned their time together, this was not the act of a stranger nor a neglectful husband. Tonight, he was her lover, one who asked what she wanted, who wanted, not to take, but to give.

Fear melted away into tremors of pleasure as his lips followed the path of his hands, the rough stubble of his chin rasping against the hard peaks of her nipples through the sheer chemise. She wanted this, wanted to know.

She felt unbearably tight, his body locked flush with hers as he inched down. His weight should be crushing her, but she welcomed it. His hands soothed any hint of panic as his knee settled between hers, opening her body for him. Her breath caught in her chest as his fingers continued their slow trail down, then up, her thighs, inching under the hem of her chemise. Upward they glided, leaving goose pimples in their wake as he moved toward her hips, then traced the indented lines at her abdomen down to her mons.

The image from Jane's naughty book flashed, and she almost stopped him, embarrassed at the intimacy. It was all too much, too fast. Before she could think, a feather-light touch brushed her curls, and her body acted on it its own, arching her back and pushing her pelvis closer to his teasing hands. He smiled, his eyes behind the mask the only thing betraying his raging desire as his hands lingered a hairsbreadth away from where she ached for him. She whimpered unintelligible words urging him on. He traced a single finger though her curls, found her cleft, and her world exploded. Heat jolted through her as he found her most sensitive nub, followed by his hot kiss claiming her, the slick heat of his tongue drawing out pleasure so intense she thought she might burst out of her skin.

He had consumed her whole and the only thing she could sense was him—his heat, his scent, his touch. Oh God, his touch was like a fire under her skin, inside her, one that burned with more intensity at each stroke. It was almost too much. She pushed her hips up to meet his hungry kisses, still in shock at the overwhelming sensation while her body began to match his rhythm. She could feel the heat pooling inside as her fears melted away. She was paralyzed by his caress, concentrating only on the slick heat of her core as his finger slipped inside her, stretching her, as he worked magic. And it was magic—he was a sorcerer vanquishing her demons of doubt and distrust by his simple attention to her pleasure. She turned her head to muffle her gasps, each released breath promising something tight, coiling within her, a tension she couldn't explain or release. One more kiss and he sucked her deep into his mouth until it was too much. With an anguished cry into the silk pillow, she arched her back to accept the thrust of his fingers, still feeling that burning building deep within her.

The cool air from the river touched her heated skin as Frances felt herself become one with the motion of the current. The constant lapping sounds at the sides of the barge aided her natural rhythm as she opened herself even more to his touch, his brand. Her body rocked with the sway of the barge, her burning flesh embraced the night sky and the soft breeze—she was connected to everything. Connected to this man. She was not in control, and she had never had more control. She was falling and it was amazing.

He lifted above her, catching her cry with his kiss, as her sensations fractured into millions of points of light; involuntary tremors rocked her body until she was replete. Tranquil. Relaxed, perhaps for the first time in her life.

Chapter Fifteen

Rule Twenty: Apprehension is the constant companion of true love.

Henry sat in his small room at the lodgings at St. Stephen's chapel wrapped in his thoughts and a steaming towel. He barely registered the sounds of the razor on leather or the whipping of the lather as his man, Browne, readied the boar's hair brush to prepare Henry's face for shaving.

"Not two evenings ago, you were invited to Queen Elizabeth's private party upon the Thames…" Browne blathered a bit about the London merchant's perspective about what fantastical things had transpired on the Queen's floating pirate island. Henry started paying attention again as Browne removed the towels and slathered thick soap over his stubbled jaw line. "…Called to court for the third time I know of since She returned from summer progress. Ye've done naught to earn ill will of late—or have ye? Well, it'll be none o'my business either way just as long as ye'r clean and yer hosen do nay fall out of the garter or any other such nonsense…"

Henry felt the steady drag and flick of the razor against his skin and marveled at Browne's ability to perform such detailed, and potentially lethal, work, all while he babbled on about paned slops, French wine, and Spanish doublet styles. Henry had grown used to the man's ramblings and found some comfort in their familiarity all the while his stomach reeled at the possibilities of why he'd been summoned for a formal interview with Queen Elizabeth. It couldn't have anything to do with Frances. No, surely not—he had given her no cause for complaint.

None at all. He smiled.

He'd come to her bed ten years ago knowing only the act of intercourse as it pertained to making an heir. Of course, his release was always a pleasure to him dimmed only by the awkwardness of using her body. He'd never dreamed relations between them could be so pleasurable for her as well. He'd heard talk between men, seductive play between courtiers that implied there was more than spending himself. But it wasn't until the book…

Thank God for the book. He'd only known what was expected up until now. The book showed him what was possible.

All he had to do was follow her responses. It was like a dance, being aware of one's partner. Funny that he'd had those instructions since he was old enough to walk, but it was now, at the mature age of five and twenty, that he applied them to something actually worthwhile. Bringing her to pure abandon with his mouth, the salty sweet taste of her on his tongue, was the most erotic experience he'd ever had. And to think, he had not even spent himself.

"Here now, stay still lest I cut ye."

Browne finished off Henry's shave with a quick swipe of the now cooled damp towel, and Henry stood up to finish dressing. Clad in his white linen collared shirt and stockings, he stepped into his slops. Browne, efficient as always, had already fastened the doublet to the waistband of the slops and attached the ornate oversleeves to the armscye so that the whole mess was able to be donned as one, with only the center closure to be dealt with. Henry, while conscious of the importance of style while in the capital, had no patience for the hundred-step dressing process. At least he didn't have to wear a corset.

Corset. Damn. He just couldn't get away from the memories of that night. Frances, his wife—*his wife, damn it!* Frances lying replete amid a luxury of silken cushions clad only in her stockings and transparent chemise. The outline of her nipples and the tantalizing shadow of curls at the apex of her thighs that showed through the fine cotton. The image alone was enough to stir his blood. His pulse pounded in his ears, reminding him of the rhythm of her heart slowing as she relaxed into a light sleep from her overpowering climax. Pride of success clashed with guilt and the sheer stupidity over all their past encounters. To think of the years they missed together when he never grew from the young idiot coached by his steward on how to bed a bride. He'd never touched her like that before, never really kissed her, not even really looked at her. They'd been nothing but polite to each other, as they'd both been instructed when they entered the marriage. It made sense, the awkwardness at first; they were children. But they'd never grown past that point in their dealings. And why would they? From the first time on their wedding night when he'd climbed on top of her, positioned himself, and drove home, nothing had changed. She'd never complained, always awaited him with her nightshirt pulled up to her waist, ready. What a fool he'd been, they'd both been.

Well, he tugged the front of his buttoned doublet straight with a self-satisfied smirk, he was figuring things out now, wasn't he? Frustration stopped him from any further congratulations with the reminder that, no matter how well he pleasured her, the separation still loomed.

She wanted to leave him, wanted him never to take his marital rights from her again. It was against her vows, against the law to refuse her husband, the husband that she had never refused before. But, as he remembered the way her body became slick with passion, weeping under his touch, he knew he didn't want mindless submission from her anymore. The barge, the ambiance, the romance, the wooing, his attention to her needs, actually communicating about it… It wasn't for naught. No, that look of bliss on her face made him feel like a god. Once again Henry found himself smiling like an idiot. Despite the dull ache in his balls.

Browne buckled Henry's dress rapier to his belt and handed him his hat. His ensemble thus completed, Henry exited his meager accommodations, flew down the stairs, and headed to retrieve his horse from the stables. It was time to see the Queen. God knew why.

• • •

Jane and Mary sat cross-legged at the foot of her bed, still in their dressing gowns. In truth, Frances did not want to talk about it at all—it was too private, too close to the heart.

"Come now, Frances, we are your friends," Mary prompted. "And it's times like these when you need a true friend."

"Aye," Jane added, "there's nothing like sharing sordid details with good friends."

"Nay, Jane. Frances can keep those bits to herself." Jane pouted. "But if you want to talk about it, sort out your feelings… I know there must be a riot in your heart right now over what comes next, and talking it out might help."

A riot in her heart—how apt. She went between reveling in the memory of each touch to shame over such wanton behavior. He saw her splayed out, even kissed her, tasted her. She knew because she tasted herself on his lips. How…what? Disgusting? Exciting? Arousing? The thought had her all warm again, a wet heat pooling at her center. And what was that about? She'd never been so slick down there. Was it healthy? Was something wrong with her? What if Henry thought it was disgusting? She pressed her hands against her eyes, fighting panic.

"God's teeth, Frances. Did he tup you or not?" Jane blurted, poking Frances in the shoulder.

"Jane!" Mary reprimanded and then looked to Frances to wait for the answer.

Certain that she was blushing from head to toe, she did her best to calm her features. Her polite mask seemed more and more unattainable of late, and it took all of Frances's focus to relax her jaw. So much for stoicism.

"Well?" Jane asked.

"No, I did not tup him. He didn't even try."

"Really? So he kidnapped you onto an opulent barge and then…nothing?"

"Well, not *nothing*…"

"Frances?"

She mocked her tone in return. "Jane?"

"So what was the 'not nothing?' You kissed, aye?"

"Aye." She nodded. "We kissed and talked and he was… considerate of me." *My only pleasure is to know that you feel it too, that you long for something only I can give you. It is as necessary to me as breath.* "He wanted to know what I wanted. He did not demand his rights as a husband." *You make me a beggar with lust, yet I only want to love you, to bring you pleasure.* "He wanted me to want him as much as he wanted me." Frances swallowed against the ache in her chest and the growing warmth between her thighs.

She looked up to find both Mary and Jane dreamy eyed and lax. Jane flopped backward on the bed and wrapped her arms around her torso.

"What a man."

Mary raised a brow at her friend, then schooled her face back into ladylike poise. Apparently her polite mask was still available to her. "So what did you tell him?"

Jane rolled over and propped herself up on her elbows. "Yes, what did you want? And did he?"

The room seemed too warm despite the lack of fire in the grate, and Frances fanned her face, trying to find the right words.

"Well, he found your book after the first masque…"

Jane interrupted her with a squeak and sat up on her knees. "He doesn't know it's mine does he? If he thinks I'm a wanton, I'll be dismissed."

"Shut up, Jane." Mary swatted her friend. "What did he think about the book?"

"He noticed the page I marked." She plucked her nightdress away from her neck, far too warm.

"He did not! But he's not even French," Jane exclaimed, bouncing on her knees and shaking the whole bed. "Did he do it, Frances? Kiss you *there*?"

"Out on the river, under the stars," Mary mused. "How romantic. I had no idea Master LeSieur had it in him."

"I am not talking about this anymore." Frances stood up and poured herself some watered wine. It was too personal, too private, too much for her to try to understand. Her husband was becoming her lover. Did she want that? She was so out of her depth here at court, pretending to be a sophisticated courtier that it went to her head, made her want things that were not for her. She should get out before things got worse. She could not afford to let herself care. There was safety in the façade of ladylike manners. "Besides," she started, after downing a cup, "I think that I should go back to the Holme."

"What?" Mary asked, aghast, right as Jane said, "Now?"

Frances struggled for her answer, sure it had to be more reasonable than the simple urge to flee. To not deal with the next step of whatever was happening with Henry. "I miss my children. I think I accomplished what I came here for, and I do not think I can, in good faith, still request a separation. If we went back to how things were, I would hardly have to see him at all anyway."

"So all wounds are healed, and you are ready to go back to being a docile country wife? You are lying to yourself, Frances."

"Henry is a good man, and I cannot shame him with the separation. I will endure."

"Oh, so you are a martyr then? Dutiful and pleasant? Frances, you have changed too much to go back now."

"But my children…"

Jane interrupted, "Require a happy, *living* mother."

"If you go back, if you resign yourself to duty, you may well sink back to whatever mire gripped you at Maria's death."

Frances thought back on those days with a sense of longing that she knew was wrong. The prospect of sleeping without waking no longer called to her. She must be past the worst of her melancholy—at least now she woke up with a sense of hope. But when she thought of her chamber back at the Holme, Mary was right; all that lay there were reminders of the darkness.

"This doesn't make sense. You've been so happy, eager, these past weeks. Even through Jane's injury, you stayed a constant strength. And this morning you woke up looking young, trouble free. So why now? Why choose to give it all up? Staying this course may give you the possibility of happiness."

"I am out of my depth here. I did not know it until this morning, but now it's clear. I do not know what comes next, and I cannot plan."

"You and planning!" Mary snapped. "Mayhap you should just take life one day at a time and see what comes of it. You never know. You may find romance, love, within your marriage."

Frances shook her head, absolutely, completely, and totally confused about what she wanted. One thing she did know for certain. "I learned long ago that romance was not something meant for me."

"Not meant for you?!" It was a miracle Jane had sat silent for as long as she had during all the meaningful feminine introspection, and her patience was used up. "Pray tell, Frances, why not for you? Are you not a woman? Do you not deserve to be loved, to have a lover?"

"A lover?" The door banged shut behind Countess of Spencer, causing a gush of cool air from the outer gallery to usher her dramatically further into Frances chamber. "Do my ears betray me? Were you discussing a dalliance? Francie, you surprise me! I have just had it from Queen Elizabeth Herself that you and your husband have reconciled—though it shames me that you let it be known you were actually quarrelling in the first place. I must say, I am confused and displeased. And, I do not like being either. Pray tell, what is going on?"

Frances closed her eyes and took another sip of watered wine. Her mother was at court.

Fie me.

Chapter Sixteen

Rule Thirteen: Public revelation of love is deadly to love in most instances.

"We are most pleased to know Our little scheme did meet with success. Our dear Henry has proven himself quite the rake. We are blessed indeed that he has not made a play for Our heart!" General laughter ensued at Queen Elizabeth's comment. "Your reconciliation warms my heart and We are feeling gracious toward the ideal of young love. Your rooms have been reassigned. Henry LeSieur is to be moved from his apartment at Parliament to new quarters here at the palace posthaste until such time as you feel need to return to the country." The queen raised one well-shaped eyebrow and flagrantly eyed Frances's form before winking to reinforce the not-so-private private joke.

Sweet God in heaven, what just happened?

"Yes, We are pleased. Come now, Frances, I see you are in shock. No need to thank Us—the true marital happiness of Our beloved subject is thanks enough. We have never had much faith in the ideal of marital bliss and, perhaps, you and your loving husband will prove Us wrong." Frances responded with a mute reverance and a dumb smile. "We do congratulate Ourselves on a job well done. Well done indeed." With an audible sigh of excited happiness, Queen Elizabeth absentmindedly offered her hand to the side for one or another of the observant handsome courtiers. Kit Hatton, almost giddy, skipped up to assist Queen Elizabeth from Her throne and on to the floor as she called for a dance.

Frances remained paralyzed in front of the dais as the dancing began behind her. Just earlier that day her mother had unexpectedly arrived, bearing the news that she and her husband had reconciled with each other. She did not know what was more upsetting—that it was common knowledge that she wished for a separation or that the Queen Herself knew about their tryst at the masque. Why was the Queen concerning Herself with Frances's marriage at all? And to take such a public position—as if the supposed reconciliation was part of some little scheme. Very odd.

Frances felt a pull on her hand and allowed herself to be led off the rapidly filling dance floor. Insipid smile still pasted to her face, Frances blinked her eyes to focus on her Mother. "You did well enough, though I can see you are inwardly reeling." When Bess received no response other than Frances's false smile, she continued, "Wake up, child! We are at court, and you need to comport yourself with due consequence." Frances jolted as her mother pinched the back of her hand. "Better. Now, come with me to gather your wits before you have to see your 'loving' husband."

She gasped. "He is here?"

Of course he is here. Hadn't the Queen just said She summoned him from Parliament to join her in their new rooms? Good God! He was here! She had managed to be a very public figure at court for over a month without ever having to interact with her husband in front of the courtiers, Kit Hatton not withstanding—and now she was to share quarters here in the palace under some façade of being a love match? This was ridiculous. Frances had come so far since leaving Holme LeSieur—she knew she had. She'd come to court insecure and lacking sophistication, yet she'd risen to become a respected, creative, well-liked, and sought-after courtier. But at this moment, surrounded by the constant motion of chains of courtiers dancing the *Montard* indefinitely, Frances felt like the child bride overwhelmed by responsibility and crushed dreams. He was here, and the charade was over. No more pretending.

"Lady mother." Henry's voice reverberated through her.

The Countess of Spencer looked up and allowed the briefest glimmer of surprise to flicker in her eyes before replying, "Henry," in a politely gracious tone and gesturing for him to recover from his reverance.

"My lady wife." Her husband's voice continued, forcing Frances to acknowledge him. Even with the formal greeting, she heard the familiarity behind the words as if he used her given name.

Frances no longer had the luxury to bask in her shock and dismay. The time had come for her to play her part. With a regal set to her shoulders and a smooth brow, she gracefully turned to give her husband a proper greeting.

"My lord husband." Frances's voice was even and steady as she dipped into her reverance.

She looked up to meet his gaze, but she could look no higher than his mouth, remembering the feel of his lips on her body. Her breath caught in her chest, and she wrested her eyes up only to find him staring at her mouth.

"Reconciliation indeed," her mother muttered beside her. "Frances, I will hear this tale from your own lips anon. For now, I pray you remember the consequence due your family and not embarrass me. Go dance."

She licked her lips, aware how the simple action brought even more tension to Henry's jaw. Was he picturing the things she could do with her mouth the same way she couldn't stop thinking about what he'd done with his? Lord have mercy. What was she feeling? Desire? For her husband without the safety of anonymity, as false as it had been? Surely not. And yet...

"Frances, the court is watching. Let your husband lead you to the dance floor."

"Nay, Mother, it is unseemly for a husband to dance with his wife." Frances's barely finished her cowardly sentence by the time Henry had guided her onto the floor in time to start with the opening *riverenza*.

Each pair of dancers moved from the opening *riverenza* into a *seguito ordinario*, turning away from their partner and then back in full circle. That measure of music was all Frances needed to compose herself before meeting the eyes of her husband once more. Her lover.

"Why is this happening?" she asked, embarrassed by the quiver in her voice.

Henry grimaced, his full lips a tight line as he took her hand once more for a series of *passi* side by side. "I did not expect this to be so public, but I knew that Hatton was bringing your plight to the Queen."

They both turned and joined hands for the next steps. Hatton... did Henry know of the kiss? All she could say was, "My plight?"

"The attack on Jane and the menace toward you." *Passo, passo* backward and two *reprise* to the right. "Queen Elizabeth was, of course, cognizant of the need for safety but did not want to force you into my arms if it was not your choice."

"She heard the rumors of the separation?" Frances almost faltered in her steps.

Henry stifled a laugh. "She hears everything. But even so, She called me to her privy chamber this morn to confirm that you were not ill-treated and to request I keep you in line."

"No!" She stopped dancing and he pulled her back into the steps, physically guiding her *continenze* to the left and the right. "She thinks I am a wanton? Am I ruined at court?"

"Nay, not after I explained it was I who secured the barge last night. Now She is enamored of our love affair, and She counts Herself as instrumental in saving our marriage."

It was all she could do not to laugh or cry, let alone keep dancing. "I fear our love affair is over now." As much as part of her wanted to make haste to their shared chamber, a bigger part wanted only to hide in a dark place and try to breathe. It was too much and far, *far* too public.

One of the rules of courtly love stated that once made public, a love rarely endures. Not that what they shared was love, but it was lover-like. Would it continue now that the masks, quite literally, were off?

Passo, passo, ordinario turn to the outside, join hands… Frances concentrated on projecting the image of the accomplished courtier and tried not to remember how the heat of his touch felt on her skin.

Facing each other for the *continenze*, Frances muttered, "I had no idea that you had the Queen's ear."

"Wife, there is much you don't know about me." Henry's voice deepened to a seductive whisper. "There is much you and I have to learn together."

Somehow they had managed to move smoothly from the promenade portion of the dance into the more rigorous final series of lively *spezatti* and *fioretti*. It was almost over. Frances was so relieved she almost crossed herself. Frances approached her husband in flanking steps and a swish of velvet skirts, her words almost lost in the beat of the music. "You presume that I wish to learn."

Frances met his eyes in an effort to show her strength of resolve and tried not to feel the touch of his fingers against hers as their hands met for the last two *cadenze*.

One final move and the dance would be finished and Frances could escape. He still had her left hand in his as they stepped in toward each other. Breaking from the choreography, his right hand snuck around her waist and splayed across the lacings on her back to press her more fully against him. Before Frances could process what was happening, Henry captured her lips in a searing kiss.

While the rest of the courtiers took a *puntate* away from their partners and gave a courtly *riverenza* to complete the dance, Frances melted into the heat of his passion not sure why she should object.

• • •

"Aye me! I thought I would die laughing when Queen Elizabeth Herself led the court to 'Huzzah the LeSieurs!'" Jane had not stopped chattering since she arrived with the last of Frances's things. Her petite figure bounced from the dressing table to the wardrobe to the trunks to the bed in a flurry of russet wool and green silk. "If not for the court watching, I think Master LeSieur would have finished what he started then and there with you not resisting a bit. Not that he seemed to care that God, the Queen, and everyone was there to see him kissing his wife like a doxy." Mary fluffed out a voluminous dove gray overskirt and hung it on a hook in the closet.

"And why should she have minded? Not many women can boast such a fine-looking husband. I do not remember his shoulders being so broad—but maybe it is just the fit of his fine courtly clothes." Jane retrieved the emerald green brocade gown from the trunk and shook it out aggressively. "I must say, I was afraid for you after your Mother told us that Queen Elizabeth had declared you 'reunited'—though I never knew that you were separated…" A garnet set in silver filigree shot across the room as Jane soundly shook the creases out of the black velvet overskirt before shutting it into the wardrobe.

Mary calmly retrieved the jewel and began digging around in her sewing basket. Needle and dark thread successfully procured, she bundled the heavy mass of black velvet out of the wardrobe and settled herself on a chaise in the window and began her task.

Jane continued to babble. "Do you think he knows about your kissing Master Hatton? Oh, if he did, mayhap the jealousy would fuel his passion. I vow they'll be no naysaying him tonight. Not that you'd want to." Jane lay the individual bodices smoothly on the shelf, completely oblivious to anyone else in the room.

Mary finished securing the jeweled piece back to the trim of the overskirt and ushered Jane out her way so she could put the overskirt back in the wardrobe. Turning to her friend she asked, "Jane, if you could find Maggie and have her bring up Mistress LeSieur's supper, it would be a blessing. Maybe you could cajole the cook to send a few extra honeyed cakes?"

Jane didn't need to be asked twice and scampered from the room, leaving welcomed silence in her wake.

Mary shut the door behind Jane and turned to face the chair in front of the hearth.

Frances, from the moment she first settled in her new rooms, occupied her hands and mind with a frenzy of needlework, compulsively creating a blackwork masterpiece. She did not move from the chair. She did not say a word. She did her best to drown out her own worries by counting out the threads in the warp and weft, but, ultimately, could do nothing but worry. The masterpiece was no better than a child's attempt and, under ordinary circumstances, would have found its home in the fire. For today though, she thought as she jabbed the needle through the linen and into her finger, it would do. Her brain was bubbling over with too many thoughts, fear and embarrassment that she could barely keep everything in order. Even a list would be of no help.

Mary sat down and leaned over to look at the blackwork that had absorbed her for the past two hours. "What will that be when you are done?"

With a forced stoicism, Frances laid down her embroidery scroll. "Rubbish."

Mary said nothing, and both ladies sat in silence, watching the fire lick through the log in the grate.

The silence stretched as the log crackled in the encroaching twilight. Finally, Mary broke the reverie. "Mistress, do you not think this reconciliation can be true? For all your fears, there is passion there and some tenderness. I do not think he would knowingly hurt you."

"No, you are correct, I think. I wish…" She dropped her needle into the pile of linen on her lap. "I don't know what I wish."

"But you know you need not fear him."

"I am not so sure." Frances pressed her cold fingers against her eyelids, willing the burning behind them to subside. "It will be worse now, because I will know what could have been. I may even surrender my body to him once more in hopes of discovering the passion I glimpsed last night. But then what? More babes and more solitude while I lay waste to myself in Nottinghamshire. What if, once I return, that darkness finds me again? It was so easy to let myself slip more and more each day, not caring. Now I care too much to let that happen again—but it feels like something out of my control. I want to hold on to who I am. I need to even more than my body yearns to play the whore."

"Knowing love with your husband does not make you a whore."

Frances looked up and saw the glaze of tears in Mary's eyes. She was worried, and should be. Frances, in her brief sojourn from the melancholy that followed her daughter's death, had been gripped by complete apathy. She hadn't meant to end her own life, but, for reasons she couldn't fathom, was well on the path to making that happen. Her mother had been right, as usual. Returning to that place where days blended into one another in their monotony, where she had no worth beside the value of her womb and even that was flawed—would it suck her back down? No, she wouldn't allow it. *No.* Not now that she knew who she was, a woman worthy of love.

"You are right again, Mary. Knowing love does not make you a whore, and I deserve to know love. Spreading my legs to my master, however, does—and I refuse to be a whore ever again."

"That is good to hear. I have no use for whores." Henry's deep voice sounded from the door that adjoined the antechamber.

Frances snapped her mouth shut as Mary rose and hurried out of the room, abandoning her to her fate.

God's teeth. And blood. And wounds. Hell, hell, hell.

With a sigh, Frances tossed her embroidery into the basket, stood, and made a graceful reverance. "My lord husband."

"Dispense the formality, I pray you. In our chamber let us be Frances and Henry."

"That implies something has changed. I still desire the separation."

He stepped closer. She would have moved back if not for the chair. "I hoped after last night, after the way you kissed me back before the entire court, you had changed your mind."

"Nay. It is as I said at the guard house; it was as if I dallied with a stranger."

"I cannot believe you really think that."

"Why is that?"

"Because…" He reached out his ungloved hand and traced the curve of her lip, down her chin, her throat. "Because when I had my mouth on you, my fingers inside you, when you shattered under my touch, you called out my name."

"Henry," she whispered as he moved closer. She longed for his kiss again but turned her head. "No, it cannot be. I won't be the harlot with you, a slave to my body."

He cupped her breast, the heat of his hand searing even through her velvet bodice and thick corset.

"So, you are saying that you don't want to lie with me?" Henry's breath caressed her cheek, his lips teasing her ear.

"I am saying that I will never again submit to my duty as a wife."

He nipped her neck just behind her ear, and she felt herself melting. "But if you were to want me?"

Heat flooded between her core, and she squeezed her thighs together to ease the ache.

"No." She pulled away, almost falling over the chair.

Henry steadied her, his gaze riveted to the rapid rise and fall of her chest. "So, should you feel desire, passion," his voice lowered to a seductive murmur, "want, need, an ache inside you, maybe then you might welcome my touch?"

With each word, Frances began to feel a tingling down her spine, spreading goose pimples over her skin and puckering her nipples almost painfully beneath the confines of her corset. "Desire is not enough."

He closed the distance between them once again and pressed his hand over the heat at her pelvis. Inches away from touching her flesh, separated by layers and layers of skirts, Frances still felt the need to press toward his hand.

"So wanting me here is not enough."

She nodded, not sure the words would make sense past the dryness on her tongue.

He removed his hand, and she closed her eyes, both grateful and needy at once.

He placed it on her once more, this time over her heart. "Until you want me here," he leaned low and placed a kiss on the swell of her left breast, "you'll not have me. Is that right?"

"Is that too much to wish for?" she asked, her voice hoarse. "If the only desire you have for me is with this," she laid her hand over the hardness beneath his codpiece, "then any woman could serve you."

He groaned at her touch, and she felt him buck even through the layers of fabric. She tightened her internal muscles, stifling a groan of her own.

"Frances, believe me when I say that I want you with everything I am, and no other woman could sate that desire." He placed his hand over hers, holding her to him. "I will promise not to press you until you want me with this." He leaned low again and placed a hot kiss on her bosom. "But if how I feel now is any indication, the two needs are connected, and I think you want me already."

Chapter Seventeen

Rule Twenty-Five: Unless it please his beloved, no act or thought is worthy to the lover.

Frances soaked in the meager heat of the late November sunshine. It had been only a handful of days since she and her husband had come to their unusual agreement. Winning her heart seemed similar to courtship, and Henry took his wooing very seriously.

"If someone had asked me a year ago if I would like to picnic with my wife, I would have thought the question absurd." Henry sat reclined on the rug, his long legs stretched out before him, his boots crossed at the ankles. Shifting his weight to one arm, Henry reached for his goblet of wine.

Frances swallowed her bite of pear before responding, "Why do you suppose that is?" Frances had not known Henry had planned for a picnic, but she was glad she assumed the day's activities would entail riding. The split skirts of her mahogany wool riding habit made sitting on a rug in the middle of a meadow much more comfortable.

Henry crossed his legs and leaned forward to talk conspiratorially. "It is outside my scope. I have always had clearly defined duties and the obvious activities that accompanied them. This is too much like leisure, something I have never sought. Wooing a woman is beyond my purview, and I have no idea what I'm doing."

Frances shouldn't be surprised. Even though their marriage had been arranged by their parents, she had never considered that he was in the same awkward position as she. The surprise must have shown on her face, for Henry raised a questioning eyebrow.

"I assumed you must be an expert in this field," her words were playful, "for you have created a wondrous setting for romance." Frances lightly skimmed the short cut grass with her hand as she gestured to their surrounds. "We are away from the palace—away from the city. It feels as if we are the only two in the world." Frances kept surprising herself at her honest whimsy. She turned her face up to catch the sunlight and allowed herself to continue her train of thought. "Winter waits just over the hill and is almost upon us. It is our duty this day to capture as much of the sun as we can."

The St. Martin's summer, the uncharacteristic warmth in the autumn, could have served as a metaphor for this captured moment of happiness—the threat of winter reminding her how fleeting time was.

"Can you feel it? The change in the wind? The change in the light? We do not have many more of these days left, and the sun is taking a final delight in gifting us with its rays. I almost feel as if I need to take stock of the sunshine before it runs out and winter cages us in the dark and damp..." Frances's voice trailed off under Henry's intense gaze. Unexpectedly self-conscious, she quickly averted her eyes and became actively interested in the lace at her cuff. How foolish of her, speaking to him like a friend.

"You have a gift with words, like a poet." The admiration in his eyes forced a blush. Frances looked back down at her now destroyed lace. "You paint a picture with them, so beautiful and so sad. Is that how you feel at the Holme? Caged?"

She looked up to meet his gaze, the dark depths of his eyes warm and welcoming. "I did not say that."

"No, you did not." Henry reached over and gently laid his hand on top of Frances's, stilling her compulsive adjustment of her wrist ruff with his warm touch. "As much as I love this time with you here and now, I have not forgotten our family and home. I have not forgotten your love and devotion to our babes. When you first arrived in London, I did not consider how difficult this must have been."

She smiled at his generous honey coating of her demand for separation.

"I knew little of the woman you were, but I did know the mother and in that you were devoted." Henry paused, awkward for once. "What drove you away? What need was so pressing that you would rip yourself away from the one thing that brought you joy?"

"The children are my happiness." Frances needed him to understand. "But I had to leave. I did not feel like I had a choice. Should I escape and reevaluate myself or stay home, isolating myself with grief? The new baby only reminded me of how I failed the ones who died. Elizabeth echoed my sadness, withdrawing even as I withdrew. Thank God for my mother. I did not know it, but I abandoned my children when I fell into the melancholy. So very alone—surrounded by my children and servants, but still alone. After giving birth to Grace and Maria, I was wasting away and welcomed the dreamless sleep that it promised, the darkness where I did not feel like a failure. Or unwanted."

Henry rose to his knees before her, gripping both her hands in his. "I had no idea."

"No, of course you did not." The soft outpouring of her soul, so necessary and so long left undone, left her empty with only anger to fill the void. Henry sitting there filled with horror and pity as if he had been powerless to help—it was laughable.

"You came home to oversee the estate books, ship off our son to fostering, attempt to sire a spare heir, and head back to God knows where to do God knows what." Frances's words gained power. She resented his apparent nonchalant attitude toward the family, but never realized how hurt she had been by his desertion—that he did not care enough about her to stay. "I was important enough to carry your babes but not for you to take a moment and actually see who I was. And then, when I failed in my role, you treated it like an everyday occurrence. Did I not know that babies die all the time and that I should thank God for my own health? How silly of me to be attached to the life growing in my womb—to mourn death. My daughters. *Your* daughters. And you did not care enough to tarry awhile at your own home with your own family. Did you feel no loss?"

• • •

Henry was dumbfounded. He had just discovered that he had missed years of precious time with his wife, but his family? Gently reared children were raised by nursemaids rather than their parents... He turned out fine without paternal involvement, hadn't he? He could understand that she would be upset over the loss, but infant mortality was so rampant that many families did not name their child until they were sure the child would survive. Was he supposed to grieve over a life he had never known? Looking at his wife, he knew the answer: How could he not grieve over a baby, his babies, who had been denied the chance at life? How could he not be there for his wife, the woman that bore his children and who was crippled by grief? How could he expect her to simply bear it because that was the socially acceptable behavior?

The answer was clear—he hadn't cared. Caring was not part of duty. He behaved honorably by the standards he had been raised to uphold, even if he had not behaved well. He had treated Frances and his family as he thought he ought. They had been an impersonal duty, an obligation...and not even very high on his list of priorities. And Frances knew it.

There was nothing he could say or do to make those years of neglect go away. All he could say was, "I am so sorry."

Frances blinked, her jaw dropping as all anger faded from her ice-blue eyes. She asked simply, "Where were you all those years? What mattered more than your family?

Henry paused a moment, removing his hand from hers to retrieve his goblet and take a long swallow. "I will tell you… I owe you that much." Henry put down his goblet and retrieved his wife's hand. "But you must promise to keep my confidence." He had much to tell of his work with Walsingham and Cecil, Norfolk's execution, and his own allegiance to the Crown.

Frances, intrigued, nodded and promised, "I will not tell anyone."

Henry smiled lightly and pulled his wife toward him. "Come then and lie with me in the waning sunlight, and I will tell you of my adventures, and you will tell me of yours."

Frances shifted and lay her head on his shoulder and warmth surrounded him at her trust. Then he started his tale of conspiracy and treason.

• • •

The afternoon sunlight drained into twilight as Frances and Henry let their horses find their footing along the rutted country roads leading to the palace at Hampton Court. Around them the fields were at varying levels of disarray, some farmers having cut the high golden grass earlier than others in order to set aside feed provisions for the winter. Autumn was almost gone, taking the last vestiges of summer with it. Despite the beauty of the day, there was darkness looming on the far distant horizon—the first winter storm on the way.

The amiable silence between them surprised Frances. To think they'd shared a bed for several nights, not even so much as accidentally bumping into each other—but today she was able to lay with him in the sun, baring her soul and finding she wanted to trust him. Could friendship blossom so quickly? Could she really put aside years of resentment and start anew?

"We should be back to the palace before full dark." Henry interrupted Frances's wandering thoughts. "I think we will be too late to change for supper."

"I am not hungry and do not relish the idea of playing the courtier tonight. I am content to make straightaway for bed." Frances, catching the innuendo too late, blushed furiously as Henry raised his brows in mock suggestion.

The steady clip clop of the horse's hooves along the intermittently cobbled roadway was the only sound to break their companionable silence. Could the perfect day end with the perfect night? And what would that be, could she design it?

He'd been every bit the gentleman, true to his word that he would not press his attentions—which was nice if not a little disappointing. He made her feel safe. Outside the glittering court she was free to talk without weighing her words, and he seemed to listen. It was almost as if he cared. *Don't be silly, Frances.*

Frances felt the heat of Henry's regard and turned to meet his gaze with a shy smile. On the back of his stallion, outlined by the amber rays of the setting sun, he cut a fine figure. His tailored doublet outlined his torso, ending at his waist and the band of his voluminous slops. Men's fashions did too much to hide their physique. His belly was flat, but did it taper down to slim hips? The way he sat a horse with ease spoke of hours in the saddle—which implied his buttocks would be hard with muscle. She gasped at her thoughts, and Frances turned away, embarrassed her husband might notice her frank appraisal of his person. Focusing her gaze on the road ahead, she calmed her breathing, remembering to be a lady once more. Letting her breath out on a sigh, she relaxed just as, with an unearthly shriek, her horse spasmed beneath her and bolted across the muddy field as if its life depended on it.

"Frances!" The pounding hooves muted Henry's panicked shout.

Trusting her instinct, Frances leaned low and gripped her horse around the neck. Her life did, in fact, depend upon staying seated.

Cursing the side saddle, Frances held on, tugging on the reins to slow the panicked mare. What happened? She watched the uneven ground race by and prayed that her mare would find solid footing. If the horse went down at this speed, Frances was practical enough to understand that the risk was great indeed.

Rumbling thunder announced the approaching hooves. Frances felt a dark shadow engulf her as Henry raced alongside her frenzied mare. His stallion was bigger and faster, but her mare was in a panic and unpredictable. There was no way Henry could stop her horse... Before Frances could finish the thought, an arm as solid as iron hooked around her middle and hefted her from her saddle.

Henry clutched her against his chest as he slowed his stallion's pace.

Calm, she must be calm. She stiffened against the shivers that threatened, grateful for Henry's strength, the arms around her. What had caused her mare to bolt like that? It seemed like a placid beast—unremarkable, yes, but definitely well trained.

If only she could stop this shivering—when had the day grown so cold?

"May-maybe she s-saw a snake?" Frances closed her eyes as her husband nestled his cheek into her curls. She must have lost her cap. What a shame—it was new. She nestled closer, needing the warmth of his body. "What else w-would have c-caused her such ter-terror?" Her teeth chattered hard against her attempt at words. Henry's arm tightened around her, and she welcomed his added warmth and comfort. "It's a shame, she will surely be disposed of for this, and it was probably only instinct—she was so g-g-gentle before..."

Henry clucked his stallion into a slow canter in the direction of Frances's errant horse. "Her behavior was certainly strange...

but I would be surprised for her to have seen any snakes in this field since it has been so recently worked…" Henry spoke with the hushed tones she would use to ease a child's night terror. Placating. Avoiding the truth.

His sudden tension made her turn to follow his gaze. There, on the stream bank some way ahead, laid the unmoving body of the horse. Henry dismounted, cautioning Frances to stay beside his stallion. She nodded, watching him step through the muck. The poor mare was close enough for her to see there was no longer any rise and fall to indicate breathing, but her stomach knotted when she saw what he had in his hand, what he'd pulled free of her mount's neck. An arrow.

This was no accident. Frances crossed herself. All the little malicious incidents compounded, and it was harassment no longer.

• • •

Frances huddled, wrapped in a quilt, on the rug before the hearth with her two ladies on either side. If not for the blame and anger on her ladies' faces, the scene would have been charming. Henry couldn't fault them at all—he blamed himself.

The small woman, Mistress Jane, all but hissed as he approached. "Why did you go out with no groom? No guards? After all the strange "gifts" and what happened to me…" Her voice trailed off.

The taller of the two, Mistress Mary, stood. "We are too close to London to pretend we're in the country. You should have stayed on the palace grounds." She leveled her gaze at him, her hazel eyes hard within the shadow of her lashes. "You should have known better."

"Aye, I should have," he answered their accusations simply and lowered himself to the rug behind Frances, drawing her to him. "Mistress Mary, Mistress Jane, pray leave us now. I thank you for your faithful service to my wife." He didn't need to see their expressions to know they didn't trust him. "Make haste to the kitchens and order a bath for your lady and have a platter of fruits and cheese sent up as soon as can be. And mulled wine, please."

The heavy thud of the oak door closing drew a sigh of relief, and Henry pulled Frances closer to him, cradling her against his chest. "I almost lost you today. I have just found you, and I almost lost you. I swear by all I hold dear that I will move heaven and earth to protect you from all harm and keep you by my side."

Nothing else mattered. She had to be safe, and she had to be with him. It had nothing to do with pride or lust. Today's attack prodded something visceral, something at the very core of his being. He tightened his arms around her. "You are mine."

If it was love she needed to agree to be his completely, then that's what he would give her, no matter the cost.

Frances nestled closer, his name soft on her whispered breath. Henry held her, unwilling to undo whatever magic encompassed them both in that moment of perfection. He had no idea how long they sat there before a discreet knock on the antechamber door signaled the delivery of her bath.

• • •

Frances closed her eyes on a sigh as she sank into the rose-scented heat of the tub.

"I have never envied water so much in my life."

She twisted with a splash and looked over the rim of the copper tub. Henry leaned one broad shoulder against the door frame, the firelight from the room beyond outlining the shadow of his arm through the fine linen of his shirt.

"You agreed to give me privacy," she whispered, her mouth dry. The idea of him striding forward and taking her in his arms took her breath away. *Hypocrite.* She shook her head and sank lower in the water.

"I came to offer my services since you dismissed your ladies. Only at your invitation, of course."

He did not move from the door, unresponsive to her wordless pleas. Of course to do so would be directly against the agreement she'd demanded…except that what she really wanted was to throw caution to the wind, to forget the reasons for her distance. She ached for his touch, and yet. And yet.

She sighed again and lowered her forehead to the brim of the tub, disgusted with herself.

"I await your instruction."

Henry's voice held just enough of a question, a hint of worry, to reassure her. He was as helpless in this as she.

"Well," she began, peering over the lip of the tub, "my ladies might help with my back and my hair."

He took a step closer and stopped. "Is it your wish that I help you? I do not want to be accused of reneging on our deal. You must be specific."

She lowered herself more, hiding behind the tub. How much of her could he see from his vantage? And if he were to come closer, did she want him to see her? It wasn't as if he hadn't seen her even more disheveled the night on the barge. A tingle ran through her chest, her breasts aching and heavy despite the water.

She swallowed against her cowardice and nodded. "Yes. You may wash my hair if you wish."

Three steps and he was at her side, crouched low so his eyes met hers over the copper brim.

"Just so you know," the smile in his eyes belied the seriousness of his tone, "you may be hiding your bosom, but I have an excellent view of your behind."

She squealed and straightened up, sloshing water everywhere.

He rose and crossed to the hearth with a low chuckle that stirred a warmth in her chest. She drew a calming breath. At four and twenty she was not a child and, married ten years already, certainly not a maiden, technically speaking. There was no reason to fear this; he had given her the reins after all. And, no matter what else could be said about her husband, he was honorable. She trusted that like nothing else.

Harnessing her courage, she forced herself to recline in her bath and let the hot water seep into her aching muscles and soothe her senses. Taking in the vision of her husband in his white linen shirt as he sat in front of the fire she let go of the tension and fear of the day, safe with Henry. He held her gaze, his deep brown eyes almost black in the shadows cast by the fire.

"Do you feel how the water is caressing you all over your body at once? I picture my hands and lips doing the same."

"Hush," she whispered.

"Imagine that I am the one cupping the weight of your breasts, skimming your nipples with my thumb, easing the growing ache."

"Henry…" She barely could speak against the tightness in her chest.

"I am wooing you, Frances."

"Nay, you are seducing me."

"What, pray, is the difference?" He rose, a pewter pitcher in each hand, and stepped closer. His jaw tensed, playful smile gone, as his gaze scorched a trail of heat down her body as if he was claiming her with his eyes alone.

She must be wanton indeed, for she could not even pretend at modesty. Her fingers itched to trace the same path, down her cheeks, her neck, over her breasts…

"What are you doing to me?" she asked, overwhelmed at the sensations.

"Well, I thought to wash your hair."

"Oh," she blinked and sat up straight, "of course." Thank goodness for the weak firelight or he would see her blush for certain. If he only knew what she'd been thinking…

She tilted her head back as he slowly drizzled the water through the masses of curls still knotted at atop her head, loosening them until they cascaded over her shoulders and down her back. Not once touching her.

"Until you give me leave, I will continue to imagine that the water is, instead, my fingers, softly caressing your hair and tickling your scalp only to stroke down your neck and find your skin heated from my touch…"

A soft moan escaped Frances's lips before she could catch herself. She closed her eyes, embarrassed at her lack of control.

"I must have your permission to touch you, which is necessary if you want me to soap your hair. Rest easy, I am not asking for more liberties."

"Oh, yes," she answered, curious as to what liberties he might request and a little disappointed. Yes, her body was turning her into the biggest hypocrite.

Henry's bare arm reached over her shoulder and into the basin. Without touching her, he retrieved the lavender soap cake and snaked his other arm over her opposite shoulder to work it into lather before he moved his hands up to her head.

His fingers traced circles of soft pressure against her scalp, massaging the soap through her wet curls. His hands moved in steady motion at her temples and behind her ears, working down toward the base of her skull.

Bliss. She closed her eyes and let her head fall back into the cradle of his hands.

With no more resistance than a puppet, she moved with him as he angled her forward, and she sighed again as he soaped the length of her hair. His thumbs left heat in their wake as they made painstakingly slow circles along the ridges at the base of her skull. The warmth of his touch snaked throughout her whole body, and she had to fight her instincts to turn into his touch, to wrap herself around him.

"If it is not too familiar, I would soap your back as well."

An incoherent mumble partnered her nod of assent. She was past words, too enthralled with his soothing touch.

His hands moved down her neck and to her shoulders, his thumbs continuing their small circles. The soap made her skin slippery so that his hot touch glided over her sore muscles as the scent of the lavender surrounded Frances in a haze of late-summer flowers. His hands moved along the top of her shoulders and down the base of her spine, kneading her muscles along the way.

During their liaisons his touch had aroused, but now every motion spoke of nurture. He sought her comfort, her pleasure, but none of his own. For the past ten years she had been the caregiver, but now Henry saw to her care—if it didn't feel so wonderful, she'd be sure there was something wrong with this role reversal. The sheer decadence of it made her smile.

His broad hands moved from her spine outward along her ribs, not quite touching her breasts but creating a swell of bathwater that caressed her nipples as the water buoyed them. A surge of heat settled between her thighs, and Frances sighed, a soft whimper fluttering on her breath.

What had she just been thinking about this *not* being arousing?

Henry continued his ministrations to her back as Frances reveled in his touch. The water itself seemed alive, vibrant with sensation, caressing her all over her body—just as Henry had said. Taking a bath seemed almost too intimate an experience. The cooling water tingled against the heat of her skin, ruffling through the hair at her pelvis and caressing her intimately… Frances closed her eyes and tightened her innermost muscles, seeking a release that wouldn't come, not without her directly asking for his touch.

"Rinse."

Henry's practical word broke through Frances concentration, and she bit her lip, embarrassed again at her traitorous body. Henry fetched a third ewer from the hearth and poured the hot water throughout her soapy hair and over her back, the trickling warmth tickling her senses.

"Stand." His word was a simple command, but his tone was husky. Did he know what she had been thinking?

Frances stood, knee deep in her bath and no longer caring about the vulnerability of nakedness, while Henry poured the remaining two ewers of heated water over her chilled skin. The water started at her shoulders flowing down her breasts in sensuous rivulets and over her belly, then though her curls, gliding over her most sensitive spots. Frances gasped at the onslaught, and her thighs parted instinctively, the water's subtle caress not nearly enough.

Frances opened her eyes to the dimly lit room when the water flow stopped. Turning her head, she saw Henry standing immobile, an empty pitcher in his hand, and his gaze locked on her. She turned to face him, her skin still rosy from the warmth of the water and the growing warmth in her belly, and opened her mouth to break the silence but found she had no words.

He stepped closer—so close that a bead of water suspended at the tips of her breasts latched onto to the fine linen covering Henry's chest. His breath mingled with hers as they locked eyes.

"You are so beautiful." The words were hardly poetry, but his deep whispered rasp was strained with passion—passion she had aroused. "Even these," his hand hovered less than an inch above the fine white marks that formed a sunburst around her navel, "these are beautiful. They are evidence of your children. Our children. They add something indescribably moving to your body. Something that makes my heart hurt."

Frances, embarrassed, looked down at her dripping body and tried to turn away.

"Wait." The single word froze her mid turn as his hand moved up to cup her cheek—and stopped, hovering, a hairsbreadth away, keeping his promise.

Frances angled her face to make contact with his waiting palm. His sigh reverberated through her as she felt the release of tension, of uncertainty. She felt it as surely as if it were her own—they were one in this feeling, this moment. She closed her eyes as he cupped the line of her jaw in the heat of his hand before settling under her chin and tipping her face up to his.

There was only a moment of hesitation. Her mind, her heart screamed "kiss me!" and she willed him to make the move, to kiss her—but, by her own rules, he could not. Taking the lead, Frances leaned toward him, allowing their lips to meet in the sweetest lingering kiss she could have ever imagined.

Their previous kisses as husband and wife had been untried and clumsy; their kisses as illicit lovers, passionate and intense. This kiss was barely a touch, but it was as if their lips fit perfectly. Soft, delicate, but hardly innocent. It was the kiss from a fairy tale between a warrior and his beloved. Frances did not want it to ever end.

Chapter Eighteen

Rule Nine: Only the insistence of love can motive one to love.

Henry woke up, surprised that the sun had risen. He'd thought he would never fall asleep. How could he last night? Frances, his surprisingly determined and independent wife, wanted to kiss him. *Had* kissed him. It was entirely her decision, and she chose to share the most achingly sweet kiss with him. In that kiss she expressed just how innocent she was—how unpracticed in the art of seduction. There was no artifice in that kiss, no attempt at sensuality. Kisses were shared at court constantly and never with any meaning. Frances's kiss told him everything he needed to know. It was pure and passionate without any pretense of being anything more. It was one of the most sensual encounters of his life. And it meant he was making headway to winning his wife's heart.

True to his word, Henry had not laid a hand on her. He was awed by her trust as she nestled into his side, safe in his warmth. He lay wide awake for most of the night, painfully aware of her heat, her scent. Morning came with her still comfortably tucked into the crook of his arm, wiggling slightly as sleep fell away. It was where she belonged, and he was afraid to move.

"You are awake?" Frances's voice was a soft whisper against his neck as she shifted slightly and unhooked her leg from his.

"Yes. How did you know?" Henry kept his voice low, afraid to interrupt the peace of the room or force her further away.

"Your breathing changed."

With a smooth roll, she moved to sit on the edge of the bed. Henry held back a curse at the sudden loss of intimacy and warmth, and stopped himself from pulling her back into his arms. Frustrated, he rose and left the room to take care of his morning needs.

When he returned, he found Frances holding on to the bedpost as Mary wordlessly laced her into her corset.

"Her Majesty has called for a hunt this morning," she called to him over her shoulder as if being dressed before him was a usual occurrence. "The gamekeeper in the eastern park has said there are two stags ripe for the hunt and Queen Elizabeth and Her party are to depart immediately. We have been invited, but it seems more of a demand." Frances nodded to the open missive lying on the coverlet.

Henry, silent with fury, grabbed the missive. Written in the Queen's steward's own hand was the instruction to join the Queen Herself on a hunt.

"This is madness. I'm certain Her Majesty knows of the threat from yesterday. There is no reason to put you in any more danger." He crumbled up the parchment and threw it in the fire. "Mistress Mary, leave us."

The young woman dropped Frances's tapes and gave him a reverance before hurrying out of the room.

Frances turned, holding her corset up over her chest. "You cannot think to deny the Queen."

He never had. Never thought he could. But here he was. "No, we are staying here. I have alerted the guard about the particulars of the attack, and until there are answers I will have you safe."

"And Queen Elizabeth will show the world she is not going to live in fear. There was an attack at Her court, yes. But will that stop Her? No. She will laugh in the face of any threat before showing weakness."

"You believe she is forcing you out into the open on purpose?" No sooner had the words left his mouth then he knew them as true. Of course the Queen would take risks with someone else's life if only to make a statement.

"There is a second missive." Frances reached into the pockets already fastened over her petticoats. "This came from my mother."

"Quite a bit happened in the short time I was gone, it seems," Henry muttered as he read the short note confirming Frances's interpretation of the Queen's behavior. All the court knew of the attack and could not be seen as craven. Frances and Henry would join the Queen for the morning's hunt, and they would make every pretense at enjoying themselves.

He cursed under his breath. His duty was to the Crown, and yet...

"No."

Frances looked up and blinked. "No? Naysaying the Queen is not done."

"Well, there is a first time for everything. You have taken ill and should not be out. I have broken my leg and cannot stand. We have both eaten bad rye and are under confinement. I do not care. No, we do not go."

His own words astounded him. Had he gone mad? *Perhaps.*

Frances snapped closed her gaping mouth and pursed her lips. "Henry, since you sent Mary out, you must help me ready."

She turned her back to him.

"We are not leaving the room, Frances."

"And we must. The Queen has said it will be so, and neither of us are fools enough to follow through on any of your silly excuses. It is no good. We are going hunting."

"Frances, I cannot let anything happen to you."

"What will happen? We will be with the elite of court. The Queen Herself and her best guardsmen will be there. Who would dare attack either of us? Yes, it makes me uneasy, but there is nothing for it. You know I am right."

He stood stiff, anger thrumming through him with no outlet. It was his duty to protect his wife *and* his duty to serve Queen

Elizabeth. But he'd made a vow to only one woman, Frances, and he'd be damned if he let any harm come to her.

"Henry," she lifted the mass of tangles over her shoulder to bare her neck, her back, "we will be safe. Together, in the bosom of the court, what could happen?"

He moved over to her, and unable to care about their agreement, placed a kiss at the base of her neck. She gasped and turned to him. Would she scold him for touching her? *I may as well be hanged for a sheep as a lamb...* Reaching up, he speared his fingers through her curls and pulled her to him in a searing kiss.

Breathless, he pulled away, staring down at her sleepy eyes, swollen lips.

"Promise me you will be cautious. Stay always aware of your surrounds. Do not go off alone. And..." He released her and crossed the room. Opening the trunk beneath the window, he found what he wanted. "Keep this with you." He handed her the bodice dagger, something that most ladies may use as a beautiful, jeweled accessory, but one he knew had a keen blade. She tucked it down the stiff center channel of her corset and he placed his hands on her face, gently cradling her cheeks as she blinked. "Promise me you'll stay safe."

She nodded. "I promise."

Relaxing his hold, he released her and stepped back, his breathing still jagged.

"My lady wife, I will call for your ladies and go ready myself." He gave a courtly reverance. "I shall see you anon."

• • •

Queen Elizabeth looked magnificent as always. Today she sat mounted on Her chestnut, Her oxblood leather doublet matching the mare's saddle and trappings. The excitement of the hunt, both in the anticipation and the kill, always added a sparkle to the

Queen's eye and a rosy glow to Her cheek. Frances had never seen Her look more lovely.

Frances, to do herself justice, felt confident in her new green velvet habit. The olive tone offered a sharp contrast to the red gold highlights in her hair and made the dark blond appear even more fashionably red. She sat, proud in her appearance and station within the Queen's party, upon her new bay mare, an unexpected gift from Henry. Persephone was stately and as responsive to her new mistress as could be expected for an untried horse and, Frances noted, a far cry above the unfortunate gray she borrowed from the palace stables the day before. The horse was an extravagant gift, but Henry had told her that was not a concern—after all, he had a wife to woo. Frances couldn't imagine when he'd found the time to find her in the hours between the invitation to the hunt and now, but she was the perfect horse. It was unfortunate her name was so pretentious. With a laugh she wondered if his own horse was named Hades. *Probably.* Men did like to feel manly, after all.

There was something exciting about the hunt, about the anticipation. She never enjoyed the kill, but the chase had always been exhilarating and it felt rewarding to serve the felled beast at the feast that followed. How long had it been? God's blood, this was her first hunt since her marriage. There was no reason for it—they had ample lands and enough titled neighbors for her to have orchestrated something over the years. In fact, she had never instigated any social activities at the Holme besides the Christmas feasting for the tenants and local villagers. With a firm nod and a cluck to the horse to move along, Frances determined that things would be different when she returned to Holme LeSieur. Planning offered the perfect foil to keep her fear over the events of yesterday in check.

...

Henry rode ahead to join the ranks of the procession, forced to comply with the positions based on precedence of rank. They should not be here. Ahead and laughing with abandon, Queen Elizabeth rode surrounded by handsome men. He'd never resented his role in court before, but then he'd never felt he was used as a tool to maintain appearances. Yes, he'd served the Crown over the Church and never once had cause to regret, but ahead rode his sovereign, a feckless woman who would risk his wife's life on a whim. Anger curdled inside him, and he forced a polite smile, girding himself for a day of hell.

He could not wait to leave court, to return to the Holme, and learn what it meant to be a husband and father.

He looked back on Frances, riding to the rear as the wife of an untitled gentlemen would, and cursed. Yes, they were surrounded by guards, but not one was in proximity of his wife, caring little about the wellbeing of Her courtiers.

Frances rode well, her seat straight and easy. Ten years of marriage and, before yesterday, they had never ridden together that he remembered. What a waste. Seeing her now as a woman and a courtier, not a burden or a responsibility, changed his perspective, and he could not help but be afraid. There was so much more at stake—perhaps that's what the unknown attacker counted on. He had been working to secure her heart but may have lost his own in the process.

Henry wasn't sure how much headway he had made over the past few days, but he couldn't think about the sweetness of her lips without grinning like an idiot. It was as if he was a smitten schoolboy and not a man of twenty-five. He, who had served his country loyally and without question, who put the interest of his estate above his own—he was not some randy adolescent.

God's wounds, maybe he was a child still to fly between rage and fear and lust and glee. His emotions were out of control, unpredictable, but one thing was certain—he had to keep his wife safe in order to win her heart.

Lord Leicester took his place beside the Queen, Her riding habit matching his oxblood slashed leather doublet perfectly. The gamekeeper signaled the party that a stag was sighted, and the dogs picked up the scent. With a quick jab of the spurs, Leicester began the hunt, and the entire party joined the chase. Henry looked back to see Frances safely at the rear of the procession beside Baroness Ludlow with one single Yeoman of the Guard bringing up the rear, his red skirted doublet a sharp contrast against the still verdant foliage of the mid-November forest.

• • •

Frances was not surprised to be bringing up the rear: she was, after all, the lowest ranking in matters of precedence. She should be honored to be in attendance at all—still, she felt vulnerable. The single guardsman was surely not enough to assuage Henry's worry, if his repeated worried glances back were any indication. She tried to dismiss the growing feeling of unease as her new mare kept pace with the party. She was surrounded by the Queen's private guard—there was nothing to worry about. The events of yesterday should not color today's enjoyment. In such a proximity to the Queen, her concerns were silly. She was safe here.

With a false confidence, she kept up her canter as she heard the horn sound—they were upon the stag. She was too far back to see, but from what she understood, undisclosed archers would take down the stag for the most part, but Queen Elizabeth would make the kill and claim the trophy. Queen Elizabeth would finish the hunt, and then they would head back to the palace. This form of orchestrated hunt had been performed a hundred times before and was more pageantry than true hunting. It was completely irrational for Frances to feel so vulnerable. It was probably only residual stress from yesterday. She reminded herself that Henry was here and she was surrounded by the Queen's guard.

Frances's bay caught up with Baroness Ludlow's just as her nerves started to get the better of her.

"You do not look comfortable upon that mount, Mistress." Baroness Ludlow looked to Frances with concern as she sidled up beside her horse. "If you are not a competent rider, you should not have joined the hunt…"

Frances was relieved to have the company, albeit sour. "No, I ride well enough. This horse is new, and I am just a little jumpy today. Besides, I feel like those clouds have the promise of a storm."

"I agree. And soon."

The two ladies rode forward in silence as they neared the group of courtiers clustered around the Queen. Baroness Ludlow leaned closer, holding her empty goblet over her mouth as she whispered, "She will have cut off the ear and claimed the kill. It was smart that She dressed in the red leather. She has spoiled too many rich gowns with this blood sport. It is amazing that She goes along with the farce. Everyone knows that it is never Queen Elizabeth who truly brings down the prey. She is only a woman and could never overpower a stag."

Frances clicked her jaw shut. Mocking the Queen was something that *was not done*. She hadn't taken Baroness Ludlow as someone so brazen. The irreverence may have been only shocking if not for the hint of malice in her voice. It was well that they were out of earshot from the next riders in the procession.

Uncomfortable silence lead into a change of subject. "How fares your husband? It was quite a spectacle for the court when Her Grace 'reunited' you." Baroness Ludlow had a smirk on her face, and Frances knew that she probably had a few opinions on the subject. Frances was used to her harsh sense of humor—and if she would jest about the Queen, no one was safe from her caustic wit. It seemed it was Frances's turn. She may as well be good-natured about the coming onslaught.

Frances let Baroness Ludlow talk a bit about how unfortunate it was that Frances should be burdened with an unwanted bed mate. It was part jest and part bitter criticism. Frances could not blame her for being so jaded—Baroness Ludlow was stuck at court with an uncertain future while her husband was being held in the Tower on the charge of treason. It wasn't a wonder that she had no well wishes for any other marriage and laced every word with biting sarcasm. Frances couldn't help feeling a little uncomfortable with the knowledge that her own husband had helped to bring down Baroness Ludlow's.

Baroness Ludlow's increasingly intimate questions were rudely, and thankfully, interrupted as Sir Harry Lee, obviously frustrated, rode up to the pair.

"Baroness Ludlow, Mistress LeSieur, Her Majesty wishes for her curved bow with the rose engraving so she may fell the next stag unassisted."

Frances assumed Queen Elizabeth had requested the task of Sir Harry and he was re-delegating the unwanted job. It was surprising he had not sent one of the yeomen for it. Then again, the way his eyes settled upon her, the quirk of his beard, she felt Sir Harry's interest might be reason for this request. She straightened on her saddle but could not see Henry ahead.

"Allow me to say that the image of you mounted is a thing of beauty. I wager you could handle something more than that mare. Nay, you are in want of a stallion."

Frances had enough self-control not to roll her eyes, but the same could not be said for Baroness Ludlow who looked as if she smelled something very foul. "You would wager, Sir Harry?" Baroness Ludlow asked. "How much? Ten pounds?"

Frances, again, looked toward Henry for guidance. He would not like her leaving the hunt, but if the Queen commanded it… "Might Yeoman Todd escort us? I fear I do not remember the way back."

Baroness Ludlow sighed. "Oh, the wee lamb is lost in the wood. Worry not, I know the way." She kicked off her mount and started back along the path.

"Sir Harry?" Frances asked, uncertain and uncomfortable with the way he watched her.

The big man smiled down on her as if she were a child. "Of course, mistress. I wish for nothing more than your comfort."

He nodded to the guardsman then looked back to her. "Go now."

"As you say." Frances bowed her head to him then kicked her mare into a canter to catch up with the baroness, the guardsman following behind.

"Mistress LeSieur," he called after her, "I knew I could count on you to fulfill my desires." Sir Harry poured so much slime into his words that Frances felt ridiculous for ever thinking him attractive.

Chapter Nineteen

Rule Five: That which is not given freely by the object of one's love loses its savor.

Henry had had enough of courtly posturing, but was not so much a fool as to overlook the honor of joining Queen Elizabeth's hunt. After the Queen had claimed her trophy and passed the bloody bounty to Leicester, the head gamekeeper announced the general whereabouts of the second stag and the party was on the move once more.

On top of it all, he was too close by far to Kit Hatton. Ever since their unusual alliance over Mistress Jane's attack and then damage control about Hatton's inability to keep himself in check around Frances, he wondered if there might actually be a basis for friendship. He abandoned that thought as his respect for the man dwindled in the face of Hatton's syrup-thick flirtation with the Queen. At least Sir Harry Lee was nowhere to be found. He hardly knew the man, and his obvious dislike of Henry made no sense. At the start of the hunt, every sentence held a taunting jibe. Henry felt as if Sir Harry were working through a list of insults: his wife, his parentage, his faith, his manhood... A lesser man would have called him out. He would be willing to bet an angel that Sir Harry *wanted* a reason to duel. Where had all this animosity come from?

Henry broke from his thoughts as the party made an about face at the direction of the hounds. After a moment's hesitation, Henry simply turned his horse and waited for his wife to reach him.

Lady Rich, Colonel Blount, various courtiers, all trotted by, but where was Frances? Glancing over the courtiers to ensure that he did not misunderstand his wife's place in precedence, he noted the other courtiers conspicuous in their absence.

Baroness Ludlow and Sir Harry Lee. The yeoman who had brought up the rear had been replaced.

Henry heeled his stallion, Petit Chou, forward until he flanked the tall ginger haired guardsman. "Yeoman, do you know where Mistress LeSieur has got herself to?"

The yeoman tugged on his cap in respect before answering, "She rode off with Baroness Ludlow. Yeoman Todd provided escort."

Damnation. She'd promised to stay with the party.

He barely ground out, "Where were they headed?"

"Back along the path to the palace, based on their direction. I do not know more than that."

"And Sir Harry?"

"He followed shortly behind."

With a gracious nod of thanks, he spurred his stallion onward and set off at a gallop after his absent wife. He didn't trust Baroness Ludlow, but he could handle her vitriol. How could a man as merry as Baron Ludlow have burdened himself with such a noxious shrew? He was probably enjoying his respite in the Tower.

As for Sir Harry, well he was in dire need of a beating.

Laying low over Petit Chou's speckled neck, Henry clenched his teeth in a fury. Damn the man. Sir Harry had his share of lovers; why seek out Frances? Certainly she was beautiful, but very, *very* unavailable. This could not be about the ten pounds Hatton placed on her seduction, could it? And now he was hunting a married lady of the court right under Queen Elizabeth's nose. *Right under her husband's nose.*

Had he no sense?

Henry was forced to slow his horse's pace in order to maneuver a muddy incline... When had it started raining? He adjusted his seat as his stallion carefully picked his footing down the increasingly treacherous slope and tried to calm his rage with reason. Why was he jumping to the assumption that Sir Harry had masterminded this liaison? What if Frances wanted a dalliance? Petit Chou whinnied at the unexpected tension and Henry forced himself to relax. There was no point in jumping to any conclusions—there may be nothing more to this than ridiculous paranoia.

Henry adjusted his cape to better cover his neck and shoulders and kept his stallion, Petit Chou, at as quick a pace as was safe in the growing deluge. The rain brought a chill with it signaling the start of winter—not a storm to be caught in without shelter. He had to get to Frances. Keeping his eyes on the path and his ears sharp for any misplaced noise, he continued down the muddy slope toward the first stream.

• • •

"By the saints, Sir Harry, do you not understand the words I am saying?" Frances lowered her voice in a way her children knew meant there was no room for argument. Of course, she had never spoken so foully to her children.

Sir Harry kept his grip tight on her reins and smiled, his teeth a flash of white against his dark waxed mustache. "I expect my quarry to give me a merry chase," he leaned closer, her horse side stepping despite his firm grip, "and you have done that, Frances. But the game is over."

"I do not give you leave to be familiar with my name. Release my reins. You are no gentleman." She looked back down the path toward the hunt, hoping to spy Baroness Ludlow and the guardsman she thought were to accompany her. No one. In fact—she looked the other direction—she wasn't certain which way was the direction of the hunt. It all looked the same. She almost cried in frustration just as rain drops began to tap against the tree canopy above her. What else could go wrong? It was foolish to even ask.

Sir Harry tugged and her horse pawed the earth in protest. "Nay, I am a hunter and have finally caught you." He released his hold and reached for her hand.

She pulled away, but he grabbed her arm. Tight. Too tight. "Sir Harry, you are hurting me."

"Then stop fighting me." He pulled, nearly unseating her. "That tepid kiss with Hatton made me angry, but I later thought on it and realized you were taunting me. It was not a kiss shared by lovers.

"Thank God for that," she muttered and tried to twist out of his grip. "I will not take a lover at court. I have tried to be plain about it, not taunting, not being coy. There has been no hidden meaning in my words."

"So many women will say that, play at virtue. But in the end, they want what I have to give." He reached down and lay a hand on his padded codpiece with a laugh. "Flirtation is a promise of more."

"I was nothing but polite to you and would have offered friendship but never more." She twisted again to no avail. Surely, he was a gentleman of the court and would not be forceful…

He was already being forceful. She would be a fool to expect anything else at this point.

"Frances, you and I have some lost time to make up for." He released his grip and reached up to cup her face. She flexed her wrist, willing the pain to ease as he caressed her cheek with the back of his gloved finger. "Come back to the palace with me, and we will have at least an hour to ourselves. More than enough time…"

She leaned back from his touch, shaking her head, speechless with shock.

"Do not deny me, Frances"

Part of her wanted to cry, another part wanted to vomit, but something powerful, something within her she never knew before, wanted to fight. Her body was hers to give, not his to take and, by God, he would not have the satisfaction of her submission.

She leaned closer, accepting his touch. His arrogant smile was that of a man who knew he had won.

Not yet. *Never.*

The storm broke overhead; a white flash from lightning sliced through the branches as she unsheathed the dagger from her bodice and drove it into his thigh.

He roared in pain, his cry covered by the pounding drums of thunder, and she urged her horse around and bolted down the path.

• • •

The wood was dark, the thick limbs of ancient trees a massive weave blocking out the light. Henry peered into the growing dark, his eyes adjusting just as a flash of lightning blinded him. His horse reared beneath him at the following thunder and then he heard it, a shout. Following the sound, he let his mount find safe footing on the increasingly muddy path.

Sir Harry bounded toward him, anger seething in his eyes. "Get your bitch under control."

"My bitch?" he asked, ready to draw his sword in defense if need be. Based on the expression on Sir Harry's face and the blood staining his buckskin breeches, it was a good bet he would. "Pray, who is my bitch?"

"Your wife. She teased me, always spurning my flirtation, and then…" He looked down at his leg and cursed again. "Banish her to the country, Master LeSieur. She does not belong here."

Sir Harry spurred his horse forward and rode back in the direction of the hunt.

Frances. Sir Harry had pursued Frances. He would deal with that whoreson later, when he knew she was safe.

He retraced the path Sir Harry left behind him and saw the diminishing evidence of a horse galloping to the east. Away from the palace. Before he could assess further, the tracks melted into mud, and he set off after her.

"Frances!" he shouted against the increasing thrum of the rain. He was on a path of sorts, but not the one back toward the palace and well off the route of the hunting party.

The underbrush thickened as his horse picked his way out of the cover of the forest and down the bank of a swelling stream.

A whinny and a splash was followed by a stream of curses he never would have believed his wife might even know, and he urged his mount upstream toward the sound.

Frances stood knee deep in the churning water, her skirts pulling at her legs as she struggled to stay upright. She was trying to lead Persephone across the water, and the damn horse was throwing her head, refusing.

Another bolt of lightning and the horse pulled back, agitated, the force toppling Frances into the stream. Sputtering, she found her feet again and reached for the reins just as Henry dismounted. Persephone whipped her head wildly, panic building with the storm around them.

"Henry!" Frances gasped, almost falling back into the water.

Henry grabbed the bridle, directing the spooked mare. Unease prickled at his nape as he soothed and walked her calmly up the embankment.

Thunder rumbled and he laid a steadying hand on the mare's neck. He could hear Frances trudging up behind him.

"Is this supposed to ingratiate me toward you? Caring for the horse and leaving me in the water?"

The horse's ears pricked at Frances's sharp tone.

Henry cooed and smoothed the bay mare's mane before explaining over his shoulder, "I had to get her away from you before you ended up trampled." His experience so far with Frances told him that speaking common sense had a better chance of success than placating her.

"Oh." Her word came out on a relieved sigh. "I was worried you cared more for the horse than for me."

"Well, I wouldn't want her hooves to tangle in your skirts—she might break a leg…"

Frances laughed and slapped his shoulder, her hand a wet smack against the sodden velvet. Lightning heightened the shadows around them, but the horse remained calm this time.

"I think we must find shelter. From this location, the palace is an almost an hour's ride in the best conditions." The rain pounded harder as Henry handed Frances Persephone's reins and recovered Petit Chou's. "If memory serves, there is a gamekeeper's cottage east of here. Shall we?"

He hoped he was correct and, even more, he hoped the gamekeeper was not in residence. They both needed to get out of their wet clothes and warm before a fire, and the possibilities that suggested were enough to make him stand at attention. Neither spoke until they broke through the tangle of branches and into a clearing upstream. No smoke came from the small thatched cottage, the secured shutters showed no sign of light inside.

Henry let the horses to the shed. Built to house only one horse and provisions, it was crammed to bursting. Aside from the LeSieurs and their two horses, it looked as though the gamekeeper was stocked for the upcoming winter.

"The horses should be safe in here through the storm. Wait here while I check the cottage."

Henry dashed into the rain, his boots unsteady in the thick mud. The heavy front door was, thankfully, unlocked.

He closed the door once more and crossed the mire to fetch Frances.

"I can walk…" she objected as he lifted her into his arms.

"I'm sure you can, but you do not wish to." He prayed he didn't fall as he pulled his boot free of the mud with a wet, suction sound. Balanced on one foot, he opened the door with the other and said, "Your palace, my lady." He set her on her feet, and a wet puddle poured from her skirts in a growing circle. "Hardly grand accommodations, but if we light a fire, at least we can attempt to dry and warm ourselves."

Frances knelt upon the earthen hearth, skillfully arranging kindling. "I saw a woodpile on the south side of the cottage. It is covered in a tarp and might be dry..."

"Let us pray it is so," Henry replied, crossing himself before he stepped outside.

• • •

Frances listened to the rain against the shutters, praying in truth for Henry's safe return. And firewood. And food would be welcome. Oh, and ale. *Amen.*

She rose and hung her sodden cloak on a peg beside the door. Her gown would have to follow if she wanted to have any chance for warmth, but that would have to wait until the fire was lit. Frances settled herself onto a stool to the side of the fire place. The walls groaned with a rumble of thunder, and a shiver of excitement ran down her spine. She was trapped in the middle of the forest, soaked to the bone—she should be miserable instead of thrilled, full of anticipation.

Henry kicked open the door as a bolt of lightning lit the sky. "Now that was a dramatic entrance." Rolling a small, muddy barrel with his foot and his arms piled with firewood, Henry moved toward the hearth. Frances helped unburden him of his load, and Henry took over building the fire.

The kindling fire caught the larger logs just as Frances finished tapping the barrel and filling the cottage's single tankard with honey ale.

"That smells delicious," Henry murmured, accepting the mug with thanks. After a deep draft, he handed it back.

Frances sat back on her stool, sipping her ale with something akin to worship as the flooding warmth soothed the tension from being lost in the wood and caught in a storm.

They both sat in silence, soaking in the heat from the hearth as it filled the dark little room. Frances stood and began to take off her sodden riding habit. "Henry, please do not take this as an invitation…"

"Worry not." Henry rose and followed suit, dropping his soaked doublet onto the rug near the door with a splat. "I know you to be nothing if not practical." His Venetians joined his doublet on the floor, leaving him standing in his sodden linen shirt and nether hosen. "I hope that I have proven that I am a man of honor. I will not ravage you." Walking over to the cot, he retrieved the worn quilt and brought it over to his wife. "That is, unless you ask me." The room was too dark to see, but Frances was sure he was smiling.

Frances, now stripped to her corset, chemise, and stockings, accepted the gift of the quilt with a noble nod. *"Unless I ask you."* Would she? Last night she cursed their blasted arrangement, longing for him to take the lead; perhaps it was not so far-fetched. The image of lying with him in their marriage bed still made her uneasy, but here, in a cottage, during a storm, it was as if they were two lovers trysting instead of a duty bound married couple.

The next bolt of lightning punctuated Frances's thought, and a frisson of awareness shivered through her body.

"Frances, you're freezing. Pick up the quilt and come to the fire. I have something I want to show you."

Frances obeyed wordlessly. She was too wrapped up in her thoughts. Come to think of it, she was still wrapped up in her corset. The quilt tucked over her shoulders, Frances reached around and deftly began picking loose lacings until the corset dropped at her waist. Henry let out a bark of a laugh as Frances pulled the corset out from under the quilt and tossed it across the room in the general direction of her hanging clothes.

"Is this your way of inviting my attentions? If so, you need to be more explicit." Henry's tone was jovial, but his eyes were piercing.

Frances smiled at his playful words. "I think the reed boning is waterlogged and doubled in thickness and weight," Frances offered before adding, "Honestly, had I wanted to enamor you with my figure I would have left it on."

"What could be more seductive than a naked woman?"

Wrapping the quilt tighter, she moved closer to the hearth to dispel the chill that shook her.

Henry rose from his stool, discovered a woolen blanket for himself, and discarded his wet shirt and hosen, wrapping the cloth about his waist like a kilt. He returned to sit on the rug in front of the hearth. "My underpinnings were never going to dry…"

"No need to explain. It's perfectly logical." Frances was intensely aware that, but for the quilt, he was naked. "Would you have more ale?"

"Aye." He nodded his assent, then gestured toward her. "Come sit on the rug with me. 'Twould be easier to share our loving cup."

Again, Frances could not fault his logic. Besides, she was aching to be closer to him, and this was a practical reason. "Just a moment." Crossing the cottage to a darkened corner, she divested herself of her wet linen chemise and woolen stockings, and wrapped the quilt securely across her bosom. Checking that she was well-covered, she returned to the hearth, joining him on the rug before the fire.

The storm continued on outside—the thunder and lightning passing on to leave only the driving wind and rain. It was still early in the day, but the sky was dark with clouds and the shutters of their haven shook with each gust. Inside, the firelight caressed

Frances and Henry with a golden glow. They were safe. They were together. They were naked.

And Henry had just risen to refill their cup for the fourth time. He returned to hand the tankard to her, then retrieved one of the saddle bags before joining her once more.

"Is this what you wanted to show me?" she asked after taking a sip. The ale got sweeter with every swallow.

"Yes. I keep it with me lest it be taken from our rooms."

"What is it?" she asked as he unwound the leather wrapping.

The pillow book. Heat flooded her face, and she looked up at him, panic taking hold anew. "Henry, I am not certain…"

"Hush. Wait." He opened the book and removed a small silk pouch from a compartment within the cover. "I learned that there are ways to prevent conception and I thought you might be interested to learn. Please, know that I am not pressuring you."

She swallowed her instinctive denial and simply nodded.

He opened the ties and upended it onto her lap—a circlet of leather so fine it may almost be silk, with two ribbons attached. "What is this?"

He took it from her and unrolled it into something resembling a glove for a very thick finger. He handed it back and said, "This is something they use in the Orient to prevent the pox."

So not for a finger then. *Lovely.* She dropped it back onto her lap and wiped her hand on the quilt. "Has it been in there all this time?"

"No, it is new. I procured it from a glover in London." He picked it up and slid a finger inside. "It fits over the male member so that a man's seed does not enter the woman's body."

Oh. She blinked at his finger. Despite his large hands, the single digit inside the sheath was hardly filling it. If that fit over him, then he must be… *Oh!* No wonder coupling had always hurt.

She looked away and shook away the thought. "So this eliminates the chance of pregnancy?"

"Lessens it, from what I was told." He rolled it back up and slipped it inside the pouch once more. "I know that fearing another babe is only part of what holds you back, but I thought if I removed that obstacle you might be more open to..." He swallowed, for a moment reminding her very much of the young boy she'd married a lifetime ago. "Me."

The nervous edge to his voice tugged at the knot in her chest. She met his eyes, her uncertainty waning under the raw emotion she saw aching in the deep brown depths of his gaze. She bit her lip and turned away. *Coward.*

"So," she cleared her throat to relieve the unexpected tightness there, "the book. You carry it with you?"

He was silent a moment before responding. "I do not know how much of this book you examined, but I have set out to become a scholar." The levity in his voice was a relief.

"A scholar on making love?" she asked, her voice edged in laughter,

He leaned closer and winked, playful once more. "I cannot think of a better thing to be an expert in."

"Well then some would call me a lucky woman."

"I would love to have you agree to that as well," he said, his voice low against the thrumming rain. "First I learned that there are multiple, erhm, access angles..."

He flipped open to a page showing a woman standing against a wall, one leg wrapped around her lover's hip. The man had an enormous... She blushed as she pictured the size of the leather sheath he'd just shown her.

Henry flipped the page. And another, she assumed it was supposed to be a man's organ but looked more like a stave, penetrated a woman who bent forward. It was intriguing and embarrassing and silly and...arousing.

"What I do not understand," Frances mused as Henry turned the page, "is why this is a good idea. It all looks uncomfortable and," she took another sip of the ale and shifted her weight to her hip so that her shoulder leaned against her husband, "messy."

Henry chuckled, his laughter shaking her softly. "I imagine there is some pleasure involved."

"Oh, for the man, certainly. I imagine there is." She leaned her head back against his chest. "But the woman, it just looks awkward." And her memories of their coupling over the years did not help, despite the unfamiliar warmth at her center.

"You seem to enjoy looking." He shifted to accommodate her position, laying a hand on her hip to move her closer. With a jerk, he pulled away. It took Frances a moment to realize why: he'd touched her without permission.

She reached over and took his hand to lay it back on her. His fingers splayed, drawing her tighter against him, the pressure of his touch hot even through the quilt. She bit her lip at the intimacy.

It felt so right, like she fit in his arms, his hands made to touch her. Drawing an unsteady breath, she looked back at the book. Henry turned the page to the one she'd originally marked. This time the look of abandon on the woman's face resonated within her. She remembered the way he made her feel, the way he loved her with his mouth that night on the barge. It was wanton, it was illicit, and it was perfect. It made her wonder what more was possible.

She looked up at him to find him focused on her. He was so close, just a breath away and all she wanted was to taste his kiss again. Her body ached with it. Please, please—she willed it, but he stayed still, his mouth a taut line, his jaw tense.

All she had to do was ask. Of course, there was that kiss this morning—that was entirely him. No permission and no apologies, he kissed her until her toes tingled. But that was different; she knew that kiss was fueled by fear for her safety, the need to confirm their connection. That wasn't seduction, it was a claim and she could not deny it. Didn't want to. *Damnation*. It was up to her.

But she didn't know what to do. She didn't even know what it was she wanted. She didn't particularly want Henry's gigantic phallus, if the pictures could be believed, anywhere near her... Except she did. A little. Really, all she wanted was a simple kiss. Maybe that would lead somewhere, maybe it wouldn't. And if she didn't like that path, she would make the right choice for herself, wouldn't she?

"Henry, I..." and "Frances, I do not..." overlapped each other, causing both to pause in order to let the other speak. Courteously, both Frances and Henry reassured each other, "No, you speak..." again, talking over each other. Frances let out a sheepish laugh, Henry sighed, the honeyed ale on his breath fanning against her cheek. After an expectant silence, both laughed again, the laughter only stopping when Frances said, "This is nonsense. Stop laughing and kiss me."

Henry did not need to be told twice.

Chapter Twenty

Rule Twenty-Six: Love is powerless to hold anything from love.

Henry leaned his head down as Frances lifted her lips to meet in a soft kiss. Just a brush of lips. Then another. He lightly kissed the corner of her mouth in a feather-soft brush. Then her lower lip. It was playful. It was not enough.

Frances wanted more. The sweet uncertainty in his touch whetted her appetite and teased her with the memory of their kisses on the barge. Abandoning her secure hold on the quilt, she reached for him with both hands, delving her fingers into his curling hair and pressing him to her. Frances crushed her lips against his, seeking something more, and Henry responded immediately. No more soft and sweet—their lips moved over each other, tasting, tempting—Frances could not get enough.

He pulled away with a jolt, his eyes heavy lidded, their dark depths boring into her. "I will not presume. Remember, you must guide this, not I."

She nodded and pushed forward to continue the kiss only to gasp as he dipped lower and pressed a hot kiss beneath her ear.

Henry's lips skated across her jaw while Frances explored the cords of his neck, the tight muscles of his shoulders. She gasped in pleasure, encouraging him with each whimper and breath, but not sure what words to say. More? What would that mean?

• • •

Henry could not lose control, but this pounding, lust-driven madness had captured the two of them. He wanted to slowly love each inch of her body. This frenzy of hands and lips on bare skin was wild and uncontainable. The thought that he should stop and ask before kissing lower, the tight peak of her breast inches below his lips, seemed insignificant, her permission implicit with each gasp. But no. He shook his head, his lips brushing the soft rise of her chest, as he regained himself.

"That feels," she breathed the words against his hair, and then pressed closer, shifting the pressure of her breasts against his bare chest, "wondrous. I want…" She moved against him. "I want…"

His entire body ached with need, so tight every muscle strained for more. Henry looked up, breathing in the heat of her panted breaths, and smiled into her passion-dazed eyes. "What do you want? Tell me."

She pressed her forehead against his, shaking her head, biting her lip. With one hand, she took his and brought it to her breast. The warm globe filled his palm, the tight budded nipple a sharp contrast to the lush fullness. Stunned, he stayed still, simply holding her. Then she pushed into his hand and cried out.

Henry leaned in, capturing Frances's waiting lips and swallowing her sigh as he shifted his hand and fit her nipple between his fingers in a soft pinch. "You want me to do this?" Henry asked, his lips still against hers, their breath mingling. "Does my touch please you?"

"Yes," she whispered. He angled his hand, his thumb steadily toying with the beautiful rosy tip. She shivered, and her skin puckered in a wave of gooseflesh.

"I did not know," she whispered as she snaked her fingers through his hair, "it could feel like this. Your touch." She kissed him again, opening herself to his mouth.

Henry felt Frances's sharp intake of breath with each caress. Her eyes closed as she leaned her head back, offering herself to him. His other hand came down, tracing the line from behind her ear, the cords of her neck, and finally resting on her other breast. The full mounds of firm, pliant flesh, with a beautiful rosebud nipple just asked to be tasted.

"I would like to kiss you." Henry broke away from her lips, the desire clear on her face not helping his restraint.

"You were kissing me," she answered and leaned in once more.

He met her mouth and then trailed his lips to her cheek before muttering, "No, I want to kiss you," he pinched her nipple between his thumb and finger, rolling it softly, "here."

She bit her lip and her head lolled back as she presented herself without words. "Tell me you want that too." His mouth followed the trail his hand had just made, along her jaw and to her neck. "A kiss is a touch…" He blew on the sensitized peak, and Frances shivered. "May I?"

"Please. Yes."

• • •

Frances had never known her breasts could give pleasure. His hands were so hot, but his touch was so light. And his lips. She wanted more, but she didn't even know how to ask. With another brush of his lips, then the coolness of his breath as he exhaled, Frances's body took over, and she arched her spine, offering him even more. The light touches became more intense, his mouth searing her nipples as he tasted her. Sensation jolted through her body. She was not in control of herself—of the small cries she let go with each spasm that coursed from her breast to her womb. It was too much to wrap her mind around, too much to feel, but she wanted more. She *needed* more.

Her hands were in his hair, cradling his head as his hot mouth moved from one breast to the next. She arched back, pressing herself to his mouth, his hands cradling her back, her head, as he lowered her to the floor. Her hair splayed out against the thick pile of the sheepskin rug, his arm wrapped around her back helping her body bow toward him. Her breasts felt heavy. She became aware of the pooling moisture between her legs and involuntarily flexed her inner muscles, sending a jolt of pleasure through her body.

She could not find the words. The memories of the way he brought her pleasure on the barge, the way he touched her so intimately, she wanted that. She squeezed her inner muscles, surprised at the sensation tingling across her skin. Frances arched toward him, pleading with her body, as he knelt over her, his arms around her, holding her to him. He shifted back, pulling her up to straddle his knees, leaving her completely open to him.

The heat of his mouth on her breasts contrasted with the cool air caressing her, making her acutely aware of an emptiness, a need to be filled. Could she be longing to couple? To feel his manhood inside her? The thought scared and aroused her, and she squirmed against his mouth, feeling too much and needing more all at once. A sharp jolt of heat at her breast shocked her out of her thoughts and all she knew were the demands of her arousal. Naked and open before him, wrapped around him, Frances was too hot with desire to be embarrassed—too wild with need to hold on to any thought other than that she wanted him to soothe the ache inside her.

She pressed her pelvis forward, her legs spread wide over his thighs, his engorged shaft just inches away.

"Frances?" he asked, lifting his head from her bosom. His eyes held a question, an innocence and uncertainty that contrasted with the tension in his jaw. He needed her permission—it would be so easy to simply take her, and yet he still needed her say. Her heart felt too large for her chest, her breath almost painful against the rapid thudding at her throat. Evidence of his need, as strong as hers, lay between them and still he honored her. He did not demand or assume.

She stilled the frantic urges of her body, asked herself what she wanted. All her arguments against marital relations seemed moot in this moment of passion. She wanted this, wanted him.

"Touch me," she said, the words a rasp from the tightness in her chest. "Touch me inside."

He remained still for too long. Was she wrong to want this? Doubt stabbed through her, but then disappeared as his mouth took hers once more. Henry's hands claimed her, gripping her bottom where she sat against his thighs. She felt soft and perfect, a woman made for love, under the strength of his touch. Ready and wanting.

His hand moved from her bottom around her thigh to her wet curls. His fingers threaded through the dark gold triangle to her cleft. Bit by bit, his questing fingers coursed their way to her warm, soft space. She bit her lip at the extreme sensation, wanting both to pull away and push closer. *Yes, this.* Her woman's center drew him in, his fingers gliding over the soft folds seeking ever deeper. She wanted him inside. Wanted to be full of him. Her body beckoned, and he followed, his long fingers finding their path inside bit by agonizing bit. His touch almost burned inside her, and she whimpered as, again, she flexed her inner muscles, gripping him tightly.

"Yes, like that," was all she could say as her body discovered the pattern his fingers drummed within her tight sheath. She rocked against him, following his motion.

She let her head fall forward against his chest, the still damp curls of her hair falling down. He winced as a cold tendril fell against his penis, and she gasped as it twitched, a dewy drop visible at the head.

All of this was for her. Her comfort and her pleasure. His fingers still stroking, that tight nub of sensation building and building, so close to a release.

Something she wanted to share with him.

With a tentative hand, she reached forward and wrapped her fingers around his steely heat.

"God help me, Frances." His words held an edge of pain. "I cannot take the torture."

"Let me," she whispered, laying a hot kiss against the straining tendon at his neck, "let me give you pleasure too." She ran a thumb over the moisture at his tip and traced a slick spiral around the pulsing crown. "Does this please you?"

"Christ, yes. I will spill in your hand." His fingers stilled inside her, their delicious pressure a promise of more. "I want to be inside you when you come apart, Frances. I want to be there with you."

She gasped at his words and tightened around him, frightened and wanting at the same time. "Inside me."

"Yes." He bucked against her hands, and her core clenched in response. He moved slowly, drawing his fingers slowly out of her sheath. "Do you want me?" Henry pressed inside once more, and Frances gripped his member, echoing the response of her body. All she could do was breathe harder as she sought out her climax. She nodded.

"Say that you want me." Henry was speaking through clenched teeth, his voice no more than a groan. "Say that you want me inside you. I swear that it will be good between us. Just say it."

"Yes." Frances's words were on a sharp intake of breath as passion drove her wild. "Please. I want you. Inside me."

In a fluid motion, Henry lifted her over him. He slowly eased her down, her body stretching around his cock, until he was buried in her. So full of him tears burned her throat, the pleasure so intense it was agony. He was so deep inside her she couldn't breathe. *Part of her.*

And then he moved. Again. A rhythmic upward thrust of his hips. How could he be any deeper? He was truly hers even as she cried out his name against his seeking mouth. He was pounding against her core, and she wanted more. More.

She wasn't sure if she said it aloud, but Henry picked up the pace, thrusting deeper and harder, his body grinding against hers. The dark hair on his lower belly was a rough pressure against the sensitive nub of flesh between her legs. Both his hands were on her hips, lifting her easily up and down to meet his thrusts. Harder and harder. Faster.

Frances felt as if her world was exploding. With each thrust of his body, the tension threatening to burst free grew and grew. She could hardly contain herself. All she could do was feel and allow wave upon wave of pleasure to ripple through her body in an exquisite torrent. She was almost there…almost to that point where it was too much and not enough and she could not hold back any longer. Her body clenched tightly where they were joined as she gave herself completely over to sensation.

Her body wracked in a shudder, Frances's womb tightened again and again as her cries voice echoed throughout the small cottage. Then he pulled away, leaving her empty as he called out, spilling his seed against her thigh, her name on his lips.

Sobbing though the last of the sensation, she pulled him to her. His lips trembled against hers. She had never felt so content. So complete.

· · ·

The rain was still a steady thrum against the shutters when Frances woke on the floor of the cottage, wrapped partially in a quilt.

Wrapped completely in Henry.

The fire sputtered low, and the artificial dark caused by the storm shifted into a very real night. How long had they been there? Frances's languor quickly evaporated and was replaced by the more familiar high-stress sensation of needing to be somewhere or do something.

Henry woke from his sleep, aware that the warm pressure across his chest no longer felt boneless. "What's wrong?"

"It's evening. We won't make it back to the palace before dark."

"Then we stay here." Henry's hand trailed up Frances's exposed back to toy with her hair. "This has become one of my favorite spots in the world. No duties, no obligations. Just us. Together. Naked."

Good God, what had happened? The remnants of pleasure still pulsed through her body, and she wanted to return to his side, curl up into his heat. But what did that mean? Confused, she got up to her knees to add a log to the fire. Henry rose and stretched his hands flat against the exposed beam ceiling.

Frances sat back on her heels and watched Henry. The flickering glow outlined his form in gold. He was a beautiful man. It seemed silly she had never noticed it before.

"We have been wed for ten years." Frances stated the seemingly nonsequitous fact plainly.

"Aye."

"We have been wed ten years, and I have never felt pleasure at your touch."

He looked back at her, his face shadowed in the dark room. "Aye."

"Why not?" The question was simple enough, but Frances realized it summed up the reasons for so much of her pain. Wasn't she worthy of love? Wasn't she desirable? What was wrong with her? She almost wished she had never learned that her husband could be so gentle and so passionate—then she could go on believing the fault lay with him.

He sat down beside her on the rug and shook his head. "I wondered the same thing. We have wasted so many years. I never knew both men and women could find pleasure in bed sport. Not really."

"I think our lack of affection limited the possibilities. Maybe we would have discovered each other. And still we only coupled roughly, out of duty." She felt tears sting her throat. "It made me feel worthless, only valued for the children I could bear. And even then, I was a failure…"

The wind shook the shutters and Frances shivered. Henry pulled her close, wrapping the quilt around them both.

"So why now? I am the same Frances as ever." Self-pity would get her nowhere. She wanted to slap herself, to shake away the melancholy that threatened.

Henry tightened his arm around her shoulders and pressed a hot kiss against the top of her head. "I knew that our marriage lacked any sort of passion or romance, but that was what I knew as normal. Why should I miss flying if it was never something I thought I should have? Passion was for other people who did not do their duty to their family, their name. I came to you an inexperienced boy and never learned that there could be something more. We had a comfortable arrangement so why question it? But then you came to London and challenged everything I knew to be right. You, not my obedient wife, but you, Frances, are a beautiful, intelligent woman. I never wondered if you wanted more. Or wanted me. I assumed you felt the same way, emotionally removed from the act of coupling." He paused and kissed her hair once more, biting back a curse. "Now I know that you simply obeyed while I used your body… It is sickening."

Wrapped in his warmth, she could feel his guilt, his anxiety, as if it were her own.

Frances could not bring herself to move from the warm haven of her husband's arms. "The stars were against us developing love in our marriage."

"We were children, devoid of choice and bound in duty. That is a weak recipe for affection. It's amazing we can even stand each other." His arms were locked around her, his muscles tensed, but she could hear a smile in his voice. "But we are not children any longer."

"No," she whispered. "We are no longer children."

He loosened his arms and splayed his hands on her back, strong and warm in the chill night. She moved into the embrace, shifting to sit between his legs. She fit there, cuddled into him as if they were made for each other. He leaned low and kissed her brow. She angled her face to give him better access as his lips teased her cheek, the shell of her ear. "Would you welcome my love? Is it something you want?" he murmured against her throat, his hands sliding up her arms to her shoulders.

Frances gasped as one hand moved down from her shoulder to lie over her bosom—over her heart. Yes. With those words, she realized with perfect clarity that his love was exactly what she wanted.

"What say you, Frances? Can we start our marriage anew?" Her breath caught as his teeth nipped her neck playfully.

Frances felt arousal build within her. Arousal and something more. Something she couldn't bring herself to trust. Part of her wanted to turn and let him claim her as his wife... She felt like she could not deny him. Somewhere between arriving at court and now her goal had changed: she no longer wished to dissolve her marriage; she wanted to love and be loved. She deserved that and strongly suspected it was well underway to happening with, luckily, her husband. And she wasn't ready.

"No." Her answer filled the cottage, clear over the sounds of the storm outside.

He stilled the soft kisses to her ear and asked, "No?"

"Not yet," Frances repeated, her voice breathy with building desire. She leaned forward, away from his soft kisses, and turned to look him in the eye. "But we appear to be having an affair while I am separated from my husband."

He laughed and pulled her back to him, but there was an edge to the sound that made his enjoyment unconvincing. "I think, in order to marry again, I need to believe that what lies between us is real. Did you not say you would woo me? Well, I want to be wooed. I do want a love match, but I do not want to force it. I think we should give ourselves the chance to find love first."

"And this is not love?" he asked.

"This," Frances gestured roughly toward his manly bits, "is proof of lust only. And I'm not certain that your only motivation is not pride. Love… I only hope I can recognize it for what it is. I wasted too many dreams on courtly love. If what we have is an indication, love is a very different beast altogether."

"I can understand why the scholars prefer to define love by rules. Anything else is too complicated," Henry murmured and pulled her closer.

Yes, very complicated. Either that or too simple by far.

Chapter Twenty-One

Rule Twenty-Eight: Presumption on the part of the beloved causes suspicion in the lover.

After a night and most of the day in a gamekeeper's cottage, Frances wanted nothing more than a bath. That, and a better perspective. Desire had a way of clouding one's vision and making ridiculous things seem like good ideas. At least the bath was something she could manage.

Frances sat submerged in a copper basin full of steaming water and ignored the knock on the door.

Another knock.

Henry came out of the chamber freshly shaven and wearing clean linens. "Surely they will give up soon?"

By the saints, he was a fine-looking man. Frances bit her lip and focused on not becoming randy again.

Another series of knocks, more insistent.

"My last set of rooms did not have a door that could be barred," Frances mused aloud as she let the heat from the water seep into her muscles. "No way to keep out unwanted guests. I had to request they fix that for me." Frances cringed at the memories of the rat and the rosary. Things at court were not as expected. She'd not anticipated fear at all—why would she?

"I can personally assure your safety now, Frances," Henry said before crossing over to the door and leaning against the hinges, presumably to listen. After a moment, he shook his head and shrugged, a clear message that he had no idea who was being so persistent or why.

When they arrived back at the palace after their night in the wood, Henry gave clear instructions for no interruptions. While it was presumptuous of him to assume she wished to stay alone with him, he was absolutely right. She couldn't face people right now. She was too raw.

The knocking continued.

"We had best answer it," Frances muttered, really not wanting to face her ladies. *Or my mother*. "Give me a moment to put on a dressing gown." And to figuratively gird her loins against coming onslaught of questions she didn't know how to answer.

"No need," he answered with resignation in his tone. "I will send them away."

Henry unbarred the door and opened it slightly. "What is the meaning…" He was unable to finish his sentence before the door pushed into him and a parade of women rushed into the room.

"No time to dawdle." The Countess of Spencer grabbed a towel and crossed the room and removed Frances from the tub while Blanche rummaged through the wardrobe. Mary followed the countess's lead and wrapped Frances in a towel while Jane stood by, chemise in hand.

"Henry." Blanche spoke curtly as she selected a gown for Frances and laid it on the bed. "Where is your man? You must dress immediately for the banquet. Dress fashionably but modestly. Understood? All eyes will be on you this evening. Do your family's consequence proud."

Frances stood in her chemise and stockings, her hair in a turban as Mary slapped a corset around her and began to lace.

"What is going on?" Frances's words felt inadequate under the circumstances. "What has happened?"

For less than a second all action within the chamber ceased, morphing into an uncomfortable silence. Henry's manservant entered the chamber, breaking the tension. Bess snapped her fingers, and Frances's lacings were, once again, yanked with full force and her feet shoved into slippers. She felt like a child, quite literally, being dressed by her mother. No answers. No control.

Ready for court, or whatever was to come, Frances calmed her breaths and smoothed the front panels of her dove-gray watered satin overskirt. Henry met her eye and crossed to her, dressed and ready, her partner in whatever was to come next.

"Now." Blanche Parry stood before Frances and Henry. "There was an assassination attempt on the Queen during the hunt. *While you were missing from the hunting party.*" Her voice lowered to a serious whisper. "There are those convinced it was you, Henry. The Queen Herself withholds judgment, but that alone does not mean She presumes your innocence."

Frances stood in shocked silence as Mary and Jane fastened pearl studded sleeves under the shoulder rolls of her bodice. "But what of his service to the Crown? His character? All he has done." *These past years where he has been more wed to duty than to me?*

Henry took her hand and grazed his thumb over her knuckles, a soft reminder of the new warmth between them. He pulled his gaze from hers and squared his shoulders.

"Have we heard from Walsingham?" Henry asked, his voice steady despite his wan face. "What do we know?"

Of course, in the moments her husband had chosen something outside of duty, everything would come crashing down.

• • •

Henry's stomach lodged in his throat, cutting off air and rational thought. An assassination attempt? While he was off seducing his wife, the Queen had been in danger. He was every sort of fool.

And they thought *he* was the perpetrator? He shook his head at the thought, needing more details to help understand. "When did it happen? Who was present? Who was not? What was the weapon?"

Her fingers stretched in his tight grip, her other hand joining his, tracing the tendons pulsing on the back of his hand and lending her strength, her faith. *Frances.* "Henry, they cannot think it is you."

He relaxed and lifted her hand to his lips, pressing a warm kiss to her fingers. "Only the ignorant would." He couldn't believe that Queen Elizabeth really suspected him. If this occurred on the palace grounds, the possibility that the perpetrator was someone welcome within the court became a fact. Someone trusted.

Sir Harry Lee came to the forefront of his thoughts. He could have used Frances as an excuse to separate himself from the hunting party… Henry shook his head and swore. Just because he disliked the man didn't make him capable of treason.

Blanche Parry laid her hand over Henry and Frances's joined hands. "You are easy to suspect. Frances as well. These incidents began with her arrival and you do have enemies. Baroness Ludlow has been a font of venomous gossip."

Frances gasped. "I thought she was my friend."

Her forehead crinkled with her look of hurt and confusion. Henry pulled her to him and kissed the adorable pucker between her brows. "Friendship at court is as real as courtly love. You cannot trust it." She lowered her head against his chest, but he could feel the tension still in her back beneath the length of her damp hair.

"No time for that now." Blanche pulled them apart and tweaked the starched ruff framing his jaw. "You'll crush his collar. Tonight the Queen calls for a celebration to show the court and the world that she does not fear death—in reality, it is the thing she fears most in the world. She shines brightest when She wants to prove a point, so tonight She will be brilliant. You two must be present in spite of the suspicion. You must show you have nothing to hide. Take a page from the Queen and put all the naysayers to shame. You are newly reconciled, in love, and blameless." Henry's stomach dropped, and he looked to Frances.

She was not ready for him to make a public spectacle of his affection. *He* was not ready. If he were to profess his love now, it would be insincere, and the last thing he wanted was to make her feel like he was playing her for a fool. Whatever they had was still too new to weather this.

Frances pulled her hands from his and crossed to stand in front of the fire, visibly shivering. Her gray gown reflected the flames, glowing gold and orange like a sunset in the firelight, while Mary brushed out the soft tangled length of her hair and began braiding, twisting and pinning.

This charade is nonsense. "There is too much to be done. I cannot simply make merry this eve."

"You cannot do anything but." The Countess of Spencer rose from her perch on the side of the bed and strode to stand beside Blanche Parry. "If it makes you feel better, you do not actually have to enjoy yourself. Just pretend. And pay attention to those around you."

He raised a brow at his mother-in-law, almost certain she was mocking him.

"Frances?" He turned to her and met her pale blue gaze. "Will you join me for tonight's festivities?" He held out his hand, unsure.

She placed her now gloved hand in his and took her place at his right. "I do not seem to have a choice." She sounded defeated, hollow.

Yet again they were playing the roles laid out for them, doing their duty.

Side by side but not together.

Chapter Twenty-Two

Rule Ten: Love cannot coexist with avarice.

Anger simmered in Frances's stomach as she once more pasted that polite veneer in place. There was no time to assimilate all the changes, and she felt too raw to pretend, to regress to the pleasant lady expected of her. Having Henry at her side only exacerbated the ache, the physical memory of their love adding confusion to her already muddled feelings.

What she wouldn't give for a quiet room, parchment, and a quill and ink. A way to organize her thoughts. Yes, a list would solve everything.

"Pray tell us, Mistress LeSieur, what is your next conceit for Her Majesty's masque? Assuming you are still welcome at court, that is."

Frances whipped around, her skirts flying. "Baroness Ludlow." She dropped into a quick reverance.

The smug look in the sour woman's face told her everything she needed to know. The baroness had put her into that situation with Sir Harry Lee during the hunt intentionally. Why? She'd never been anything other than kind to the lonely woman, even when it wasn't the easy choice. Come to think of it, she'd forced friendship on Baroness Ludlow, and it had never been easy. The older woman always left her with the impression of being judged and found lacking. For a moment Frances smiled, impressed with her own saintly compassion. The thought brought out an involuntary laugh, turning Baroness Ludlow's already puckered anus of a mouth into an even tighter vise. Likening her mouth to an arse made a lot of sense; she'd always thought she had the expression of someone who had just gotten a strong whiff of a bad smell. She laughed harder, the busk in her corset pressing against her abdomen with each guffaw. Really, court dresses were not designed for anyone to enjoy themselves.

"Are you quite well, Mistress LeSieur? Mayhap the night spent in the wood has addled your mind."

She stilled her laughter, squaring her shoulders within the confines of her bodice, the rolled details at the caps pulling taut against her upper arms.

"Is that what you expected?" she asked, quirking a brow.

"Of course, I had hoped for the best, but after you went off into the wood with Sir Harry Lee, I did not know what to think." Baroness Ludlow blinked in all innocence, spreading her hands wide, the rings on her gloved fingers sparkling in the flickering light. "Odd that you should say that. I recall expecting a Yeoman of the Guard's escort back to the palace. Imagine my surprise when I found myself on the wrong path with only Sir Harry at my back."

This time Baroness Ludlow laughed, a bitter bark. "Come now, Mistress. You claim to be a lady of the court but play at virtue. You cannot live in both worlds."

"Funny, you claim to be above it all, and yet you engage in intrigue and courtly machinations more than I have ever done. What pious woman would facilitate a fellow gentlewoman's fall from virtue? Put a *friend* into such a precarious situation? I thought you had some regard for me."

"I do, of course." Baroness Ludlow reached for Frances's hand in an awkward show of kinship. The rough edge of the Ludlow signet caught on Frances's glove, tearing the delicate leather, and Frances bit back a curse. At least she would be returning to Holme LeSieur soon and would have no need to impress anyone with her courtly sophistication. In fact, the pretty gloves would be impractical there. She ran a finger over the small hole, frustrated nonetheless. Baroness Ludlow noted the movement and gasped, "I tore your glove? How clumsy of me." She reached forward once more and turned over Frances's palm to examine the damage. "At least it did not break the skin."

"Yes," Frances responded. There was something about the way the baroness held her hand this time that seemed less for show and more a familiarity, a disturbing familiarity.

Baroness Ludlow held on to Frances's hand, tracing the tear at her palm. "I saw how horribly unhappy you were to be reunited with your husband."

"So you thought to aid me in my ruination?" Frances pulled her hand away.

Baroness Ludlow shrugged. "This is court. Everyone is debauched. No one will judge your actions." And yet she stood right there, judging away.

The tone of the exchange had shifted from confrontational to almost conspiratorial and something else she couldn't quite name... Something that made Frances feel more uncomfortable even than when under Sir Harry's leering scrutiny. It smacked of ownership and a right to her person that Frances would, never again, concede. From her own mother to Queen Elizabeth, now Baroness Ludlow and all the hungry onlookers... God's teeth, she was finished with this.

"So you would forgive my bad behavior, for dallying with Sir Harry in the woods?" Frances asked, curious and disgusted.

Baroness Ludlow smiled, an unnatural expression on her face. "It is not for me to forgive, but I do not hold you accountable."

"Would you also forgive me for stabbing him in the thigh?"

"What?" Baroness Ludlow gasped, the shock on her face the first sincere expression of the evening. "Surely you did not."

This time Frances affected a face of pure innocence. "What would you do if a man refused to take no for an answer?"

She stammered, "Surely he misunderstood…"

She interrupted. "I was very, very clear."

"Well," Baroness Ludlow blustered in a superior tone, "perhaps you are used to country ways and not sophisticated enough to be part of the Queen's entourage. Dalliances are the rule, not the exception. As I said before, it is the way of court."

"Is that so?" she asked, unable to help herself. "Who are you tupping?"

The baroness's jaw dropped as she exclaimed in a high whine, "Mistress LeSieur!"

"Me? Goodness Baroness Ludlow, are you telling me I am a Sapphist? I had no idea. No, if you are in search of a lover, I have it on good authority that Sir Harry Lee is ready and not all that particular, though he may be suffering from a bum leg. I assume you have the requisite body parts."

"Mistress LeSieur!"

Frances smiled at the eavesdropping courtiers attempting to be inconspicuous. Queen Elizabeth wanted to spotlight the inconsequential LeSieur family drama and pretend the very serious assassination attempt was of no matter. Well, Frances was good at nothing as much as staging a spectacle. And this time she was doing it without lists.

And to think she had sunk back into herself, played by the rules, and tucked tail.

Why bother? Whom did it serve?

Queen Elizabeth, she was certain, was watching the scene unfold, even though She appeared interested in the poet reciting before Her. Blanche Parry, however, was rapt. Her mother, by comparison, was pale, her lips drawn tight. No approval there.

Well, Mother, watch this.

Frances turned back to Baroness Ludlow in time to hear the end of whatever horrible thing she was saying about Henry, something about him being a Papist bastard. And then Frances slapped her right across her face.

• • •

Henry kept his hand firm against Frances's lower back, the bulk of her skirts pleated just below his fingers. He could feel her shaking through all the layers, but still she held her head high and her shoulders straight. Without a word, she accepted his lead through the great hall and into the gallery.

Then outside into the darkening night. The courtyard gardens glowed under the dim flicker of torchlight, beaded mist on the shaped foliage burnished the garden with gold. Down one cobbled path and left, toward the long gallery, he directed her with the steady pressure of his touch and she remained silent. Thank goodness for small mercies, he wouldn't know what to say. Couldn't tell if her continued trembling was from anger or excitement. Or the growing cold.

In that moment, the hazy mist thickened into heavy rain. The sound of it thundered against the tiled awnings overhanging the confines of the courtyard, and Frances shrieked and made a dash for cover back in the direction of the main hall.

He wasn't ready to face the court again. Not yet. He grabbed her wrist and pulled her behind him, ushering her into the relative dry of a brick archway, closed off at both ends only by the threat of the start of another English winter.

"Henry, we must find shelter," she muttered, barely audible over the roar of the onslaught.

"This is shelter." He pulled her close. She was only a silhouette against the torchlight glowing through the curtain of rain that sluiced off the roofline. "And we need to talk."

He wished he could see her face, read the expression in her eyes. Henry reached out and splayed his hands on either side of her waist and traced them up her torso. He heard her catch of breath, the surprise at his touch, and then her soft sigh as he found her shoulders, her neck, her jaw.

She was unspeakably soft, her cheeks warming under his hands in a blush.

"I am sorry if I damaged your consequence with my actions in the hall," she muttered and lowered her head.

He tightened his hands on her jaw and lifted her, urging her to hold her head high again. "Do not do that. Just…don't."

"Do what?"

"Shrivel." He almost spat the word. A drop of moisture slid down her cheek and pooled on his hand. Tears? He brushed the trail from her cheek with a soft caress and asked, "Frances?"

"I am afraid I have disappointed you and my mother. Again," she muttered. "No matter where I go, here at court or home at Holme LeSieur, I cannot seem to balance on that fine line. In order to be calm, to be that perfect lady I have to plan out *everything*. It gives me security, and without it I am not moored. Like I cannot keep the wild part of myself at bay. God help me, I actually hit Baroness Ludlow." She laughed nervously over a sob. "I should be better able to control myself. I have behaved impeccably for ten years—why can I not now? There are better ways to solve disputes. Civilized ways." She groaned the last sentence and leaned forward, resting her head against his chest. The pearl pins on her headdress scratched his chin.

He'd seen many aspects of his wife during these weeks at court, but she was always composed. Even last night in the cottage, she was in control of herself. He'd always admired her strength, but this crack in her armor gave him a glimpse of the girl he remembered from before their betrothal. A girl who sailed upon the wave of her emotions, who was unexpected and passionate. Someone who could love him. Who he could love.

"A proper lady, a proper wife is serene." Frances's voice fell flat and emotionless against the autumn rain curtaining their enclosure.

"So," Henry asked, "a proper wife would not have slapped Baroness Ludlow for calling her husband a Papist bastard of a pox-riddled whore?"

She smiled and turned her face, pressing her lips to his palm. "No."

"And she probably would not draw blood from the Queen's champion..."

She looked up with a start. "I had to get away from him! If you only knew..."

He interrupted her with a soft kiss and whispered, "I suppose it's a good thing, then, that you already informed me you did not wish to be a proper wife."

She pulled back. "That is not what I said." He could not see her face but heard her smile.

"Is it not? Mayhap this is what you really wanted rather than an end to our marriage, you wished for a release from expectation and appearances. Freedom."

"That is not possible. I have the consequence of my family name to think about. It isn't done to indulge in flights of fancy. There are expectations within our circle of peers. I was raised to be a lady."

"Yet being a lady, following your mother's rules, I suspect that is at the root of the melancholy. You do not have to end our marriage in order to be yourself. I want you, the real you, as my wife, not some complacent cypher."

"The wanton wench who slapped a baroness just now? You think I should be that woman?"

"If that is part of who you are, then yes." He leaned in, finding her mouth in the darkness as if drawn home. Her lips parted beneath his in a gasp of surprise; her hands clutched the collar of his doublet in either entreaty or resistance. He pulled away, afraid he'd overstepped himself, but she followed him, holding on to the kiss.

"If I'd known slapping Baroness Ludlow would draw you to me thusly, I would have done it years ago."

"A month ago you did not want me." He spun her in his arms and pulled her back flush against his chest, her bottom level with his groin. "Thusly." He pushed his hips forward, cursing the layers of fabric between them.

"But I did. At first." Her voice was softer now, an alto whisper against the bass of the rain. "I wanted to be desired. I wanted courtly love. I was too ignorant, though, to know what it meant and simply did what I was told."

"As did I." He gathered up her skirts, the heavy satin cold against his fingers, the layers of her boned farthingale acting as an inverted ladder for his hands to scale.

He reached below the yards of fabric and grazed the back of his fingers over the soft skin of her bottom.

She shivered and pressed back, grinding against him.

"For example, I would never have thought to touch you," he slid one hand down the sweet curve of her arse and in between her thighs, "here."

She gasped and spread her legs for him, the slick entrance to her core ready for him. "God's blood, Frances," he moaned her name and leaned forward, biting the tender pulse at her shoulder lightly. "You've made a beast of me."

She whimpered, arching her head to allow him more access. He dragged his lips up her neck and nuzzled her ear, then nipped her again.

"Better that than the proper gentleman."

His fingers found her opening and probed gently forward, afraid she might be sore from the night before. She bowed her back and leaned forward, opening herself. He speared his fingers deep, stretching her as he caressed.

"God, Frances, I wanted to take you next in a proper bed. Our marriage bed."

She pushed back and tightened her muscles around his fingers. "I'm finished being proper." She clenched once more, shivering. "This. Now." She wiggled and then jolted as he brushed over the sensitive bud at the front with his finger. "This is right."

The darkness of the November night blinded him to all but sensation as he unlaced the placket of his slops and freed his ready cock. He rubbed the sensitive tip against the slick heat of her opening as she cried for more.

His wife, the woman of passion he'd taken for granted for too long, wanted him the way he'd always wanted her.

With that thought he drove home, her body stretching to take him. All of him. She called out his name as he held her hips steady, afraid to move, afraid to breathe. He fit so perfectly within her, her heat branded him, making him hers far more than she'd ever been his.

Slowly he pulled back and then pressed forward, setting a slow, grinding rhythm. One hand on her leg, he guided her back to meet each thrust. The other hand snaked around the front, again finding that little nub that drove her mad.

He came apart inside her as she clenched around him in spasms, drenching his cock in her pleasure.

Chapter Twenty-Three

Rule Twenty-Nine: Aggravation of excessive passion does not usually afflict the true lover.

For Frances, everything was different now. Could others see the change in her? It felt so colossal surely it must be branded on her face. She loved her husband. She wanted a future with him. And he wanted her as she was, less than perfect.

She'd come to London in search of freedom, and she'd found it. And that freedom was going to lead her straight back to Holme LeSieur and her children. Where she would run the estate and simply be herself.

And she didn't care what her mother thought.

The banquet was over now, but the dancing and entertainments were only beginning. Queen Elizabeth hosted with all the aplomb of a generous monarch who was not in fear for Her life. Such a charade, with every courtier present no different than a hired player at a masque. Practiced wit, conspicuous costumes, and petty dramas.

Henry sat beside her, a secret smile playing on his lips just for her. She wanted to disappear with him to their rooms and find out more about each other and, perhaps, seduce him with the actions from page one and twenty of the book.

Baroness Ludlow approached and dropped into a low reverance, her olive-green velvet skirts pooling at Frances's feet. Baroness Ludlow, a baroness, outranked Frances and owed her no courtesy, still the woman waited.

Frances, uncertain, waved to give Baroness Ludlow permission to rise.

"I owe you my apologies, Mistress LeSieur. In my vanity and anger I insulted you and your family, and that was ill done."

Her jaw did not drop open, nor did she gape like a codfish at this surprise. Her proper lady persona, it appeared, had one more job to do. "Baroness Ludlow, you do me great courtesy. I pray you will accept my own apology for my untoward response."

Baroness Ludlow's face creased into an awkward smile. "Yes, of course. Then will you continue to count me among your friends?" She extended her hand.

Frances rose and placed her gloved hand in Baroness Ludlow's. "If you will count me among yours."

"Mistress LeSieur?"

Frances turned, surprised. "Master Hatton." She dropped into a small reverance in response to his.

"And Master LeSieur." Hatton nodded, still holding the gesture of respect.

Henry reveranced and they both rose up. "Pray pardon, mistress, but I have matters to discuss with your husband." He cocked a brow at Frances and she nodded.

Yes, he was attractive, but she did not respond to him the same way she did with Henry. Even before she and Henry had begun their game of seduction and she entertained the possibility of a flirtation with Hatton, it was only in play. With Henry, she glanced at her husband, his jaw stern at whatever Hatton was saying to him, there was a tug at somewhere inside her, a visceral pull to him.

"Mistress LeSieur?" Baroness Ludlow called out her name again, drawing her attention back.

"I am so sorry, Baroness. I did not mean to be rude."

"Of course not." The woman's lips pinched into her regular facial expression, essence of chamber pot. "Would you join me in the next dance? One of your ladies," she gestured to the two women Frances had been all but ignoring since her return to the hall after the tryst with her husband, "could make the third in our set." Frances almost laughed at the thought of what Jane would say if she ever told her.

"Mistress LeSieur?" Baroness Ludlow did not look contrite and friendly any longer.

"My apologies. My mind was wandering. The excitement of the past days must have taken their toll. Allow me to beg off dancing tonight. I think it is time I left."

Left the hall. Left the court. Left forced pleasantries.

"Baroness Ludlow and Mistress LeSieur," Sir Harry Lee approached, his step uneven, a Venetian glass goblet in each hand, "How now, ladies? Allow me to be of service." He presented both goblets, one to each of them.

They both accepted, but Frances could not bring herself to take a sip, although a strong drink seemed just the thing at the moment.

"Mistress LeSieur, I came to beg your forgiveness for my forward actions yesterday."

Frances stiffened. "Assuming I wished to dally with you? All but forcing me?"

"Aye, it was badly done. I do not blame you for your," he looked down at his leg, the injury covered by his voluminous breeches, "actions. When you did not return during the storm, I feared for your safety."

"How gentlemanly of you."

Baroness Ludlow snickered and lifted her goblet to hide her smile.

He continued, "It *was* ill done, and I wish to make amends."

"How would you suggest doing that?" Frances asked as she placed the goblet on the banquet table behind her. She'd already slapped one peer of the realm tonight. She'd best avoid having a potential weapon in her hand whilst dealing with Sir Harry, the Queen's favorite. She rather liked the idea of splashing the spiced mead into his face and that, in itself, unnerved her. She was developing a violent streak.

He stepped closer and took her gloved hand. "By saving you from further abuse."

"By leaving my presence?" She pulled her hand from his. "How thoughtful."

He grimaced, his mouth tight beneath his waxed mustache. "I certainly shall if that is your wish." He reveranced once more, his hat over his heart. "But first let me give you some information."

She raised a brow and waited. Baroness Ludlow drained the remains of her mead then pressed closer to listen.

"There has been a prize on bedding you since you arrived at court."

Frances sighed. Of course there was. Why would she expect any less? Tired, she asked, "And?"

"The wager was set up by your husband, Master LeSieur."

She straightened her shoulders and looked up sharply, meeting his eye. "I do not believe you."

"I see that, but ask Master Hatton. He has pursued you as well."

"Henry would not do that."

"Oh, but he did," Baroness Ludlow added in *sotto voce*. "Even I heard of it. Ten pounds on bedding you. Some might be flattered to be worth so much."

There had to be a mistake. Henry, even before their time together, *especially* before their time together, would not be so callous to lay a bet on bedding his wife. She had no words.

She glanced around the great hall but could not spot him. Had he left with Kit Hatton? Mayhap to collect on the wager. He had certainly won.

Baroness Ludlow picked up Frances's discarded goblet and pressed it into her hands. "Drink. You look pale."

Frances took a sip of the sweet mead, the honey spiced with nutmeg sending a feeling of warmth through her. She did not know how to process the information, how to behave. She needed a quiet place to write it out and think.

"The musicians are starting a new song. Baroness Ludlow, Mistress LeSieur, I pray you, join me."

Maybe a dance would help reel in her riot of emotions, focus her thoughts. She took a deep draft of the mead, almost emptying the goblet and then accepted Sir Harry Lee's hand, too numb for anger or self-righteousness. "I am honored, sir."

The drummer beat out the rhythm as Frances took her place on the floor and reveranced her partners. Stepping lightly from side to side and then a spin, she lost her bearings and crashed into Baroness Ludlow.

The woman reached out to steady her, concern in her eyes despite the disdain in the set of her mouth. It must be a miserable thing to be Baroness Ludlow. No friends…

Her thoughts trailed off, and she tried to stay upright. "I do not feel at all well. Pray excuse me, Sir Harry, Baroness Ludlow." Frances stumbled off the dance floor. It was simply too hot in here. Suffocating.

"Allow me to escort you." Sir Harry placed a possessive hand on the small of her back and ushered her toward the door.

"Mistress," Jane appeared before her. A sense of relief speared through her. At least she did have friends she could trust. Mary. Jane. Frances offered a silent prayer of gratitude as Jane took her hand and guided her to an empty bench. Sir Harry Lee followed but Baroness Ludlow… Where was she? Still dancing?

"You are not well, and I am not the only one to notice. Here," Jane pushed a heavy goblet into Frances's weak hand. "Drink this. It will warm your blood."

Frances took a deep gulp of the ale and grimaced. Sir Harry sat beside her with every appearance of genuine concern for her wellbeing. He was probably just concerned that she recover herself enough for him to be able to get under her skirts in some dark corner. Men were all the same—they would only value her for the juncture between her thighs. Sickening. She had never felt so worthless in her life. Frances could hardly think straight. She was so angry but couldn't remember why.

Jane sat beside her in silent companionship as Frances sipped the strong ale and tried not to cry. She was such a fool.

"Jane, I think we should go home," Frances muttered and laid her head on Jane's shoulder, grateful that she could sleep.

Jane's arms wrapped around her in time to hold her steady as the world went black.

Chapter Twenty-Four

Rule Two: A man in love is always apprehensive

Henry LeSieur burst into the room. "What has happened?" His voice broke the concentrated silence of waiting. He hurried across to join Blanche and knelt by Frances's unconscious form. He had no words as he gently laid his hand in his wife's hair.

Blanche Parry, more maternal than Frances's mother, answered. "Only time will tell. I have purged her, but do not know what the poison is or how long it has been in her body…"

"Poison?" He spoke the word with a sharp rasp. "Poison?" Anger burned in his throat, and he tried to calm himself, to be the man Frances needed right now.

Blanche said nothing, watching him patiently as the tide of Henry's anger won the battle over his efforts.

"Have I done my duty? No! When I should have been protecting the Queen, I was wooing my wife. When I should have been wooing my wife, I was protecting the Queen! I have failed on all accounts, and I can only blame myself for being fool enough to play the games of courtly intrigue." He turned and punched the plastered wall, crumbling flakes sticking to his damaged hand.

Blanche Parry smiled sadly. "It's not over yet, my dear. This has to stop, these attacks, all the violence. Catch this criminal. Frances lives still, and that is a good sign." Henry looked down at his fevered wife and smoothed a tendril from her brow, the oozing red on his knuckles hardly enough of a punishment for his failures. Blanche continued, "The villain has made a mistake—both of his victims are alive, and now he will be forced to step out of the shadows if he wants to finish the job."

"I will not use my wife as bait …" Henry began, hating himself for thinking the same thing, only to be interrupted by Bess.

"Frances is safe as she can be for now. I am here, and her ladies will not leave her side. Go and bring this evil to an end."

Henry sat back on his haunches, thinking aloud. "Who could have done this? A courtier, definitely. Someone with a vendetta against Frances—or against me? Frances was last dancing, healthy, with Sir Harry and Baroness Ludlow." He swallowed against the bile rising in his throat. "Sir Harry wants her and does not lose well. Where is he now?" He did not look up as he asked the question, sure in what must be done. He had no time to consider the right or wrong of it; he needed to take action. Now.

"Hatton called for a meeting at the guard house to discuss the investigation into the events during the hunt," she answered. Henry was certain she would not, that she'd rein him in as deftly as she'd always done with the Queen. She finished, "He crowed like a cock about it as he left, so very proud to be included."

"Pride?" he said, quietly. It made more sense, Sir Harry's motivation. "Pride?" He stood, drew his rapier, and bounded to the door, almost skewering the two ladies entering. "That is it. He could not win her. She embarrassed him, brought his manhood to question. Ha! That bastard thinks to assuage his pride by harming her?"

"Henry, that is not what I said," Blanche stepped forward and lay a staying hand on Henry's sword, pressing it down as both Baroness Ludlow and Lady Howard of Effingham shrieked at the drawn steel and huddled next to the wall. "Use your wits. I know you are angry. Afraid."

"Afraid?" He spat, pushing past her into the corridor. He needed to take action. He couldn't simply stay here and watch

Frances waste away. "It is Sir Harry Lee that best be afraid. He is a dead man."

The galleries were dark, lit only by candle sconces in the alcoves, but Henry knew where he was going. Down past the great hall, through the kitchen courtyard, the clock tower arch, on across the cobblestone path through the gardens... He ran like a man possessed toward the guard house. He pounded on the oaken door with his hilt, demanding Master Hatton. Henry had no patience and filled his wait with oaths and threats until, at last, he appeared, sword also at the ready.

"To what do I owe this visit?" Master Hatton asked amicably, his hand poised on the hilt of his rapier.

"Sir Harry Lee tried to kill my wife. Is he here?"

"He just left. And he does not wish to kill her, Henry. He merely wished to fu..."

"Where is he!" Henry had no time for games. He was sick to death of games. Games had put him in this position, and he would no longer be anyone's pawn. "Tell me, now, if you please."

Kit Hatton was far more of a courtier than a warrior and did not vacillate. "He and the Earl of Leicester just returned to the Queen's presence chamber. They should be there; the night is young still."

Henry turned on his heel and headed back toward the palace major, his sword still clenched in his gloved hand. With a curse of exasperation, Hatton followed close behind.

"Henry, is Mistress LeSieur in danger truly?" he called after Henry.

He answered, calling back over his shoulder, "Poison."

"And you think Sir Harry is to blame. Henry, he is neither that passionate nor that foolhardy. Hell, he has probably already forgotten any perceived slight, with some wench's lips wrapped around his co—"

Henry held up left hand, silencing Hatton with the gesture just as Sir Harry Lee stepped into the darkness of the Queen's Privy garden, a young girl tucked under his arm as he, playing the gentleman, shielded her from the light rain with his cloak.

Devil take the bastard; she was barely more than a child.

"Sir Harry, a word, I pray you," Hatton called out.

"Kit, I am past words." Henry lifted his rapier and bared his path. "Draw your sword, Sir Harry."

The strong words broke through the darkness and his reverie. Slowly moving his hand to his rapier, he shifted his weight only to pivot and draw in one fluid motion.

"Who goes there? Hatton? And, ah, I see. Master LeSieur." Sir Harry's voice held a warning.

Sword at the ready and knees loose to jump into position, Henry held his stance. "You are a cur and a knave, and I will have justice for my wife! *En garde!*" His challenge rang throughout the courtyard, getting the instant attention of those leaving Her Majesty's presence chamber for the night. It looked like he would be giving court one more spectacle.

Their swords clashed, Sir Harry careening back to gain his balance at the unexpected strength of Henry LeSieur's blow.

"Stand down, Master LeSieur. I am the better man here!"

"Stand down, says he!" Henry's mocking words were edged in restrained fury. "The better man?" Henry's footwork brought him close enough to deliver another blow. "I say that you tried to kill the Queen and may well have killed my wife!" Sir Harry, again, blocked Henry's blow with a loud crash and pushed him back.

"A murderer? I? No, I say it's you who are the murderer here. Who here is the foul Papist who disappeared so conveniently during the hunt?" Sir Harry parried the barrage of blows from Henry LeSieur's sword. "You are guilty of attempted murder and treason, and I will see you dead for it!"

Henry moved forward, trying to break through Sir Harry's defenses with a powerful strike. "You poisoned my wife, and you are a worm to deny it!"

"What good would that do me? I cannot bed a corpse!" Sir Harry misjudged Henry's feint and overcompensated to defend his position, rolling onto the cut grass of the garden. Righting himself quickly, he met Henry's blade, steel hissing along steel—sparks in the dark night. Grunting with the effort of holding back Henry's surprising force, Sir Harry muttered, "Besides poison is a woman's weapon."

Poison is a woman's weapon. Sir Harry's words rang true, and Henry staggered back, lowering his guard as he realized it may not have been Sir Harry. Then who?

Sir Harry Lee moved to strike at the distracted Henry when four armed yeoman of the guard stepped from the shadows to disarm both Sir Harry and Henry LeSieur as a voice boomed out of the fallen silence.

"Huzzah, gentlemen, for the entertainment. I find nothing as riveting as grown men acting like children."

Both Sir Harry and Henry LeSieur dropped to their knees at the sound of their Sovereign's voice.

"Your Majesty, I believe Sir Harry Lee has tried to murder my wife."

Sir Harry interrupted, "I protest! It is Henry LeSieur who was the assassin at the hunt, and I fight for Your honor, Your Majesty."

"Enough!" Queen Elizabeth was in Her full glory, the meager light provided by the sliver of moon gilded her features with a supernatural glow. "We have heard about dear Frances's illness, and We are most saddened."

The courtiers in the shadows stopped breathing in a collective hush as they waited for the show to continue. To them this was one more game, one more entertainment. He prayed Frances would fight this and cursed himself for letting anger and panic send him after Sir Harry. His place was by her side, especially now.

"Sir Harry, as you have publically accused Henry LeSieur of treason, We ask you to state your evidence." Queen Elizabeth calmly finished her statement, and folded her hands at her waist in a position that screamed, "We are waiting."

"Your Majesty. Master LeSieur is a known Papist. Secondly, he was one of Your party upon the hunt and went missing right before the arrow was fired at Your person." Sir Harry waited for the Queen to respond.

"This is true. There were many witnesses, Ourself among them." Queen Elizabeth's voice was severe. "What excuse can you give to save yourself, Master LeSieur? For the evidence is only mildly damning."

Henry knew, better than most, the possible consequences of this makeshift trial. After all, it was due to his word that Norfolk and Ludlow had been sent to the tower. At least it took a formal hearing to justify execution.

"Your Majesty, I left the party to follow my wife, who had ridden off. I was concerned for her safety." Henry did not add his concern for her virtue.

"A likely excuse, my Queen!" Sir Harry bellowed indignantly. "And his wife is not here to speak on his behalf. Or she may be involved in the plot as well!"

"God's teeth, she may be dying, and you still malign her!" Henry LeSieur glowered. "There is no time for this. I do not know if she still lives."

"Master LeSieur," Queen Elizabeth began calmly. "It appears you have no one to vouch for your innocence, and the entire court is against you. We may have need to remove you to the Tower for your own protection pending an official investigation..."

"Ahem." The sound of a soft cough filled the silence like cannon fire.

"Master Hatton, have you something to add?"

Immediately he was down on one knee, his hat over his breast. "Your Grace. I humbly beg forgiveness."

The Queen sounded surprisingly patient, given the circumstances. "What have I to forgive? This time?" The court erupted into titters all around, followed by strained silence.

"I should have spoken sooner, put an end to this madness. Mistress LeSieur was indeed lured away from the hunt. Sir Harry Lee knows this very well as it was he who tricked her. He told me this much just an hour ago."

"Your Majesty, I merely offered her escort…"

"You," Hatton interrupted, "misled her so that she would leave the hunt, and then when she rejected you, you left her lost in the wood in the rain."

Sir Harry stood, his fists balled at his sides before lowering to a respectful knee once more. "Your Majesty, the wench led me on, sharing her favors with Hatton and I am sure others. I had every reason to believe her willing."

"She shared nothing with me but a laugh, you poxy sod! She simply had not yet learned that men of the court take ever kindness as an invitation. She hadn't learned to be a bitch yet, but that did not mean she wanted you mouth-breathing down her bodice. Besides, if you believed her to have already been had by myself, you would no longer qualify for the winnings."

"And did you have her, Master Hatton?" Queen Elizabeth's eyes blazed, either with fury or humor—and no wise man would dare to guess which one.

"Not I, my Queen. Although the prize of ten pounds and the prestige that went alongside it was tempting. Mistress LeSieur is a virtuous and lovely woman. I am only a man, am I not?" Kit Hatton was still on one knee, but gesticulated so grandly, he put on quite a performance to the eager audience of courtiers. "She would have none of it."

"Smart girl," was the Queen's only response. The court held still in a hush, waiting on the Queen's good humor. Henry knew better than to call attention to himself as the silence dragged on.

"As you can see, my glorious Queen, my pursuit of Mistress LeSieur had naught to do with desire and only the goal to remain Your champion." God's teeth, Sir Harry was a fool.

Queen Elizabeth laughed and held up her fan to shield her smile before continuing. "You lured a married woman off to a dalliance in effort to please Us? How noble of you."

"I did not place the price on her, Your Majesty. My pride demanded success."

"And yet Mistress LeSieur recently pointed out that pride was a sin, Sir Harry. We suggest you think hard on your next words for you are not speaking in your own best interests." She turned her gaze on Henry, the moment he'd dreaded. "So, Master LeSieur, who did wager against your wife's virtue?"

"I did," Hatton answered.

"But I did not naysay it." Henry spoke up, unwilling to let Hatton take this blow alone. Were they friends now? "I had faith in my wife's virtue," or lack of interest in dalliance, "and let them exhaust themselves."

"So you threw her to the wolves. I expected better of you. And now you challenge, as Sir Harry pointed out, Our own champion without any proof but your own anger. And this, instead of staying by your ailing wife's side? We wonder at your devotion. And, frankly, your intelligence."

Sir Harry heaved a sigh of relief. Too soon.

"All of you, men I counted among the best at my court, are no better than children." Sir Harry straightened once more. Hatton never even flinched. Henry fought a lump in his throat, his lungs tight at the thought that Frances lay sick as he, idiot that he was, distracted his own fear with anger.

"Your Majesty." Henry leapt to his feet, not waiting to be recovered. "Pray allow me to return to my wife. I am a fool."

"Yes, you are. Hold a moment," She answered. "Sir Harry, what have you to say?"

"Master LeSieur, accept my apology for my disrespect to you and your wife. I placed her in danger by separating her from the court during the hunt."

The garden was so silent Henry imagined he could hear the grass grow. The entire court waited in the doorway from the Queen's presence chamber, fearing to move lest they disrupt their firsthand viewing of what promised to be the gossip of the decade. Only Queen Elizabeth made any motion, elegantly gesturing to rise up the kneeling gentlemen.

"Master LeSieur, it seems you are absolved in any perfidy. Go to your wife and get to the bottom of this."

Jumping to his feet, Henry blurted, "Your Majesty, I thought Sir Harry Lee the culprit behind her poisoning..."

"And now you do not?"

"No, and I beg his forgiveness for my accusations. I am sure that he is beyond blame on the assassination attempt on You, Your Majesty."

"We vouch for him," the Queen responded, waving a gloved hand at Sir Harry, giving him leave to stand.

"You have reason to believe the same villain behind both attacks?" Sir Harry interjected without thought about courtly niceties or his previous enmity with Henry.

"Aye, and the attack on Mistress Jane at the St. Luke's Day masque. Someone has been terrorizing my wife."

Hatton asked, still on one knee at the Queen's will, "Who do you suspect then?"

"Something Sir Harry said—that poison was a woman's weapon. Perhaps it is a woman we seek... Many women practice archery."

"I can aim and shoot an arrow as well as any man." Queen Elizabeth nodded and glared around at her ladies harshly for a moment or so as if to read their souls, and then back at Henry. "In this case Sir Harry and Master LeSieur are excused for their sword play and charged to find the culprit at once."

A cry went up from the covered walkway approaching the Queen's gardens. Two yeoman came forward bearing between them, two crying gentlewomen.

Kit Hatton ever Captain of the Guard though contrite on one knee before the Queen, addressed his men. "What is the meaning of this?"

"We found them running this way, talking of poison. Thought as we'd bring 'em to ye."

"Speak, ladies."

Mary ushered Jane forward before they both dropped to one knee before the Queen. "Oh, Master LeSieur! I have done a terrible wrong! I took Mistress LeSieur a goblet of ale after her dance, and she was ill after." Henry could hardly contain himself as Jane continued to babble. "I knew she was tired and sad and thought naught of it, but the Countess of Spencer says it was poison. So then I thought maybe it was you at the dinner table, feeding her each bite and all…"

Henry urged, "Get to the point, Mistress!"

"But you ate from that plate too, so it must have been the ale. But I did not poison it!"

"Then who did?" he asked.

"I did not suspect malice. She was always a friend to our Frances, and she said my lady looked overtired and should sit and have a sup…"

"Who!"

"The Baroness Ludlow," Jane answered, her face pale. Mistress Mary patted her gently on the back, as Jane began to sob once more.

Many audible gasps filled the moment, but none such as the stalwart Countess of Spencer. "Henry, Frances awoke, so Blanche and I came to check that all was well with you." Bess gathered her breath. "My son, I left her in the care of Lady Howard and Baroness Ludlow."

Chapter Twenty-Five

Rule Nineteen: When love grows faint its demise is usually certain.

Lights swirled. So much noise…buzzing pressed on Frances's ears. Louder and louder, choking her. So much pain—the wrenching in her gut tore her in half. Stop! Stop touching me! She tried to fight the hands, but she couldn't move. Where were her arms? Why couldn't she feel her arms? The lights moved too quickly, too bright, too loud. Too much…

"There, there my dear. Mistress Parry said you had to get fluids into you to restore your strength." Lady Howard of Effingham may not be terribly bright, but she sounded genuinely concerned.

"Your husband had best get you with child quick so you can use your nurturing tendencies where they would be appreciated." Baroness Ludlow's censure was not uncharacteristic, but really out of place in a sickroom.

Lady Howard must have agreed with Frances's unspoken thought. "Lady, Mistress LeSieur has just escaped the clutches of death, and you mock me for being tender?" With that, young Lady Howard of Effingham rose and crossed the room to refill her cup.

Frances felt as if her stomach and throat were on fire. The incessant pounding behind her eyes made it hard for her to follow the conversation. If Frances could have found the strength, she would have smiled at Lady Howard's nerve. Who would have thought such a sprite of a girl would stand up to sour-faced Baroness Ludlow? Frances started to fall into sleep again as she wondered why she had ever wanted to befriend such an unpleasant woman.

She woke from her dozing state to Baroness Ludlow lifting her head to bring yet another goblet to her mouth. The contents were vile, and Frances did not have the strength to force herself to swallow. The liquid dribbled across her face as her head hit the pallet of her bed with a thump.

"Why can you never do as you ought?" Baroness Ludlow's voice penetrated the thick fog of Frances's mind. She opened her eyes at the harsh tone, only to find her face away and drenched with tears.

"Baroness Ludlow, you are distraught. What troubles you?" Frances croaked her words. What was going on, and why did she hurt so much? And why was the baroness clutching her so tightly and weeping.

Crying? Baroness Ludlow? Impossible.

"It was so simple... Then you had to spoil it all!" Her voice was a sobbing wreck.

Frances shifted to raise herself and laid a hand on the back of Baroness Ludlow's head. Whispering soothing sounds, Frances looked around the room for the first time, trying to take in her surrounds. They were in her chamber...the chamber she shared with her husband. She was in her bed but wrapped in flannel blankets. What happened? Fighting the pain, Frances whispered, "All will be well, lady. All will be well..."

Frances's soothing ministrations were interrupted when she caught sight of a heap of clothes on the floor that somehow looked wrong. Were those her clothes? She didn't recognize them. Looking closely, she thought they were moving...

Baroness Ludlow sprang up from her prostrate position on Frances lap and scurried across the room to the pile and started kicking at what Frances now recognized as the unconscious form of Lady Howard. Baroness Ludlow was screaming and screaming... Frances couldn't make out actual words.

"Stop!" Frances croaked. Baroness Ludlow ceased immediately and turned her malevolent stare upon her. Pure evil replaced the baroness's regular look of disdain. The evil stalking her, Jane's attacker, the Queen's attempted assassin, it was all Baroness Ludlow...her friend.

"Why?" she struggled to whisper as she shifted her weight and slid her feet to the floor.

"Why?" Baroness Ludlow laughed at the word. "Why? Why what, mistress? I do not know what you mean."

"Why harm Lady Howard?"

"That answer is simple. She refused to leave so I could finish with you. Silly bit of fluff, no one will miss her."

Frances could not have anticipated that answer. "But why do you wish to harm me? I thought you were my friend."

Baroness Ludlow had inched closer during the short conversation and was now just an arm's length away. At Frances's question, she stopped for a moment, taken aback. "Friends? Oh, yes. I have never had a friend such as you. You were like a shining angel in this dank cesspool...." Baroness Ludlow reached out her hand as if to stroke Frances's cheek. "I tried to lead you on the righteous path. You were swayed by the glittering deceit of this blasphemous court, but I knew what was right. I gave you signs."

"The rosary?"

"Yes, you were too calm in your acceptance of the English church. And your forepart was a reminder of what happens to sinners."

Frances wrapped the flannel sheet closer around her bosom, careful to keep her arms free. "My sin was my cooperation with Queen Elizabeth's Mass?"

"No! Your sin is that you are a *whore*!" Baroness Ludlow spat the words. "I gave you the jasmine to tempt you, to learn for myself that you were beyond reproach, and the temptation was too much! I saw you at the masque, seducing every gentleman you partnered and finally, a willing wanton in the arms of your husband."

"So you taught me a lesson." Frances prayed for her strength to return. If she could just keep Baroness Ludlow talking for longer, perhaps she had a chance.

"It was a mistake to attack your gentlewoman, although she was a doxy in need of punishment."

"Mistress Radclyffe?" *Poor Jane.* "You mistook her for me?"

"Yes, and I was glad of the error. I could not have stood to see you suffer as she did." Again, Baroness Ludlow reached lightly toward Frances and softly caressed her hair.

Frances held back the urge to flinch away and instead pasted on a warm smile. *How do you rationalize with an insane woman?* "I am honored to know you call me friend." Baroness Ludlow wavered where she stood, uncertain. Frances continued, "I have never been able to call such a great lady a friend. I am blessed indeed. And now, you can show me the righteous path and help me not be tempted by sin…"

"NO!" The voice was from one possessed. "You must die! It is the only way!" Baroness Ludlow's light touch shifted into a violent fistful of hair as she pulled her head back, forcing her to look up.

Frances read the violence in her eyes and knew she was running out of options. "The only way for what?"

"To punish your husband! Henry LeSieur is a bastard who charmed the court and weaseled his way into the noblest houses with his false faith."

Frances just wanted to keep her talking, but she was out of time. In a panic, she responded, "My husband? What did he do?"

"He was a pretender! A servant of that heretic, Walsingham. He lied his way into my husband and Norfolk's trust, then betrayed them. Norfolk is dead at your husband's word. My husband will die in the tower, and it is Henry LeSieur's fault!"

Frances tried not to gasp as the pressure increased, drawing her head farther back, exposing her throat. Baroness Ludlow continued her tirade. "He has taken all I love. My husband, my home, my honor… So I will take all he loves." Frances heard a knife being withdrawn from a sheath, then saw a silver blade sparkle in the baroness's right hand. Her own bodice dagger.

"But he does not love me!" she protested. "The last time I saw him before court was at the birth of the twins. One died, and still he left me to grieve alone. That is not love!" Frances spoke nothing but the truth, and she knew Baroness Ludlow could tell.

Her grip on Frances's hair loosened, but she still held the weapon. "But he loves you now."

"Loves me now?" Frances forced an easy laugh. "You mean he lusts for me. He wants me only because other men want me. He wants me because I do not want him. And as soon as he is finished, he will ignore me again. I am nothing to him but a wager." Frances wished she did not feel the words so keenly. They were only to convince Baroness Ludlow, weren't they? "The only thing important to him is his duty."

Baroness Ludlow let go of Frances's hair with an exasperated gasp. "His duty, you say? Misguided duty. And when I am done with you, I will not fail again with Queen Elizabeth. He will lose everything and suffer as I have suffered. And I will serve God's will."

The door crashed open, distracting Baroness Ludlow and giving Frances the moment she needed to roll to the other side of her bed and fall to the floor to take cover.

Henry burst into the room followed close by Sir Harry and Master Hatton. Baroness Ludlow screeched her hate like a demon, raising her dagger high and charging blindly at Henry LeSieur. Master Hatton took her obsessive focus as an opportunity and simply stepped up beside her and conked her on the head with the hilt of his sword. Her limp form crumpled to the ground as Henry rushed to his wife's side and Sir Harry revived Lady Howard.

Standing useless in the middle of the chaos, Hatton remarked with levity, "Gentlemen, please do not let it be known that I struck a woman."

Chapter Twenty-Six

Rule Twenty-Four: The lover's every deed is performed with the thought of his beloved in mind.

Frances inhaled the icy breeze from the open window as she rested her forehead against the velvet upholstery. Drab, sleet-coated scenery jolted by as her carriage continued its northern trek from London to Nottinghamshire. Winter was in full force, and the recent frost had robbed England of the last vestiges of green.

Frances closed the heavy blinds against the cold at Jane's request. Darkness once again enveloped the close confines of the carriage, and it took a moment for Frances's eyes to readjust. Smiling softly in response to Jane's accusing glare, Frances closed her eyes and attempted to sleep.

As if reading her thoughts, Jane spoke up. "I do not begrudge missing the work involved with moving the court to Whitehall for Christ's Mass… I just don't understand why you insisted on leaving in such a rush." Jane shook her head as Frances opened her eyes in frustration. "And without a word to anyone. Not Mistress Parry or your mother—not even to Master LeSieur…"

"I left him a missive. I will talk no more of it." It was true, she had left a note. Of course, it said as little as possible. She just hoped it was enough so that he didn't feel obligated to follow her. Frances had been honest when she told him that she needed time away from him to think. Besides, as soon as she'd gain her strength after the ordeal with Baroness Ludlow, she had been struck by an overwhelming need to hold her children. She loved them so much, every thought of them brought an ache to her chest. To think she had left them behind…

No. Frances would not feel guilty over her decision to go to court. She'd needed that time to herself. Time to figure out who she was. It was ironic that her time away had made her realize that being a mother *was* an integral part of who she was. But she also had to be a woman, to be proud of herself for her own sake. Yes, she was going home to be a mother, but things were going to change at Holme LeSieur. The Holme would no longer be stagnant, waiting in expectation of one of the master's visits. No, the Holme would no longer be her cage… It would be her home, alive with love, laughter, and friendship.

Oh, yes—things would definitely be different. She would have to make a point of that. She didn't know if Henry planned to return to the way things had been or not. Even though she knew that she had fallen in love with him, she couldn't trust he would feel the same once they returned to their country routine. She owed their marriage effort. She now knew she could not blame him entirely for the loveless first ten years. Where they went from here, well that was up to both of them.

She had to know if what they shared was real or all mixed in with an ill-placed wager and courtly conspiracies. He was too much of a gentleman not to come with her if she'd asked, so she didn't ask and left the choice to him. No duty or obligation, just him choosing what he wanted.

I must be sanguine about the possibility that he may not choose me.

Of course, sneaking out of their chamber at the palace and running home was not necessarily a show of good faith. She was a coward—she was aware of that.

Jane cleared her throat abruptly. "Mistress, if you'll pardon my saying so… You are a coward."

Apparently, Jane was aware of the fact as well.

Frances leaned across the center of the coach to press Jane's hand. "You are completely right." Jane lifted one eyebrow in surprise. "I just needed time to acclimate to my home, my position... I needed space to think."

Jane considered Frances's words. "Aye. It would be a hard task indeed to stay levelheaded with a man like Master LeSieur in your bed." Jane paused a moment as if to say more, then, as she realized what she had said, blushed furiously and began to stammer, "Oh mistress! I didn't mean..."

Frances opened her mouth to speak and stopped herself. Of course, what Jane said was true. It was hard enough to know her own mind without it being clouded by her husband's hard body cradling hers intimately. Blinking away the memory and the yearning, Frances nodded with a smile to her companion, "Jane, you are quite right." Frances had become closer to Mary during their stay at the palace, but only Jane had elected to return to the Holme. Frances ached for the pain that still lingered behind Jane's smile. This time at court had changed her, brought her back to the timid young woman who'd joined her service years ago. In those years, Frances had seen Jane gain a spark and, in the space of mere months, lose it once more. Fear shadowed her decisions and was probably the only reason Jane chose service in a boring country house over the palace's Christmastide revelries and the company of her best friend. Frances could recognize a woman in need of escape when she saw one. Perhaps Jane would open up to her in time...and maybe Frances could help Jane along by being forthcoming herself.

"I had to leave. I did not want Henry to have to share my bed out of obligation or convenience. He can come to me when he is ready, if he really wants to. In the meantime, I will have some time to myself to sort through all that has happened."

All awkwardness out of the way, the mood in the carriage lightened, and the two women began to talk about how they would set up Holme LeSieur for Christ's Mass and the following twelve days.

• • •

Henry woke that morning to an empty bed and a scribbled note. He had stayed by his wife's side throughout her recovery. The poison that Baroness Ludlow had given Frances had taken some time to work through her system. Each day had shown improvement, and she had finally held down a solid meal two days past. Henry's relief was almost tangible.

The whole week following Baroness Ludlow's capture had been difficult. Frances, while on the mend, drifted in and out of consciousness for the first several days. She would wake up and seem almost normal for short periods, then start to ramble and eventually close her eyes in a restless sleep. Mistress Parry told her this was all part of her body's natural reaction. As Frances fought hard to expel the poison, Henry had helped regulate her fever with his own body heat, dripped honeyed tea into her mouth, and stroked her back to lull her into a more comfortable sleep than the fever and poison driven delirium. It was a shame to have had to miss the trial and sentencing of Baroness Ludlow, but he was needed by his wife's side. At last he knew where he belonged.

If Henry had forgotten how loved his wife was, the steady stream of visitors and gifts would have been a constant reminder of the fact. Even Lord and Lady Howard of Effingham had spent a lot of time keeping Henry company in Frances's sickroom. Mary had stayed with Henry and Frances during the day, helping in any way she could. With so many prominent courtiers paying their respect, Master Hatton had been conspicuous in his absence. Henry assumed he was making himself scarce for a while to allow the Queen's temper to cool over the matter of the wager.

And then he woke to an empty chamber and all sense of balance in his world crashed and burned.

Frances's missive explained that she wanted to head home ahead of him in order to give herself time to collect her muddled thoughts. She said she couldn't think when he was around, and she was not sure what direction her marriage was heading. What direction? Hadn't he made it clear to her that he desired her above any other? Didn't she know that he was turning his back on his perceived "duty" to the Crown in order to be a real part of his family? Didn't she know that he loved her?

It took Henry less than an hour to ready himself for the journey.

• • •

As the landscape became more familiar, the knot in Frances's chest tightened. Had she done the right thing leaving Henry, forcing him to choose? Frances wanted to believe him when he told her their passion had been real—but believing that would awaken a hope that best lay dormant. She had some serious thinking to do before she ever let herself hope that he loved her as much as she loved him. She had been nothing but one of his duties for the past ten years—their courtship was so fresh that she did not want to taint it by forcing him to accompany her home simply because it was his job. She wanted him to *want* to be there. She refused to simply be one more responsibility in his life.

Frances took a deep breath to steady herself as the wheels rattled against the familiar cobble drive to the house. This was the start of her new life, and she would take joy in it.

Frances sat with Jane in silence until the carriage rolled to a halt. Frances accepted the aid of her coachman and stepped into the courtyard. Raising her head, she surveyed the red brick symmetry of the modern home. She would be happy here.

"Welcome home, Mistress LeSieur." Mistress Cooley dropped into a squat reverance as she neared the entrance. Frances raised her up and, on impulse, embraced the matronly housekeeper in a warm hug.

"I am glad to be home." Releasing her, Frances quickly wiped happy tears from her eyes. "I would like to see the children immediately, Mistress Cooley."

• • •

"Mama!" A squealing bundle of a warm and snuggly almost-seven-year-old hurled herself across the room and into Frances waiting arms. Cheek to cheek, Frances inhaled the scent of lavender soap and sweetmeats that clung to her daughter and murmured, "Mama's home, Moppet."

Frances could not have detached Elizabeth's vice-like hug if she had wanted to. Settling herself onto the floor of the nursery, Frances welcomed Elizabeth as she crawled into her lap and more firmly ensconced herself in her mother's arms.

"I missed you so, Mama." Elizabeth muttered her words into Frances's shoulder, the sounds muffled by her ornate shoulder role. Elizabeth pulled back to look at the bejeweled puff, then moved further to take a better look at her mother.

"Oh, Mama! Did the Queen turn you into a princess?"

Frances laughed, crying happy tears, as Elizabeth offered her hands and gave her best effort to help her mother rise from the floor. Frances twirled, her lavender velvet skirts making a soft whooshing sound as they flew out about her. Elizabeth clapped in delight. "Mama! Such a pretty dress. Oh! You look so..." Elizabeth's eyes widened as she tried to select the right word. "...exquisite." Her small mouth cinched in a pout. Apparently "exquisite" wasn't exactly the word she was looking for, but was the best she could do. Frances knelt down once more to scoop her daughter into her arms.

"Where is the baby?" Frances loved the feel of her big girl but longed to reacquaint herself with baby Grace. There was a lot of lost time to make up for.

"Gracie is with Papa in his chambers." Elizabeth spoke as if this was the natural occurrence in the world.

Frances was dumbfounded. "Papa?" Surely Elizabeth was confused…but then, how could she be confused about something like that? Frances removed Elizabeth from her lap and gave her kiss on the forehead. "I shall be back in just a moment."

Frances made a slight note of Elizabeth's perfect reverance as Frances rose to leave. Her baby was turning into a little lady. Smiling to herself at the recent memory of Elizabeth's soft cheek pressed against hers, she prepared herself for whatever she would find in the master's chambers.

So Henry had followed her… Her heart skipped beneath the confines of her corset. What was his motivation? Why? Pride or desire? Duty or love? The time she had given herself to sort out her muddled thoughts had run out and she had to face him—ready or not. The main question had been what she wanted. Now she knew that she wanted him to be a part of her home. All she had to do was tell him.

Frances descended the grand staircase, taking time to look around for the first time since her return. The balustrade was wound with vines of ivy, every finial capped with wreaths of holly. The scent of the evergreens mingled with a perfume of cloves and citrus… The retainers at the Holme had certainly been hard at work to make the manor house ready for Christmastide festivities. The Holme glowed with the cozy warmth of the season. To think she had dreaded winter here.

This is no longer a cage. I am home.

Frances alighted on the first-floor landing and opened the door to her chambers. The last time she had seen her room, she had just finished packing and was starting on her grand adventure. She laughed to herself as she realized that this moment was perhaps the grandest adventure of all. She had served the Queen and Her glittering court. She had been accepted and admired…yet all she really wanted from life was here at the Holme. Knowing that the fulfillment of all her hopes and dreams hinged on this moment made it even more intimidating. All she had to do was have the courage to open the door to the adjoining chamber…

Never a timid woman, Frances gripped the handle and opened the door.

Chapter Twenty-Seven

Rule Eighteen: Good character is the one real requirement for worthiness of love.

Henry had ridden directly from London, stopping only to change the horses. He knew Frances was traveling by coach and with a baggage train, so she would take at least four days to travel, weather permitting.

Henry made the journey in two.

He arrived exhausted and unexpected at his ancestral estate. Too tired to do much, he satisfied himself with giving Mistress Cooley leeway to prepare the Holme for Christmastide in Mistress LeSieur's absence. He dispatched a courier to his sister-in-law's home in Spencer, requesting that they send young Robert home as soon as may be so he could spend time with his family. Then he pulled off his boots, leaned back in his chair, and fell asleep.

He awoke some time later to find himself eye to eye with a tiny female. He moved to sit up but was encumbered by quilts.

"Well met, my lord father. I have tucked you in." Little Mistress Elizabeth dropped her father a sweet reverance and continued, "I did not mean to disturb you...but you were snoring quite ferociously..."

Henry blinked the sleep out of his eyes as he followed her words. "Ferociously? That is a big word for a little girl."

"Mama knows so many words. Nurse does too." Elizabeth sat at her father's feet and pulled a carved wooden ship out of his boot. She must have been here for some time.

She played happily with the boat and the boot while Henry silently observed the little human that he had helped create. What an amazing creature. His duty had been to breed an heir ... He'd no use for daughters and had never paid much attention. What sort of man had he been to be so detached? What sort of father would not delight in watching his child grow? He had a lot of lost time to catch up on.

"Elizabeth, where can I find your sister?" For the life of him, Henry could not remember the baby's name.

"Gracie's up with nurse. Baby Frances and Maria are outside the chapel. They died." Elizabeth gave a very straightforward, if morbid, answer.

"I think it would be best for me to see Gracie first." With that, Henry stood in his stockinged feet and offered his hand to his daughter.

If Elizabeth felt intimidated by her stranger of a father, she never showed it. Her small, warm hand slipped into his, gripping his first three fingers. Henry slowed his pace to allow Elizabeth to walk comfortably as they ascended the main stair toward the third-floor nursery.

By the time Henry left baby Grace sleeping and went into the main house, Yule decorations were well underway. At this rate, the Holme would be completely decked by the time Frances arrived. He must not forget to speak to his steward about issuing an invitation to the villagers for the feasting and revelry. What else did Frances usually do for Christ's Mass? Of course, there was the actual three Masses themselves, but those were the responsibility of the Holme's priest. This would be exciting—sharing the twelve days of revelry with his family. He hadn't celebrated the season at the Holme since he had become lord of the manor. Duty had always kept him elsewhere.

Lost in his thoughts, Henry was surprised to find himself at his destination already. Before him lay the little gate into the consecrated ground behind Holme LeSieur's chapel. Beyond that lay generations of LeSieurs, all enshrouded with the dignity and honor of their station. Swallowing the lump in his throat, Henry picked his way between grave markers, looking for the more recent additions—two very small graves belonging to the daughters he would never know.

• • •

Frances stepped through the door to her husband's adjoining chamber and was immediately embraced by the warmth of the room. She was not expecting the vision of her husband in his shirtsleeves, lounging on the bed. In the center, cradled in the crook of his shoulder, baby Gracie slept contentedly, still gripping Henry's thumb. With a slight nod and a sleepy smile on his lips, he wordlessly welcomed her home and invited her to join him and the baby. After a moment of uncertainty, Frances crawled up onto the massive bed. She lay on her side, her head propped up by one arm, and delicately traced the curve of the baby's cheek with a finger. Leaning forward she placed a soft kiss on the downy crown, closed her eyes, and inhaled the sweet baby scent. Oh, she had missed her baby. What a beautiful girl. She almost wanted to wake her to see if her eyes had changed color in her absence, but this scene was too touching to disturb. She could never have pictured this in her wildest dreams. The image of her husband cradling their sleeping babe, the love that radiated from him... Her heart felt like it would burst. Blinking the mist from her eyes, Frances moved her hand from Grace's cheek and laid it over her husband's.

"Did you have the time you needed to sort through your thoughts? I could not stay away from you any longer." His husky whisper brought back memories of stolen moments on the barge.

"I did." She could feel the heat of his gaze, and her anxiety lessoned as she met at her husband's heavy-lidded stare. He wanted her. He wanted to be with her. "I am glad you followed me."

Henry smiled and removed himself from Grace's grasp and interlaced his fingers with Frances's. "I am glad to be home." Lifting his head gently, he bridged the gap between them brushed his lips tenderly against her forehead.

Frances spoke first. "I never expected to find such joy, such contentment, at the Holme."

"I never expected to find such love." Henry pulled away to look Frances in the eye. "I love you. You do know that, don't you?"

Frances smiled as her misty eyes gave way to true tears. Leaning forward again, she brushed her lips over his as she whispered. "Yes. I know that now."

Henry's lips engulfed hers in a kiss she would never forget. More than words, it promised her a lifetime of love, of honest friendship.

Baby Grace made a soft cooing sound in her sleep and nestled deeper against her father's chest, inadvertently reminding her parents that this was not the time for an amorous encounter. With a sigh of resignation, Henry laid his forehead against his wife's.

Frances knew she was complete now—she had found the missing part of who she was. She was a woman who was loved, and she was so happy, she didn't know if she should laugh or cry. She felt Henry's hand brush away an errant tear... It appeared she was crying. The realization made laughter bubble past the knot in her throat.

Still cradling her cheek with his hand, Henry asked, "What is so funny?"

Still laughing, Frances answered with a random thought, "Did you know that I've never been in your bed before?"

Henry barked a short laugh and then stopped her with a quick kiss before he smoothly rolled out of bed, taking Grace with him.

"Where are you going?"

Henry padded on soft feet across the room to summon the nurse. "I just thought perhaps I should remove Grace to her own cradle for a while." His voice was a whisper for the baby's sake.

"But this was so sweet…" Frances felt his absence like a missing part of her.

"Yes, but I would rather introduce you to the comforts of my bed without the company of our baby." Henry handed the baby out the door to the waiting nursemaid. "You'd best get used to the bed since you won't be leaving it for some time."

"Is that so?" Frances could think of nothing she'd like more.

"Yes. I figure that if I keep you here long enough, I can convince you that you love me." Henry met her eyes as he lowered himself back on the bed until they both lay on their sides, facing each other. Without the baby between them, there was nothing keeping them apart. Except for their clothes.

"But what if I don't want to leave your bed?"

Smiling, he said, "Well, that in itself says something, doesn't it?" He moved to pepper her face with kisses while he undid the lacings on her bodice.

"Yes, yes it does." Frances sighed her words. Henry could not undress her fast enough. "May I still stay in your bed even if I were to say that you I love you?" Frances's voice lowered to a husky whisper on the last three words.

Henry let out a boyish laugh before he finished with her bodice and moved on to nuzzle her neck. "I may never let you leave either way."

"That sounds wonderful to me." Frances sighed as Henry's teeth nipped at her ear.

Frances could hardly contain the sense of wholeness, the feeling of family and love that came with Henry and her children. He was home, truly home for reasons other than the quarterly income reports or the obligation of siring a babe.

Henry nuzzled her neck and whispered, "This is everything I have ever worked for and not known it until now. You are my wife, and it awes me that I'm worthy to touch you, that you want me."

For the first time, they were equal. She wanted everything he wanted…or at least she thought so. It was almost silly how much she needed to hear him say that he loved her, that it was real, before she made herself more vulnerable to him by expressing her love. Then again, she had to trust what she felt, what she felt from him.

"Wanting to stay in my bed—*our* bed," he murmured, "is no excuse to avoid saying it."

Frances felt the heat of his words against her skin. Didn't every breath she took scream it? Every sigh? Every kiss? No, it was not the same. Saying it now would be more meaningful than the vows they spoke out of duty ten years ago.

Shy, Frances whispered, "I do love you." Her heart fluttered in her chest, and she felt as giddy as a young girl.

Henry paused his sensual torture of her neck to gaze at her with a beaming smile. "And I love you more than duty. More than the Crown. You are everything." He leaned down to kiss her softly on the forehead. "I love you," he kissed her on the tip of her nose. For a moment, Frances thought he looked very much like the boy she had wed… Only now her dreams of love and romance had actually come true.

His eyes burned with intensity as once more he said, "I love you." He finished, claiming her mouth with a passion that made his words unnecessary.

Author's Note

This story is entirely fictional. All the actual historical noble characters are at the approximate age and stage of their life they would have been in 1572. The Duke of Norfolk had just been executed. Francis Walsingham was in Paris following the St. Bart's massacre and had not yet been knighted. A very young Anne Cecil had just married the self-centered and licentious Earl of Oxford. Robert Dudley was nearing the end of an affair with Baroness Howard and was picking up with Lady Essex. I originally wrote this to fill in the missing history of Frances and Henry Pierrepont, Frances being the eldest daughter of Bess of Hardwick, Countess of Shrewsbury. Because this is historical romance and not historical fiction and I was inventing so much of the story, I opted to change Frances and Henry's names to LeSieur.

The real Frances and Henry Pierrepont were indeed married young and had a number of children, some who survived, but that was all I could discover. Their descendants, however, did make a name for themselves, and Holme Pierrepont is open as a historical home for tours in Nottinghamshire.

To all the history and costume buffs out there, please give me some allowance for poetic license. Some things needed to be adapted for the pacing of the plot. It was much more exciting for Frances to have her new dress right away instead of waiting a more realistic time period. I have been as accurate as I can within the scope of the flow of my story and my resources. The dances referenced throughout the story were accurate in choreography and were created and used during the Elizabethan era—but *late* era. They would not have been danced at court in 1572. For this historical inaccuracy, I apologize. I love the Italian dances too much to limit the story to French.

In this story, Frances is taking action to lift herself out of depression. In Elizabethan England, she would have been diagnosed with a melancholy and an unbalance of humors. Apothecaries may have prescribed any number of treatments, from bleeding to inventive suppositories. A wise woman may have created a tincture of St. John's wart—an herb used today to battle depression.

In modern society, depression is taken seriously. Frances managed to solve her problems with positive attitude, a change of scenery, a shopping trip, and some good lovin'. Not everyone is so fortunate. I think the most important step of Frances's transformation was that she allowed herself to have needs of her own—that she didn't dismiss her thoughts and feelings as silly simply because they may have seemed irrational. She became the master of her own destiny by acknowledging that she had a valid problem that she needed to address.

Thank you for choosing to read this book. I hope you enjoyed it as much as I enjoyed writing it.

About the Author

Erin Kane Spock lives in Southern California with her husband, two daughters, an old-lady dog, and a puppy. She is a teacher and an active Irish dance mom.

Find Erin Kane Spock at her blog at courtlyromance.blogspot. com, on Facebook at http://www.facebook.com/Spockromance, and on Twitter at @kanespock.